NOBODY'S ANGEL

LINDA FREENY

NOBODY'S ANGEL

ARPress
45 Dan Road Suite 5
Canton MA 02021
Hotline: 1(888) 821-0229
Fax: 1(508) 545-7580

Ordering Information:
Quantity sales. Special discounts are available on quantity purchases by corporations, associations, and others. For details, contact the publisher at the address above.

Printed in the United States of America.

ISBN-13:   Softcover   979-8-89330-468-8
           eBook   979-8-89330-469-5
           Hardcover   979-8-89330-470-1

Library of Congress Control Number: 2024902552

TABLE OF CONTENTS

CHAPTER 1

She was eighteen, maybe twenty; young in some respects, old in that most of the hookers who frequented this dubious section of New York City were often under sixteen. She wore only a cheap ill-fitting leather dress and a black lace bra, and in the pocket of her dress was a filthy wine soaked note that read:

IVE BIN KILD

Detective Dave Kincaid and Brad Monroe stared down at the dead girl, exchanging weary glances. They rubbed their hands together to warm them in the unseasonable cold weather. In the two years that they'd been partners they'd come to anticipate each other's moods, become close enough to be considered friends, and yet still be as different as two men could be and still maintain that kind of bond.

Dave was boyishly good-looking, belying his thirty-five years, his thick sandy hair disguising a few premature grey hairs. Brad, younger, blonder, had earned his reputation as a "stud" honestly. Most of the guys in the precinct envied his skill with the ladies. One of the reasons that he and Dave got along so well was because Dave wasn't among their number.

Brad yawned. It was 4:00 a.m. It had been a rough night with two gang-related murders, a suicide, and now what looked like an overdose.

He glanced over at Dave. He cursed under his breath. Dave had that "look" he knew only too well. There were those in the department who called Dave's intuitiveness uncanny. Others who called him just plain lucky when he called a case long before anyone else got close.

Brad slapped his hands against his sides hoping to distract Dave's concentration. "Damn! Three more hours and we'd be off-duty. She'd be someone else's problem. She should have been, anyway," he said with disgust. "Would have been, if Rogers and Chernak hadn't called in sick. What does it take to get one lousy day off? I don't know about you, but I have enough fucking paperwork to decorate the squad room wall."

Dave continued to stare down at the girl, silently echoing his partner's outburst, but with more reason. He reluctantly tore his gaze away and looked up and down the alley. They were in a seamy downtown section that bordered skid row. Prostitutes in this neighborhood overdosed on cheap heroin and crack with depressing regularity.

He scanned the alley again, this time more slowly, his blue-green eyes acting as a camera. Litter and garbage hugged the graffiti-scarred walls. The girl was slumped up against a dumpster that spilled its foul odor into the crisp night air. One arm was stretched out toward the dumpster. Her legs were drawn up underneath her. She hadn't died easily or quickly.

It was an ugly place to die, Dave thought, and there was something else he couldn't yet define. Something about the girl that made him feel like someone had shoved a knife in his gut.

⌘

The next day, a few minutes after 10:00 a.m., the county coroner Sid Carter, was leaving the morgue when Dave Kincaid walked in. Carter's chosen career seemed tailor made for him because he was as cold-eyed as his charges, and just about as lively. He looked up at Dave, who at six-feet-three towered over his own diminutive frame.

"Working late, Dave? I thought you got off at seven."

Dave was way past tired. Last night had been no less taxing than the one before, or the one before that. "I came about the Jane Doe. What did you find?"

Sid yawned. "I just sent the report upstairs to the captain." "Humor me. Tell me what's in it."

"All right. There's nothing earthshaking about my findings. She died about 11:00

p.m. of an overdose of heroin. There were recent tracks on both arms, though she hadn't been using long, but the doses were heavy. She was eighteen to twenty, in basic good health, and she'd had quality dental care in the last month."

"Sex?"

"Not in the last twenty-four hours."

"Anything else?"

"Nothing to help you." Sid sighed. "Don't you ever get tired of chasing shadows, Dave? She got a hold of some bad stuff. Let vice find out where it came from. That's what they get paid for."

"You said she hadn't had sex in twenty-four hours?"

"That's right."

"Then she wasn't a hooker?"

"That's a label your people put on her. Personally, I don't judge them, I just examine the medical evidence. Why don't you go on home? That's where I'm headed." And when Dave didn't move, "It's a matter of priorities. We'll hold her, hoping someone claims her, but you know as well as I do that a lot of them are never identified."

Dave ground out his cigarette on the spotless white tile floor, ignoring Carter's frown of disapproval. "I want to see her."

"You got a reason?"

"None you'd understand. I had a feeling when we found her that she was out of place. That she didn't belong in that filthy alley." He sighed. "It was just a feeling. And I keep thinking about the note. Something just doesn't add up."

Carter shrugged, nodding at the door behind him. "Be my guest. She's in number twelve."

Dave entered the inner room. The sound of cold steel filled the air as he pulled out the drawer labeled number twelve. He lifted the sheet and stared down at her. Who in the hell was she? And what was she doing in that alley? He started to close the drawer. What was he doing here? Captain Herring had made the department's position clear. It was a clear-cut case, pending anything unusual in the coroner's findings, which apparently wasn't forthcoming. No I.D., lousy neighborhood, hypodermic by her side. That, and too few cops for too many incidents made it prudent in the eyes of the higher- ups to forgo a detailed investigation. The fact that she was a Jane Doe" was going to make it easy to write her off.

Dave was finding that he couldn't write her off. It was as if he knew her, or at least he should. Almost as if finding her in that alley was inevitable.

He shook his head to clear it. It was at times like this that what his mother considered a gift seemed more like a classic symptom of mental instability.

He turned his gaze back to the girl. She'd been pretty, Dave thought. Even the heavily applied make-up, smeared and caked, couldn't hide that fact.

For expediency's sake, the official records would show that she was a hooker. Then why am I not buying it? Dave wondered. Better yet, why does it matter?

He thought about the note in her pocket. A hoax, as Captain Herring maintained? Placed there by a wino as he suggested?

Herring was a good enough cop, Dave acknowledged. He was a large man, no fat or flab, all muscle, with shoulders like a wrester. Herring took pains to keep himself in good shape. In fact, at fifty-nine, he was in better shape than some of the guys in the department half his age. His bushy salt and pepper moustache was his pride and joy.

He'd stroked it, a sure sign of his impatience, when using departmental logic, the kind Dave had little or no tolerance for, he'd said, "Forget the note, Kincaid. It's stained with cheap wine, and it was written on a paper napkin. It was barely legible. Probably the work of an illiterate."

"Or someone who knew she was dying. You don't think there's a chance the girl wrote it?"

"No."

"Why?"

Herring gave him an exasperated glance. "Jesus, Kincaid, don't you have something important to do? The girl was barefoot, she wore no coat. It was below forty degrees out there. Whoever took her coat, shoes, stockings, and underpants left the note as some kind of sick joke. Why can't you accept that? That whole area is crawling with derelicts, some of them not too bright. She was a hooker, Kincaid. She overdosed herself with bad dope. It was an accidental death. Case closed."

"I'd like to follow it through, anyway."

"Forget it. We have other cases. The nut who's blasting collage kids in the face with a shotgun for one."

"But…"

"No buts. I said forget it. Some of them really are hookers, Kincaid. Most of them by choice."

"And some of them aren't," Dave remembered answering him.

He disappeared into the morgue's bathroom and emerged with a wet towel. He wiped the make-up from the girl's face. He stood back and looked at her. Why couldn't he accept the fact that she was a hooker? And why, when everyone else wanted to treat her death as an accident, was he trying to make something more of it?

The answer he suspected, lay in his past.

❧

Katie had been near death when someone unceremoniously dumped her at the emergency entrance of a New York City hospital. Her face was a patchwork quilt of bruises and cuts, and every rib was either broken or cracked.

She was seventeen. A New York City hooker. A cop's sister.

Katie had run away once before. Dave brought her back home that time. This time he just hadn't gone out of his way to look for her.

Now, eighteen months later, he was still blaming himself.

Katie was barely fifteen the first time she got herself pregnant. She came to Dave because she was afraid to go to their mother.

"There's this doctor…" she began.

"A quack," he shouted. "Jesus, Katie, I can get you a legal abortion if that's what you want."

"They'd tell mother." There were tears in her voice.

"I'll take care of it," he growled.

And he had.

Right after that she ran away. Dave found her and brought her back. She promised him she'd straighten up.

For almost two years she kept her promise. Then, a week before her seventeenth birthday, Dave found out that Katie was pregnant again, and that she was taking drugs. He threatened to turn her in if she didn't quit using, and he arranged for counseling. He also agreed not to tell his mother about her pregnancy, her subsequent abortion, and her drug addiction, though how in the hell she could overlook Katie's obvious symptoms was beyond him.

When he found out that Katie was skipping her counseling sessions, he laid down the law.

"Get it together, Katie. I can't, no make that I won't cover for you anymore. Not with mother, and not with the law. What's wrong with you anyway? You have everything a girl could want."

"Sure," she snorted. "But you're the one mother thinks is so special. Davie, my son the policeman. Davie, my son who sees things before they happen," she mimicked her mother.

"That's so untrue, it's sick. You're blowing mother's fantasy about my so called "gift" as out of proportion as she does. It's not much of an asset to "see" things I can't explain or prevent."

"Really? Well maybe you're right. After all, I'm the fuck-up in this family. That is what you see when you look at me, isn't it? A fuck-up?"

Dave slapped her. "I should have done that a long time ago. It might have done us both some good. I've been so busy resenting you all these years, it never occurred to me you felt the same way about me." Yet I should have known, he thought, angry at his oversight. None so blind as those who refuse to see, he conceded.

They held each other, and in that moment, all Dave could think about was that in spite of everything he loved Katie. It was a good and cleansing experience.

And a short-lived one.

He'd expected things to get better with Katie. When she took off just a few days later, he felt betrayed.

Six months later, the night before someone dumped her in front of aNew York hospital, Dave experienced an uneasiness that was now familiar to him. He dreamed about Katie that night. She was running through the woods. Someone was chasing her, throwing rocks at her back. Her flesh was bloodied. Her screams filled the air as she called out to him for help.

Before he could act on what he now knew was an omen, or a "vision" as his mother liked to call it, it was too late for Katie.

⌘

It was the night after they'd found the girl in the alley.

"I want to follow the "Jane Doe" case," Dave addressed Captain Herring again.

Herring barely looked up from his cluttered desk. "There is no case, Kincaid." "

Because you say so?"

Herring raised his head. He liked Dave Kincaid. He was that rare kind of cop whose instincts were as good as the man himself. At least they had been until his sister…It really was too bad about her. Worse still was what it had done to Kincaid himself. "There is no case because we're understaffed, under-funded, and overloaded. There is no case because it was an accidental overdose. And, yes, Kincaid, there is no case because I said so. You got a problem with that?"

Dave respected Herring's loyalty to the department, even if privately he thought it was excessive. Most of the time he even liked him. Today, he was having a hard time remembering that.

Herring came from behind his desk. There was sympathetic undertone that softened the harshness of his words. "Listen to me, Kincaid. You can't justify what happened to your sister through every dead or beaten hooker that passes through here."

"I don't think the Jane Doe was a hooker."

"Until something changes my mind, that's how the record will read."

Dave moved closer to him, his square-set jaw like hard steel, his eyes, more blue now than green, cold and unrelenting. "Tell me Captain, wasn't there ever a time that you wanted to follow your instincts instead of living by the book? Didn't you ever want to take that goddamn book and toss it out the window?"

Herring's expression hardened. Funny Dave should mention instincts when he was just thinking about his own. The pain of something he thought was buried in his sub- conscious came rushing back. There was that time, ten years ago. He hadn't listened to a voice from inside that clamored to be heard. Because he hadn't, two people died. No one had blamed him, and he'd quit trashing himself about the incident years ago. He'd made a wrong call, he'd justified. Cops, good and bad, made them all the time. He stared back at Dave. He wasn't happy with him for making him remember something he'd rather forget, nor was he about to tell Dave what was running through his mind.

"I can't okay it, Kincaid. However, if you want to follow it on our own time…"

Dave grabbed Herring's lead. "Thanks, Captain. I have three weeks' vacation coming."

"Fuck you, Kincaid. You know damn well that the only excuse for pulling instant vacation is death, yours in this case, or a family emergency."

Dave gave him a broad grin. "A family emergency, you say? Well, there's always Katie."

The captain was still yelling as Dave left the room, but behind Herring's exterior exasperation was a stirring from within. Dave was the kind of cop that he'd started out to be. Time and the rigors of the job had changed him. They would probably change Dave. Or maybe not, he considered, because Dave was different. He envied Dave his convictions. *If only I were twenty years younger,* he lamented.

⚬⚭⚬

Dave propped his feet up on the desk he shared with Brad, doing his best to block out the noise in the squad room. He studied the "Jane Doe" file. It was a slim one. Besides the medical examiner's report, there were a few brief notations. The hypodermic needle hadn't been tested for prints; no one had deemed it necessary. There was one notation made by the crime lab crew. Fresh scratches had been found on the trash dumpster that spelled out the letters BR. Of course anyone could have placed them there, but a nail file had been found by the girl's body. What if she had been murdered? If she had been, and if she'd scratched out the letters BR, what did they mean? Was she trying to name her killer?

Dave ran his fingers through his hair, thinking distractedly that he needed a haircut. Sandy strands dusted his collar. He was missing something. What was it? He had a sense that it was something so simple that when it came to him, he'd be angry that he hadn't gotten it sooner.

"Think, damn it," he said out loud.

All he got for his efforts was a giant headache.

⚬⚭⚬

"Are you out of your mind?" Brad Monroe exploded, causing questioning glances from other detectives in the squad room. He lowered his voice. "We don't need to invent cases, Dave! It's Katie, isn't it? Don't bother to deny it." A frown etched creases in his face. "Did it ever occur to you that I might get stuck with Prentiss while you're off playing private cop?"

Dave grinned. Sheila Prentiss was new to the squad. She filled in for sick or vacationing personnel. There were few men who relished the thought of a women for a partner in this crime-ridden city, and Brad's own opinion of women on the police force had nothing to do with fair play or equality.

Dave was spared an answer when Herring strode into the room. "You got a week, Kincaid. If you stay away any longer, I'll assume you're turning in your badge."

A week! It was more than Dave had dared to hope for. "Thanks, Captain."

"Don't thank me yet. I'm going to work your tail off when you report back for duty, and that's a goddamn promise." He started to walk away, then whirled around. "And you, Monroe. While Kincaid's gone, I'm assigning Prentiss to you."

Dave grimaced, anticipating Brad's reaction. He slapped his partner on the back. "Smile, Brad. Look on the bright side. Prentiss just might teach you some manners."

Dave left, a grin spreading across his face as his partner struggled with sputtered curses.

⌒⟁⟁⟁⌒

Dave was apprehensive as his car neared the apartment he shared with Laura Richards. Laura wouldn't understand his motives in the "Jane Doe" case anymore than Brad had.

Home was an apartment on the third floor of a modern six-story building located in the better part of town. Best of all, it was convenient to both their jobs.

Laura had taken a stereotypical apartment and made it special. "Very unlawyerlike," he'd teased her as she'd worked on it, taking a playful jab at her position on the D.A.'s staff. "It has warmth," he said, referring to the seascapes and country scenes that decorated the walls, and to the browns, yellows and oranges of the furniture and drapes that gave him a sense of well-being every time he came home.

It was one-fifteen a.m. Leaving Laura at night was the toughest part of pulling the graveyard shift.

She was in bed. He opened the door to their bedroom and stared down at her in the moonlight that filtered through the window. Her shoulder-length blonde hair caressed her pillow. Not beautiful in the sense that so many of the women in his life had been, she was for so many other reasons, the best thing that ever happened to him.

He remembered back to when they'd met three years ago. It hadn't been love at first sight. It had taken time. Months. She claimed to have known long before Dave had that what they had was worth building on. Or maybe he'd known, too, he thought, and been afraid to trust the feeling. She was so normal. So together. Everything he wasn't. He wasn't sure he deserved her back then.

He was even more unsure of that tonight in light of what he was about to tell her.

They had planned to be married. Then the incident with Katie had happened. It had been Laura's idea to wait. He could still hear her saying, "If we got married now, it wouldn't work. You're too full of guilt about something that wasn't your fault. I love you, Dave, but you have to learn to feel as good about yourself as I do."

They'd retrieved the down payment they'd placed on a house outside the city limits and taken this apartment in town instead. It was supposed to be a temporary move, but they were still here.

Dave flipped on the beside light.

Laura stirred, opened her eyes, and sat up. She glanced at the clock on the nightstand. "What's the matter?" Alarm crept into her voice.

Dave took off his jacket and carelessly dropped it on the floor. He loosened his tie. "Sorry to wake you, but I need to talk. I'll go put on some coffee."

Moments later she joined him in the kitchen, tying the sash to her silk tangerine- colored calf-length robe. He loved that color on her, and he loved this room the best of any in the apartment. Laura had given the room a country atmosphere by placing wooden plaques on the wall, some with raised straw figures so lifelike they seemed to leap off the wall. There were quaint wood-framed sayings like "Keep your hands off the cook's buns." It was the kitchen they'd planned to have in their home. Plan to have, he reminded himself.

He placed a steaming cup of coffee in front of her. "I took a leave. I had time coming."

Laura gave him a puzzled look. "Why didn't you tell me about it before? I could have tried to get time off."

Dave sighed. He'd known this wasn't going to be easy. "It's a working leave, Laura."

"Am I supposed to know what that means?"

"No. It's the "Jane Doe" we found the other night. I want to follow the case. The department doesn't. Herring gave me a week, but on my own time."

She frowned. "I thought it was an accidental overdose."

"Maybe it was. There's just something about the whole thing that doesn't feel right."

She took a sip of her coffee. She grimaced. "Now I know why I make the coffee. Working for the D.A has its advantages, Dave. If there'd been a case to follow, I'd have heard about it."

"I've listened to all the arguments against what I'm doing, Laura. They even make sense. It's something I have to do."

"It's Katie, isn't it?"

It was the second time in less than an hour he'd been accused of using his sister's tragedy as a catalyst for his actions. "I don't know. Maybe."

"Oh, come one, Dave. At least face up to your problem. It's time."

Dave rose. He pulled Laura to her feet. He placed his hand on her shoulder. She shook it off. "I need your help on this, Laura. I want to know that you're with me."

"I'm saying I'm not sure I am." Tears of frustration added to her sudden lack of composure. "God knows I've tried to understand what it is that makes you want to self- destruct. Truth is, I don't understand any of it."

He stared past her, unable to alleviate her distress. When he finally spoke, he said. "I'm not sure it really is Katie."

She moved toward the kitchen door. "Then find out what it is.I hope we can get past this new crisis, Dave, I really do." She cried

"So do I. I love you, Laura."

"And I love you. You can't know how many times a day I wish I didn't." She looked upward, brushing away tears that she resented. "I'm very tired. I have to be at work early in the morning. We'll talk later."

Dave finished his coffee alone. He went into the living room and flipped on the television, setting the volume very low. He sighed. It was going to be a long night. Not only was his body used to staying awake all night, but his mind was on full alert.

☙

An hour after Laura left for work, Brad brought the file on "Jane Doe" by Dave's apartment. Everything that was known about the girl was summed up on a few pages.

As he handed Dave the file, Brad said, "Herring told me to bring this to you. He thought you'd need it. I ought to punch your light out instead of playing errand boy. Prentiss! The son of a bitch gave me Prentiss!"

"I'll make it up to you, I promise," Dave said.

"You bet your ass, you will. Did you tell Laura about your knight in shining armor act?"

"Yeah."

"How did she take it?"

"She wasn't crazy about it. We barely spoke before she left this morning." Standing at the door of the apartment, Brad said, "Well, what did you expect, for Christ's sake?'

He slammed the door as he stormed out of the apartment.

Dave slumped back in the rocker/recliner. He ran his hand through his hair. Laura claimed he only did it when he was frustrated or worried.

Laura.

What had he expected from her?

He'd shut her out when she tried to help him after they found Katie. And now he was shutting her out again, even if it wasn't intentional. She had a right to be upset.

He thought back to when Katie had taken off that last time. Dave, tired of the ritual of bringing her back, only to have her screw up again, hadn't done more than file a missing person's report.

He remembered Greg Mahoney, head of that division, saying, "You want priority again, Dave?"

Dave shook his head. "No. Not this time. You've heard of bad seeds, Greg.

That's Katie's problem. I think it's time she found out how cruel the world can be when she's got no one to bail her out. My mother and I have been making it easy for her to fuck up. But thanks for the gesture."

They were words that later Dave wished he hadn't said.

"Speaking of your mother," Mahoney said. "How's she taking it?"

"My mother makes pain go away by pretending it isn't there. It's an art form she developed when my father died. She was a rock when my step-father died last year. But I've always known that underneath all that pretense is a vulnerable human being who bleeds inside. Katie hasn't helped by being a…hell, no sense in calling her names. But I have to admit something, Greg. This time I hope Katie stays gone. Maybe then, Ma can get on with her life."

And I can get on with mine, he'd thought.

How wrong can you be? He questioned now.

Then, they'd found her. No I.D., just like the "Jane Doe," but with one difference. She wasn't dead. Before she went into a coma, she'd uttered Dave's name and where to find him.

It was ten days before his wedding. Wallowing in his own guilt, Dave had almost been relieved when Laura postponed the wedding. She believed that in time he'd get over the tragedy of Katie.

Except he hadn't gotten over it.

And they hadn't gotten married.

Dave shook his head to clear it of painful memories.

He opened up the "Jane Doe" file once again. Had someone written her off, too? Why hadn't Missing Persons been able to place her? A call had gone out to the National computer bank.

He read the file over and over. He thought about the scratched letters, BR. What did they mean? Initials? Part of a name? He slapped the side of his chair. Why couldn't he figure it out? What was he missing? Why in the hell hadn't someone claimed her? Tomorrow, he'd make a tour of the downtown area. Flash her picture to prostitutes, pimps, known users, and informers.

Dave threw the file to the floor. There it was again. The nagging feeling there was something he was overlooking. He pounded his fist on the arm of the chair. Laura would be home soon. He didn't feel like facing her right now. She'd still be angry, and he had no reasonable defense for his actions. Hell, even he didn't understand his own actions.

Besides, he had to go see Katie.

Every time he came here, Dave asked himself why. It was depressing and futile.

Katie stared glassy-eyed beyond him, just as she always did.

The sound of soft-soled shoes and the swish of crisp white uniforms served to remind him that this was an institution, for all the attempt to create a home-like atmosphere.

"Damn it, Katie," he said, hating himself for the harshness in his voice, but unable to harness it. "I wish you'd snap out of it. There's a life to be lived out there. Yours and

mine. What is it about us that puts us at the beginning of two roads, the hard one and the easy one, and we always choose the hard one?"

He moved toward the large picture window, staring out at the manicured ground beyond. He thought about his life before Katie. He'd been fifteen when his mother married his stepfather, Ted Damont. Sixteen when she got pregnant with Katie. Dave already resented Ted for taking his father's place. Now there was going to be a new baby to take his. He'd resented Katie even before she was born. When she began to screw up, it seemed like poetic justice at first. That was before he began to worry about her. Then he'd met Laura, the only woman he'd ever asked to marry him. He didn't want to mess that up, so he hadn't gone after Katie when she ran away again. He'd messed everything up anyway. He and Laura never talked about marriage anymore.

He turned back to look at Katie. He took her hand in his. It was limp and unresponsive. Last he'd heard, the doctors were, at best, pessimistic. Chances are, Katie would live in her own private hell forever.

And so would he.

☙

Dave went back to the morgue.

Sid Carter made, what was for him, an attempt at a joke. "I've heard of people trying to get kicked upstairs, but down here! Tell me, are you after my job?" He nodded knowingly when Dave didn't respond. "She's still in number twelve."

Dave pulled out the drawer and lifted up the sheet. "Who in the hell are you?" He said. His words echoed in the cold chamber of death.

A shiver ran down his spine as he once again sensed that he should know her. He lowered the sheet and closed the drawer. Too many years on the force, and too many dead bodies, he thought. After a while, they all looked familiar.

He turned to leave. The chill he'd experienced a few seconds ago came back, but now it was more intense. His eyes were drawn to the closed drawer. It was if she was trying to reach out to him. To tell him something.

And then it hit him. BR! It couldn't be! It was too wild a coincidence!

18

Daveemailed the Sheriff's station in Briarwood. He paused several times before completing it and a longer pause before he actually sent it. It read:

"Have a dead girl in the morgue, possibly from your area. Eighteen to twenty.

Dark hair, hazel eyes, five-feet-seven. No distinguishing marks. Please advise if this fits a description of any girl who could be presumed missing in your area."

He added his precinct number and location. He knew he should have gone through channels, but what if he was wrong?

Now, all he had to do was wait for a reply and hope he was wrong about the girl's origins, because, if he was right, his life was about to take on complications he didn't even want to think about.

CHAPTER 2

The day after Dave sent the wire to Briarwood, Brad stopped by the apartment. Dave was on his way out, on his way to another depressing expedition to the downtown area.

Brad gently pushed him back inside. "You know, I'm really starting to feel like a messenger boy. Don't you believe in checking in?"

"I've been busy crawling in the gutters," Dave said. He scowled. "None of the pimps claim to have known the dead girl, but then getting anything out of them was a long shot. Even if one of them knew the girl, they wouldn't be likely to admit it now."

"Then I think I can make your day, my friend. There's news about your "Jane Doe." We received a call for you from the Sheriff's office in a town called Briarwood. They said they received an email from you.Of course, you wouldn't know anything about that, would you?"

"So, I sent an email. I had a hunch."

Brad's eyes narrowed. "It was more than a hunch, wasn't it Dave? Why didn't you let me in on what you were doing?"

"Because I could have been wrong. You said you had news."

"Okay, keep your secrets." Brad's tone held a trace of resentment. "What was it, Dave? Another one of those revelations your mother brags about?"

"Screw my mother and her fantasies, and damn her for running off at the mouth." Dave ran his fingers through his hair. "Sorry, Brad. It's just that I'm tired of hearing about what my mother calls "the power." You know what those so called visions are?

They're distortions. They're dreams I sometimes get before a tragedy happens. I had one the night before my father died. Because of my dream, I felt uneasy. I begged him not to go out that night. A few hours later he wrapped his car around a lamp post. He was killed instantly. They said he was drunk. For a long time I refused to believe that, but it was true." He shrugged. "No kid likes to face up to the fact that his father is an alcoholic, and I'd been avoiding that nasty little truth for a long time."

Dave sighed. "My mother heard about this psychic. She was into that kind of bullshit back then. She dragged me along with her when she went to see the old bitch. The woman was a candidate for Belleview in my opinion. If I close my eyes, I can still see her. She was ugly as sin itself, with long black hairs hanging from her chin, and a moustache that covered her entire upper lip. She convinced my mother that I "saw" things. The old hag said I had the power. All because of one lousy dream."

"That one dream isn't an isolated incident, is it, Dave?"

Dave hesitated for a second. "No. Over the years there have been others, nightmares really. But, like I said, they're distorted. If they really are signs of the future, I never learned to understand their significance until it was too late. The last time I had one of those dreams was right before Katie got hurt and a lot of good that did me or her."

"None lately, then?"

Dave smiled. "You're referring to the "Jane Doe." No, just an uneasiness." Dave slapped Brad on the shoulder. "You didn't come here to discuss my dreams. You came here with news about the girl."

Brad plopped himself down in a brown velvet swivel rocker. "A few hours after your wire arrived in Briarwood, a woman by the name of Margaret Gray walked into the

Sheriff's office to report her sister missing." Brad looked up at Dave. "The dead girl was named Ellen Gray. She was eighteen."

Dave felt sick, but not surprised. From the moment he'd made the decision to contact Briarwood he'd known that there was a possibility the girl came from there. "Any other relatives?" Dave held his breath. He had no idea if Trinity Gray still lived in Briarwood. She could even be dead.

Brad answered his question. "A mother and step-father living in Briarwood. And a boyfriend, the sister thinks."

"Why didn't her mother report her missing?" Dave asked. "And why did the sister just now come forward?"

"The sister was overseas. She's an embassy clerk. She just came back to the States. I don't know about the girl's mother. Margaret Gray will be here later today to officially identify her sister. There seems to be little doubt. We faxed a picture of the girl to Briarwood. Margaret Gray gave a tentative I.D. You want to be there when she comes in?"

Dave shook his head. "No. You take care of it."

Brad gave him a hard look. "You're planning on taking your investigation to Briarwood, aren't you?"

Dave tried to muster a smile. It didn't reach his eyes. "Now, who has visions?"

It wasn't until after Brad left that Dave faced the enormity of the task ahead, and the folly of going back to Briarwood.

⚭

Dave was sixteen that spring almost eighteen years ago. His mother was acting like a teen-ager in love for the first time, her belly swollen with her new husband's child.

There was no room in her life for Dave. At least, that's the way he saw it. He didn't feel welcome in his own house anymore, so he began thinking of reasons not to spend time there. He took a job after school delivering groceries for the only market Briarwood boasted. It not only occupied his time, but the extra money came in handy. Dave's father, Paul Kincaid, hadn't left much, just a small insurance policy, and Dave's new step-father barely made enough to cover the expenses.

Trinity Gray was a regular on his delivery route.

Mostly, she waved him into the kitchen and gave him a dollar tip. It was hard to remember later when the wave and passing glances turned into something special in his life, because it happened so gradually. It began with an offer of a soda, fresh-baked cookies, and then conversation. He loved their talks around her small wooden kitchen table. She talked to him like a man, not a boy, and he responded with fervor. She madehim feel like he counted for something. At first, he couldn't believe she would be interested in anything he had to say, but she really listened when he talked about his ambition to study law, and she sympathized when he expressed his frustrations with the changes at home. He came to depend on her as a sounding board for his feelings. It wasn'tuntil much too late that he realized while she was learning an awful lot about him, he was learning nothing about her.

As time passed, her dress subtly changed from Levis and casual print dresses, to shorts with sweaters or blouses that hugged her full breasts. He began to break out in a sweat every time he pulled up in her driveway on his delivery bicycle. His world narrowed because of her. He awakened each morning, sat through blurred days in school, he ate, he drank, and he slept, performing each function like a well-trained robot. He only came alive when he was with Trinity. He was in love with her long before he owned up to it.

He'd known Trinity ever since he could remember. Or known of her. She was like an exotic flower in the desert, and just as out of place. Briarwood was a small farming community. The women here for the most part, looked like farmer's wives. But then Sam Gray wasn't a farmer. He was what his mother called "a traveling man." He was a salesman.

Sam Gray had brought Trinity home with him after one of his sales trips. Dave was five years old at the time. Trinity was eighteen, twenty years Sam's junior. She earned herself a reputation that in later years, Dave realized she didn't deserve. It wasn't her fault that half the men in Briarwood lusted after her. It was a fact that not one of them could prove they'd come close to having her, contrary to a few drunken brags in the local tavern.

That warm spring day when she led him, without preamble to her bedroom and closed the door and pulled down the shades, he had no real inkling of what was about to happen to him, only overworked hormones, and a desire that this day end in sexual satisfaction. What followed was pure magic. In less than two hours, she all but spoiled him for any other woman.

She leaned forward and kissed him. Her tongue meshed with is. Dave felt as if she was sucking the very life from him, drawing out feelings he never knew were inside of him. If I die now, he'd thought, this moment will have been worth it.

She stepped backward, pulling him with her until they were within inches of the bed. She placed his hand on her breast, still encased by her blouse. His fingers strayed to the buttons. When she didn't stop him, he slowly undid them and slipped the blouse from her shoulders. She smiled and unhooked her bra. Dave stared at her full breasts.

Stupidly, he thought about Jennie Kramer. He and Jennie had almost gone all the way. Jennie's breasts were small, like tennis balls, the breasts of a girl. He swallowed. This wasn't Jennie. This was a woman. And not just any woman. This was Trinity Gray. And for some strange reason she seemed to want him, Dave Kincaid!

If this is one of my dreams, he thought at the time, then I never want to wake up.

Trinity removed her shorts and stood for what seemed like an eternity in just her bikini briefs. When he reached for her, she stayed his hand and slid her panties down her legs and gracefully stepped out of them. She slipped down onto the bed. She fondled her breasts, then trailed her fingers up and down her sex.

Dave's mouth was so dry he couldn't swallow. He could only stare.

She smiled "Take off your clothes, Davie. I want to look at you." When he started to turn around, "No, face me and look at me while you undress."

Afraid to speak for fear that his voice had raised a pitch or two, Dave obeyed, his fingers trembling. When he was naked, she pulled him down beside her. Dave experienced excruciating warmth that traveled the length of his body. His palms were wet from fear and desire, his sex erect. He stepped out of his shorts and, for the first time in his life, he worried about the size of his penis. Was it big enough? Oh God, if it wasn't, could he satisfy her? Please, he remembered praying, don't let me lose it before I'm inside of her.

She placed his hands on her breasts and then moved them downward. She reached for him. He shuddered. His eyes begged for release, but she continued to fondle him. When he thought he couldn't contain himself for a moment longer, she smiled and pulled him on top of her. Then he was inside of her. A moan, like that of a wounded animal, passed his lips as his juices filled her.

He rolled away from her, his body drenched with sweat.

He had barely caught his breath when she said, "That was good, Davie. Very good. Now lie there and let me teach you the pleasures of sex I imagine you've only talked about in whispers."

A sob escaped his throat as she took him into her mouth and caressed him with her tongue, stroking his testicles with her fingertips. He fought to keep control and, right before he lost it, her mouth left him.

Before he could react to those magical moments, she guided his head to the mound between her legs. The sensuous musky odor of their sex act still lingered. His groan turned into a low moan as he tasted her. She arched her back and spread herself so that no part of her was denied him. It was she who finally pulled him away and led him inside her once again.

Afterward, she said. "You've never had oral sex, before, have you, Davie?" "No," he whispered, terrified that she would accuse him of never having had any kind of sex before.

The affair lasted from spring till the end of summer. Sam traveled a lot. When it was safe to see her, Trinity would leave the red flag on her mailbox at half-mast. On the days and nights when he passed by and the flag was down, Dave was desolate. On those days, he would often go home, lock the door to his room, and masturbate to relieve the pressure.

Dave adored Trinity. He was obsessed by her. An A student, his grades dropped to a passing C. His friends seemed like children, so he avoided them. His mother, thank God, was so engrossed with her new husband and baby, she didn't notice the changes in him. Oh, she'd ask how he was doing every once in a while, but in a distracted way. She failed to see his inner turmoil.

Then, as quickly as the affair began, Trinity ended it. She did it without ceremony and with little in the way of explanation. "It's over, Davie," she said. "I can't see you anymore."

"You can't do that," he yelled. "I love you." He knew he sounded desperate.

She touched his cheek with her fingertips. He wanted to hold her hands there forever. "What we had was a precious wonderful moment out of time," she whispered. "We'd be reaching for the impossible, if we tried to make it more than that. Trust me, I'm right."

There was a sadness in her voice that gave him reason to hope. She didn't really want to end it!

"Please," he begged. "Don't send me away. I'll come less often. I won't ask anything of you. You don't even have to love me. Just don't send me away."

"I do love you, Davie. Don't you see? That's the point. That's why it has to stop."

Desperation drove him on. "It's the age difference, isn't it? It doesn't matter.

You're only thirteen years older than me. That's not so much."

The sadness that had been in her voice was now reflected in the smile she gave him. "Thirteen years can be a lifetime, and no woman likes to be reminded that she's older than her lover, Davie. Why don't we just say that I'm wiser than you are? Wise enough to know when something is over."

He'd called her. He'd begged. He'd pleaded, but to no avail. He thought briefly about suicide and how badly she'd feel if he were dead. When his step-father was transferred to the city, a month after she ended their affair, Dave barely protested. If the affair was really over, he didn't want to be in the same town as Trinity, to see her every day, to know he couldn't have her.

But he would never forget the black-haired, black-eyed woman, who made him a man and broke his heart. Until Laura came along, every woman in his life had been a poor imitation of Trinity. Trinity was the reason that when Ellen Gray had been tagged a mere "Jane Doe," something more than a need for justice nagged at his subconscious.

With few exceptions, like her hazel eyes, Ellen Gray was almost a mirror image of the woman he'd loved so blindly, so very long ago.

෴

Laura entered the apartment as Dave was zipping up his suitcase. She tossed her briefcase on a chair. "I saw Brad. He told me they identified the girl in the alley and how it happened. He also told me about your conversation with Captain Herring, or should I say confrontation?"

"Brad has a big mouth," Dave said. He thought back to his conversation with Herring earlier in the day.

"Since when," Herring had asked, "do you contact Sheriff's stations without checking with me first? Why in the hell, if you knew where this girl came from, didn't you tell me?"

"I didn't know. It was a feeling I had. I could have been wrong. There were the letters BR, remember?"

"Oh, yeah? Out of all the towns and cities, not only in this state, but in the whole goddamn country, you happen to get a feeling about Briarwood?"

"Right. It made sense. It's less than a hundred miles from here." "I'm not buying it."

Dave sighed. "I didn't think you would. All right. I was born in Briarwood. My family left there when I was sixteen. The girl reminded me of someone I knew."

"And based on that you contacted the Sheriff there?" Dave nodded.

"That's bullshit. Jesus, Kincaid, what am I going to do with you? I suppose you want to go to Briarwood?"

Dave nodded again.

"Ask me why I'm not surprised? Your week is almost up, Kincaid. Then I want you back here. You're running out of time, and I'm running out of patience. Do we understand each other?"

"Yes, sir. We do." "Good."

Laura brought him back to the present. "You might get away with telling Brad your fairytale about the girl being from Briarwood was just a hunch, but this is me, and I know better. You were raised in Briarwood. What's happening, Dave? What is it you're not telling me?"

Dave evaded her eyes. "Nothing. The girl reminded me of someone I knew in Briarwood. So I contacted them. I'm a trained professional. I'm trained to think.

Contacting Briarwood was good police work. So what's the big deal?"

"This someone? She must have been very special," Laura said, her voice tight with emotion.

Dave hated to lie to her. Now was a perfect time to tell Laura about Trinity. But he couldn't. He hadn't told anyone. Ever. "Not special," he said, "Just someone I knew."

Laura stared down at his suitcase. "You're going to Briarwood." It was more in the nature of a statement than a question.

Dave gripped the handle of his suitcase and lifted it. "Yeah." "Why? What do you hope to find there?"

"Answers. I didn't think Ellen Gray ended up in that alley of her own volition. I don't think she was a hooker, and I don't think she was a junkie."

"Not even when all the evidence points that way?" she asked quietly.

"I don't happen to share that opinion. But then," he added sharply, "I don't work for the D.A.'s office. I still believe people are innocent until proven guilty."

Laura flushed. "That's a cheap shot, Dave."

He rested his hand on her arm. "You're right, I'm sorry. I'm on edge. I shouldn't take it out on you."

Laura sighed. "I know you're on edge and that's what worries me. I don't know why you're so up-tight, but I think you do."

When he didn't respond, she said, "I want to be angry with you, Dave, and I'd like to stay angry. But I can't. I'm concerned. You came from Briarwood. You don't think that one simple fact is clouding your judgment where this girl is concerned?"

"No, because I thought she was murdered before I knew where she came from. I admit it's one hell of a coincidence that she's from my hometown, but that's all it is."

"I thought all you wanted was for the girl to have an identity," Laura said quietly. "Why not let the authorities in Briarwood take it from here?"

What she said made sense. Then she didn't know everything. She didn't know about Trinity. What was he supposed to say to her? He could imagine Laura's reaction if he said, "There's a possibility that Ellen Gray was my daughter?" Even thinking about it made him sick. How could he say the words out loud? "It's something I have to do, Laura. It's true, the girl has a name now. I want to know why she was in that alley, what kind of person she was, and why no one cared enough to report her missing until her sister showed up. There are others who should have cared. She has a mother, a step- father, and a boyfriend."

Laura bit down on her lip. Now was not the time to bring up Katie and his willingness to write her off before she'd gotten hurt. "There's nothing I can do to stop you from going, is there?" she asked.

He pulled Laura to him and tried to kiss her. She avoided his lips. She was stiff to his touch. He sighed. "I'll call you when I get settled."

"How long will you be gone?" Her tone was curt.

"Just until I get some answers, or until my week is up. I want to talk to people who knew the girl. Maybe if I know more about her, I can find out why she died in that alley."

Admit it, a voice from within shouted. You want to see Trinity Gray again.

⚭

Before Dave headed south to Briarwood, he made a stop downtown.

Loretta Kramer was sixteen and looked thirty. She'd been a prostitute for three years. Dave had unsuccessfully tried to help her by getting her decent jobs, and he'd been instrumental in placing her in a halfway house on one occasion, a private home another. Both times, she'd returned here to the streets and to prostitution.

She and Dave maintained an arm's length friendship. She often helped him out by keeping an ear to the ground for him. Once, she'd tipped him off about a small-time drug dealer who was trying to widen his horizons by dealing in guns. He knew that she helped him at great risk to herself, just as he knew she helped him as a way of saying thank you, even if his efforts on her behalf had failed.

When he pulled up to the curb, Loretta tossed back her long frizzed bleached hair.

She approached his car and leaned inside through the open window. "Slumming, Kincaid?" She laughed. "Or are you still trying to reform me?"

"Not a chance, kid. Two strikes and you're out." He reached inside his jacket and pulled out a picture of Ellen Gray he'd taken from her file. It was one of the pictures taken by the crime lab people. "Did you ever see this girl around here?"

She shook her head. "I don't think so. She don't look so healthy, Kincaid." "She's dead. An overdose. She may have been a hooker. New to the area."

Loretta shook her head more vehemently this time. "She didn't turn tricks in this neighborhood. We have an unwritten code down here. We look out for each other. Hell, if we depended on the cops or pimps, we'd all be dead. What makes you think she was a hooker?"

"I didn't say I did."

"You sure as hell implied it." "So you never saw her?"

"Never. You said she was new around here. How new?" "Two, three weeks."

"That's a long time down here, Kincaid. A lifetime for some. You want me to check around for you?"

Dave smiled. "Yeah. I'll see you're taken care of."

She stepped back from the car. "Okay. But do me a favor, Kincaid."
"What's that?"

"No more social work. Deal?"

Loretta was what she was, and she was doing exactly what she wanted to do. Once Dave had accepted that, he'd been able to live with the reality of it. He'd quit seeing Katie in her eyes a long time ago. "Deal. I'll be out of town for a while. If you get anything, contact Brad. He'll know where to reach me."

She leaned back inside the car. "This girl? Is she special?"

Dave shifted the car into gear. "They're all special, Loretta. Don't you know that?"

⣿⣿

Driving into Briarwood was like stepping back in time. Dave felt out of his place in his two-hundred-and fifty dollar dark blue suit, a Broadway sale special that Laura had bought him for Christmas. He loosened his tie and slipped out of his jacket. He had a sudden sense of well-being in spite of the tragedy that was bringing him here. Trees lined the streets, shrubbery and rose bushes bordered houses. He'd lived in a concrete world for so long Dave had forgotten how good it felt to breathe crisp clean air. He took a deep breath and exhaled. The air even smelled good.

A storekeeper sweeping the sidewalk waved as Dave drove by. Dave smiled. The guy didn't know him from Adam. A pleasantry like that could only happen in a small town like Briarwood, where a friendly gesture was a watchword, the norm rather than the exception, not like in the city where suspicion was an excuse for rudeness. What a cynic I've become, Dave couldn't help thinking.

Progress had been slow in reaching Briarwood. Downtown was only five blocks long. Dave recognized the same old buildings, though some of the names on the storefronts had changed over the years.

A familiar sign caught his attention.

Dave pulled up in front of "Ozzie's Ice Cream Parlor." It had been a popular hangout for Dave and his friends. He wondered if kids still came here.

In answer to his question, three youths and three young girls exited the building, laughing. The girls wore mini-skirts that barely covered their buttocks. The guys wore faded Levi's.

Dave felt old and tired. He wondered why he'd come back here. Ellen Gray meant nothing to him, even if it turned out she had been his daughter. Add to that the fact that the memories here were, at best, painful. You can still turn around and go back, a voice of reason persisted. No one will care.

Dave sighed and started up the engine. Since not much had changed, the Sheriff's office should still be at the end of the last block of buildings.

Even the faded brick structure that housed the only law enforcement in the immediate area brought back memories. Dave had spent the night in one of its four cells. He'd been charged with being drunk and disorderly at the age of sixteen. Like father, like son, a few malicious people had observed. It had been the night that Trinity Gray had told him she didn't want to see him again.

Dave entered the building through a faded wooded double door. A woman in her late fifties at the reception desk asked, "Can I help you?"

Dave noted the contrast of this woman and the woman who staffed the big city precincts. She reminded him of his mother.

Dave pulled out his badge. "Dave Kincaid. I'm not here in an official capacity, but I'd like to speak to the sheriff. I called him. He's expecting me."

She shook her head. "You came about Ellen. Poor little thing. The sheriff is fishing." She flashed him a wide smile. "He always goes fishing this time of year. Has done ever since I can remember."

"But I spoke to him!"

"Sorry. Nothing gets in the Sheriff's way when the trout are biting. He'll be back in a few days. You can see him then, or you can talk to Bill now."

Waiting was out of the question. His week was dwindling away. "Who's Bill?"

"Bill Lackland. He's one of the deputies. You want to see him?"

As if I have a choice, Dave thought. "Yes, of course, I'd like to speak to him."

A few moments later, a large man about Dave's age emerged from a room in the back. He extended his hand. "I'm Bill Lackland."

Over the years he'd put on fifty pounds and his hairline was receding, but Dave remembered Bill Lackland well. He'd been Briarwood High's best hope for a football championship against neighboring Greensville. A real super star. Dave also remembered that Bill had planned to capitalize on his athletic prowess to secure a college scholarship. Several talent scouts were already looking at him with interest when Dave and his family left Briarwood.

Dave took Bill's extended hand. "Dave Kincaid. I was born and raised in Briarwood. I doubt that you remember me, but I sure remember you. What happened to your ambitions to be a football star? You were one hell of a player as I recall."

Bill frowned. "That was a long time ago. I got hurt, and then it was all over for me. Stupid part was I didn't get hurt on the field. I got busted up in a fight. But that's ancient history. Sorry. Your name doesn't ring a bell. When did you leave Briarwood?"

"Almost eighteen years ago."

"It's been a long time. You're here about Ellen, of course. Nasty business.

Nobody around here knew Ellen was on drugs." "It was supposed to look like an overdose." "Supposed to?"

"She may have been murdered."

"Why would anyone want to kill Ellen?"

"That's what I came here to find out."

Bill scratched his head. "Tilda said you were here unofficial." Dave nodded.

"Mind telling me why?"

"My department tagged it as an accidental overdose. Have you ever been around big city law, Bill?" And when Bill shook his head, "It's not like Briarwood. For every hundred crimes, we have one cop. A lot of stuff gets shoved under the rug. This case was one of them."

"You have proof it wasn't an accident?"

"No. It could have been an accident. It may very well be that she left here, got connected, and really did overdose. Then again, she could have been murdered."

"I'd like to help," Bill said. "I dated Margaret Gray for a while. Ellen's death was hard on her, especially since she was the one who had to identify her. I liked Ellen. She was moody and standoffish, but she was a nice kid."

"She was moody and standoffish?"

"Well, moody anyway. She wasn't a joiner, if you know what I mean. But it could have been she was just shy. Margaret told me that Ellen was happiest when she was locked up in her room playing highbrow music."

Not exactly a description of a hooker, Dave thought, even as he silently acknowledged that prostitutes came in all shapes, sizes, and temperaments and many came from small towns like Briarwood. "I'd like to talk to her family. Her sister…" he barely hesitated. "And hermother. You have addresses?"

"Sure. You want me to take you there?"

Dave shook his head. "I have to get settled in a hotel first. Is there still only one?"

Bill smiled. "We're big time now. There's a new motel just outside of town. It's clean, modern, and not expensive. Just keep going for about a mile. You can't miss it.

You sure you don't want me to go with you to see Ellen's family?"

Seeing Trinity again was going to be difficult enough. Dave didn't want an audience. "Thanks, again. I'll call you if I need help."

He accepted the addresses from Bill. Margaret Gray was unmarried. Trinity, as he'd found out before he left the city, had remarried. She was now Trinity St. John.

Dave wondered what manner of man her second husband was and if he was able to satisfy her as her first husband never had been able to. Or maybe, he considered, no man ever had or could.

He felt a burning sensation deep in his gut. Coming back here was forcing him to face up to the fact that he had never really gotten over Trinity Gray.

CHAPTER 3

Margaret Gray lived alone in a small well-maintained house two blocks south of Briarwood's main thoroughfare. She answered Dave's knock on her door almost immediately.

Dave introduced himself, wondering if she had any recollection of him. "I came about your sister."

She motioned him inside. "Of course. Come in. Bill said I should be expecting you."

Eighteen years of living in the city had all but obliterated Dave's memory of the effectiveness of a small town grapevine. "I suppose everyone in Briarwood knows I'm here, and why?"

She attempted a smile and almost made it. "Probably. You were raised here. Are you really that surprised?"

Dave studied the woman and her surroundings. The living room was tastefully decorated in browns, beiges and pastels. It was pleasant, but it didn't look lived in.

Butthen, according to Brad, her job kept her away most of the time. She was beautiful in a strange, almost ethereal way, not earthy and seductive like her mother. This wasn't the Margaret Gray he remembered. She'd been nine years old the last time he'd seen her.

She'd worn braces on her teeth, and she'd been thin and painfully awkward. Did she remember him? Or was she just quoting Bill when she referred to his roots?

Margaret indicated a rose-beige couch. "Please. Sit down." And when he complied, she followed suit and placed herself in a matching swivel chair.

"You think Ellen was murdered," she said.

It was more forthright than Lackland's approach. "I think it's a possibility," he answered. "But only that."

"I remember you," she said, answering his earlier silent query. "You delivered groceries to my house." She tilted her head to one side. "You look exactly like I imagined you'd look after eighteen years."

What else did she remember? He wondered. Trinity had been very careful to keep her distance when her nine-year-old daughter was around. Had Margaret seen something to suggest her mother was sleeping with him in spite of Trinity's precautions? Or guessed, with the intuitiveness of an inquisitive child?

He was being paranoid, and he knew it. "I liked your mother." This time the smile reached her eyes. "You weren't alone."

Don't pursue it, a voice inside him warned. You came here for a purpose. Don't get sidetracked. "Tell me about Ellen."

"What do you want to know?"

"Everything. Her friends. Men in her life. What kind of person she was."

Margaret got up and stood by the bay window. She parted the curtain an inch and looked out. "These last few years, my job has kept me away a great deal, and there were a lot of years between Ellen and me. Ten to be exact, but nonetheless we managed to stay close. She was brilliant. She sailed through school with straight A's. She was blessed with a photographic memory. I always thought she'd go to college. You know, one of those big ones. Instead, she went straight from high school to working at the bank. Such a waste. Ellen said she wanted to wait for college, to get a feel for the real world first. That's why I was surprised when she stayed in Briarwood. This is hardly the real world."

Dave could attest to and sympathize with that after spending half his life in the city.

You asked me what kind of person Ellen was," Margaret went on. "How can you sum a person's life in a few sentences?" She smiled. "When I think of Ellen I think about Faust. She loved opera music. I guess you could say she was highbrow."

"Who were her friends?"

"That's a tough one. Ellen was a loner. She didn't make friends easily.

AmySpring is probably her best friend. They both work at the bank."

She paled. "I keep doing that. Talking about Ellen as if she's still alive. I can't believe she's really dead. I identified her body and yet I still can't believe it."

This was the part of his job that Dave hated most, dealing with bereaved relatives.

He'd never felt comfortable doing it.

Margaret moved away from the window. "I keep asking myself why she left here so suddenly. I don't get any answers." The muscles in her face tightened. "I only know that Ellen wouldn't have left town without telling me she was going unless someone wouldn't let her. We stayed in touch even when I was out of the country. I have outrageous phone bills to prove it." She clenched her fist. " I know, as sure as I know the sun will rise tomorrow, that Ellen didn't take drugs or sell her body."

"You seem real sure of that." "I am."

"My partner said you mentioned a boyfriend."

"I did, but I don't know who he is."

"You said you and Ellen were close. She didn't discuss her boyfriend with you?" Margaret flushed. "Am I being chastised? Or are you calling me a liar?" "Neither. Just trying to get some answers."

"All right. Ellen went out with Chris Briggs for a long time. They broke up. Her idea, not Chris's. He adores…I mean he adored her. Recently, she was seeing someone she didn't want to talk about. Not even to me. All I know is that he's married."

"She told you that?" "In so many words."

"You think this guy is local?"

She nodded. "You might ask Chris about it. They had a big blow-up when Ellen broke it off between them. I think it had something to do with this other man."

"I'll talk to him. If you think of anything else, call me. I'm staying at the motel outside of town."

Margaret walked with him to the front door. He was halfway down the front steps when he turned and said. "I'm curious. Why didn't your mother report Ellen missing?"

"That," Margaret said, "is something you'll have to ask her."

Dave walked to the curb and slid onto the front seat of his car. He looked back at the house. Margaret was at the window, watching him through parted curtains. He waved. She abruptly closed the curtains.

Dave had no idea what the relationship between Ellen and her mother had been.

One thing was sure, there seemed to be little love lost between Trinity and her oldest daughter.

☙

Acting on impulse, Dave drove in a direction that would take him by the house Trinity used to live in. He'd intended to just pass by the place, until he spotted a "FOR SALE" sign out in front of the house.

He pulled over to the curb across the street from the house.

40

The house was in need of repairs. The lawn was overgrown. The hedges that separated it from its neighbors, the same ones that had made it easy for Dave to slip in and out of the house all those years ago, were ragged.

It looked abandoned.

Dave got out of his car. He leaned up against the vehicle, staring over at the house. Emotions he'd thought he'd conquered came rushing back in a wave. His eyes were drawn to the weather-beaten mailbox. The flag was down. He thought about the nights he'd paced his room because it was down. It seemed like only yesterday. A gut wrenching groan escaped his lips. It had been a mistake to come back here.

A car drove up and parked behind his. He quickly composed himself. Damn it! In a town this size, soon everyone would know he'd been here. I have a right to be here, he rationalized. I'm a cop. Ellen Gray used to live here. What could be more reasonable than for me to want to see the house she was raised in?

A plump woman in her forties emerged from the other car. She extended her hand. "Hi there. You're new in town, aren't you? My name is Dorothy Bussman. I'm the realtor for this house. Would you like to look at it?"

Dave glanced back at the house. The for sale sign proclaimed: "OFFERED BY BUSSMAN REALTY."

She's a real estate agent! Not some nosy passerby! He breathed a sigh of relief. He took her extended hand. "Thank you. I'm not a buyer." He showed her his badge. "I'm here because of what happened to Ellen Gray."

"That was a terrible thing," she said. "Rumor has it she was murdered."

Dave wondered who in the hell was spreading that rumor. It could only be Bill Lackland, Margaret Gray, or Tilda, the Sheriff's receptionist. He opted for Tilda.

"That's all it is, Ma'am. A rumor."

"Would you like to see the house, anyway?" she asked hopefully.

It was an offer he couldn't refuse. "Strictly from a cop's perspective, yes, I would. I don't suppose you could just open it up and let me browse around the place by myself?"

It was obvious she'd hoped to stay and gossip. She sighed. "Of course. Just be sure to lock it up after you."

Dave waited while she opened up the front door. "Which one was Ellen's room?" he asked.

"The one in the rear. She shared it with her sister until Margaret left home. What are you looking for in her room?"

"Nothing special. Just curious."

She reluctantly turned to leave. "There's nothing left in Ellen's room," she offered. "Ellen hadn't lived here for a year. When her mother married Steven St. John, they moved to the farm. I rented the house for Trinity for a while. Transients," she said with disgust. "Look what they did to the place. So Trinity decided to sell it. You sure you're not in the market?" She added hopefully. "It would be a good investment. Trinity would take just about any decent offer right about now."

"No, thanks. I'll be sure to lock the house," he said, anxious to get rid of her.

After the woman left, Dave slowly wandered through the dwelling. His footsteps echoed on the dirty wooden floors. The walls needed paint. Cobwebs hung from the ceilings. He stood in the room Ellen had once occupied. There were no vibrations, no feelings, only silent emptiness.

It was a different story when he entered the master bedroom. This was where he'd learned how to satisfy a woman, and where he himself had been satisfied. He closed his eyes. The image of him and Trinity locked in each other's arms was a vivid one. He could almost feel her hands on him. The pain of remembering was intense.

It hadn't been just about sex, he remembered. Sometimes, they'd just lain naked in the bed and talked and laughed. She was ticklish. Dave had often driven her to near hysteria when he'd gently squeezed her sides until she begged for mercy.

Funny, the things you remembered.

He placed his hand over his ears to drown out the sound of Trinity's laughter.

He fled the room and stood on the threshold of the kitchen. More memories. The imagined smell of freshly baked cookies assailed his nostrils.

I have to get out of here, he thought.

He obeyed the warning voice from within and strode briskly to his car. He sucked in his breath and filled his lungs with air.

On the drive to Trinity's new home, Dave made a half-hearted attempt to concentrate on the landscape. Trinity lived on the extreme outer limits of Briarwood

now. Dave passed lush green fields that dotted the countryside. It was peaceful and uncluttered. You could go as much as a quarter of a mile between homes and farms.

The St. John home was easy to spot. It was an impressive white two-story colonial-style dwelling. It was a far cry from the house he'd just left. Horses, thoroughbreds, Dave guessed, occupied well-maintained corrals that lined the driveway leading to the house.

In a town like Briarwood, this was real opulence. It was more like a dude ranch than a farm. The only kind of farming done here was the gentlemanly kind.

Dave slipped on his jacket and knotted his tied before he got out of his car. He patted down his hair. Annoyed at his action, Dave thought, you're like a kid on your first date. But then he felt like one. Silly, he cautioned himself. It's been eighteen years.

She's forty-eight. She's not the woman you remembered.

The front door opened before he could ring the bell. Dave held his breath. He'd been preparing himself for this moment for years, just in case their paths ever crossed. Yet, he wasn't at all prepared, he realized, because time had only enhanced her beauty, not detracted from it. She looked wonderful. Her hair, worn long the last time he'd seen her, was cut short. Dark curls framed her still lovely face. She was slim. Her dark eyes sparkled. She wore a long black sheath with a mandarin neckline. That modest touch was offset by the fact that the dress featured huge slits at both sides that almost reached her thighs. She still had great legs.

He was momentarily struck mute.

Trinity smiled. The years rolled away. He felt sixteen again. "Sorry if I startled you," she said. "I saw your car drive up. Margaret told me you were coming."

Briarwood had an effective grapevine, Dave had to admit. He was angry at himself for his reaction to her. What right did she have to look like this? To place him off guard? He made a supreme effort to gain control. After all, he told himself, this is a possible murder investigation, and you're the man in charge. Act like one.

"You look terrific," he told her. "Nice place you've got here. I'm sorry we had to meet again under these circumstances."

That's better, he told himself. You sound pleasant but authoritative.

Her voice was still as husky and as inviting as he remembered, but now it was laced with sorrow. "So am I. Please. Won't you come in?"

He followed her to a huge room with wooden vaulted ceilings. The walls were rough cedar, the floors red brick tile covered here and there with scattered throw rugs. A huge stone fireplace dominated the far wall, a wet bar another. There was a pool table, a ping pong table, a pin ball machine, a soccer game and a juke box. And, almost intrusive in the room, was a ten-foot long mahogany and leather couch.

Trinity took note of his frown. "We call it the playroom. Appropriate don't you think?" She moved behind the bar. "What can I get you, Davie?"

Only two people had ever called him Davie. His mother, and Trinity. "It's Dave."

She raised an eyebrow. "I see. I stand corrected. Does that mean you don't want a drink?"

You're on duty, he reminded himself. Even if it is unofficial. But he needed a drink. God, how he needed a drink. He sat in one of the backless wooden bar stools. "Scotch on the rocks."

She smiled. "A change from coke and cookies," she said, evoking memories of she and Dave around her kitchen table eighteen years ago. She mixed his drink and passed it to him and then poured herself a glass of wine.

Dave took a swallow of his drink. "Where's your husband?" "Away on business."

"What does he do?"

She leaned her elbows on the bar top. "He's a consultant for a large corporation.

You already know that, don't you? You didn't come here uniformed. You're a cop. Probably a good one."

Dave downed his drink. "Right on all counts. I do know what your husband does, and I am a good cop. A damn good one. So, let's cut the crap. I'm here about Ellen, and not just because she's dead. I've got to know. Is there a chance that Ellen was my daughter?"

Trinity's tanned skin turned almost grey. "I knew you'd think that, but I hoped you wouldn't ask the question. Of course, she wasn't yours. My God, Davie, you were only sixteen. I was almost thirty. Do you think I'd have let that happen? I wore a diaphragm when I was with you. No exceptions. No mistakes."

"She was born six-and-a-half months after I left here. I checked."

" I had a husband, Davie. I slept with him every time he came home. What did you think? That I only made love with you? With Sam I wasn't always so careful.

Before Ellen, and after Margaret, I had three miscarriages. Ellen was Sam's daughter. Believe it, Davie, because that's the truth."

"Why didn't you tell me about the miscarriages before?"

"Because we never talked."

"We did! We talked all the time." "No, Davie, you talked and I listened."

He thought back to the days when they'd sat at her kitchen table and talked, sometimes for hours. How selfish he'd been. They'd discussed his problems, never hers. He looked into her eyes, seeking the truth about Ellen, hoping to catch her in a lie. He found only pain reflected there.

"Then she wasn't mine?" "No."

He searched his heart for his own feelings. He confessed that a part of him had wanted Ellen to be his and Trinity's child. It would have given them a link from the past to the present. He admitted it was better this way. Now he could investigate Ellen's death without emotional attachment. Even that wasn't realistic. She'd still been Trinity's daughter. "I loved you so much." The words were unwittingly wrenched from him.

Tears filled her eyes. For him or for Ellen, he wondered. She started to place a hand on his cheek and pulled it back. "I know."

Dave was disgusted with his outburst. "I'm sorry," he said. "I swore I wasn't going to do that. Can I have another drink?"

She seemed relieved to have something useful to do. "Of course."

After she poured them a drink, Dave said. "I'm sorry about Ellen. It must have been an awful shock."

She wiped the moisture from her eyes with a Kleenex. "It was, and you're making it worse. Why are you making it sound like she was murdered?"

The grapevine was still working. "Because it's possible. Like I told you, I'm a good cop. I've got a better question. Why didn't you report her missing?"

"Because she just didn't disappear. She came to me the night she left. She said she had to leave Briarwood. It was Margaret who insisted on reporting her missing, even after I told her that I talked to Ellen the night she left here."

"I guess I'm with Margaret on this one," Dave said. "Ellen told you she had to leave, with the emphasis on had. Your word, not mine. You didn't want to know why?" His tone was incredulous.

"Leave it be, Davie. Go back to the big city and leave us alone. You're making a case where there is none." She stared at her empty glass. Instead of reaching for the wine bottle, she poured herself a straight bourbon. She swallowed it in one gulp. She poured another. Dave caught her hand as she raised the glass to her lips. Amber liquid spilled on the mahogany counter.

"Just what in the hell is it you're hiding?" he accused. "Hiding?"

"Yes, hiding. Your daughter takes off, ends up in a filthy alley shot up with heroin in a neighborhood full of hookers, dressed like a hooker, made up like a hooker, and you're trying to act as if she was run over by a truck!"

Trinity's hand trembled. She rescued her drink and swallowed it. "Damn you, Davie. She's dead. What difference does it make now, how or why? It won't bring her back."

Dave grabbed her arm. "It makes a lot of difference. There's a file back in the city that says Ellen Gray, eighteen, Caucasian, was a hooker and a drug addict. It's not a nice epitaph." He jerked his hand from her arm. "And for Christ's sake, quit calling me Davie."

Trinity shuddered. "All right. You win. Ellen was frightened when she left here." "Of what?"

Trinity shook her head. "I don't know. She wouldn't say."

"And when you didn't hear from her, it never occurred to you that she might be in trouble?" He clenched his fist and waved it in her face. "You should have reported her missing. Why didn't you?"

She suddenly looked her age. "Because, damn you, if Ellen really was murdered, it's possible that someone from Briarwood was responsible for her death."

Her words hung in the air. Dave sucked in his breath. He'd come here to find out who Ellen Gray was, and what had led her to that alley and her death. He hadn't expected to be looking for her killer here.

He placed his hand over Trinity's. The contact caused shock waves to run through him. "I'll find whoever killed her, if indeed someone did. I promise you that, no matter where he came from."

She abruptly removed her hand. "It would be better for everyone if you didn't.

You could end up hurting a lot of people. I meant it when I said you should leave. There are people in the city who need you. By the way, I'm sorry about Katie. How is she?"

"You know about Katie! How? The gossip machine in Briarwood is good, I grant you, but it's impossible that you could know about my sister."

"When you left here you didn't look back, which is as it should have been. I didn't have that luxury. I cared about you, about what happened to you. In a way, I felt responsible for you. I made a point of knowing about your life."

"Why?" He was incredulous. "How? Who have you been talking to? My mother?"

"It doesn't matter who. It doesn't even matter why, anymore. I am sorry about law school. I know how much that meant to you."

He was still shaken by the fact that she'd kept tabs on him. "There wasn't enough money," he said absently.

A sad smile touched her lips. "Oh, Davie. My sweet Davie. Where were you six years ago when I needed you? Where were you when Sam died?"

His heartbeat faster. She cared about him. She'd said so. It changed everything. Then again, he thought, it changes nothing. "Six years ago, I was still looking for you in every woman I ever met. That was your legacy to me. Besides, you seem to have landed on your feet with St. John. This is hardly tenement living."

Dave's mind wandered. If Trinity knew about Katie, she must know about Laura. He tried to conjure up Laura's image. If ever he needed her, he needed her now. Today, here with Trinity, he knew she was still his weakness. Only Laura could shield him from that weakness with her goodness and her stability.

He came to with a start. Trinity was staring at him. "Are you okay?" "I'm fine."

"I'm sorry. You're still bitter, aren't you?" "No. I'm indifferent," he lied defensively.

The look on her face told him she didn't believe him.

He wanted to take her in his arms. He wanted to turn back the clock so they could have a second chance. He wanted to be sixteen again.

You can't go back, a voice inside him said. And if you could, would you really want to?

He left her without saying another word.

Re-living his encounter with Trinity, moment by moment, on the drive back to his motel, it occurred to Dave that Trinity had very deftly turned the conversation away from Ellen by making him think about the two of them. It had certainly worked. It also occurred to him that Trinity Gray knew a hell of a lot more about Ellen's tragic death than she was telling.

⚬₥₥⚬

When he arrived at the motel, the desk clerk handed him a message. It was from Captain Herring.

Dave reached him at the precinct, glad of the diversion. "What's up, Captain?" He asked. "You promised me a week."

"Forget that," Herring answered. "Loretta Kramer tried to call Brad. He wasn't in, so she asked for me, said she had important information for you. She came up with a wino who was in the alley the night the Gray girl died. The wino claims a man dumped her there. She also claims to have seen him stick a needle in the girl's arm."

Dave heard Herring's heavy sigh. He pictured him stroking his moustache. "We're going to open up the file," Herring said. "You're on official business now. You finding anything?"

"I think so. The girl's mother thinks that someone from Briarwood may have killed her. That means Ellen Gray was followed when she left here, maybe stalked. I need time here, Captain. Any problems with that?"

"You've got it. At least, for now. Do you need Brad?"

"No, not yet anyway. There's a local lawman I can use. I knew him in high school. He knows the territory, and the people. What about the wino?"

"She won't talk to anyone but you. You're going to have to come back here to talk to her. You can be back in Briarwood late tomorrow night or early the next morning."

"I'll leave right away. And Captain?" "What?"

"Thanks."

Herring's voice was gruff. "For what? I can't ignore eye-witness testimony.

We've got a murder on our hands."

Dave knew that Herring could have washed the case. The word of a wino could easily be discounted and ignored.

Dave called the desk clerk and told him he'd be gone for a day, but not to give up his room.

He knew that by morning everyone in Briarwood would know he was going back to the city for the day.

CHAPTER 4

Her name was Wilma. She was fifty, maybe fifty-five. She no longer remembered or cared.

She and Dave met on her terms and at a place she designated. Her clothes were old and torn, her gray hair laced with a few stray brown wisps, remnants of her youth. Her teeth were yellowed and uneven with huge gaps in the back. Her brown eyes were dull, surrounded by red, bloodied streaks, battle lines placed there by a war with alcohol she couldn't, or wouldn't, overcome.

They were in a downtown diner. The food was hot, which was the best that could be said of it. The place reeked of grease. None of this bothered Wilma as she gulped down a plate of unappetizing-looking meat, potatoes, and gravy.

"You sure you're not hungry?" she asked Dave, her mouth disgustingly full.

Dave swallowed his distaste. What brought a woman to this? What brought any of them to this for that matter? "How long have you been on the streets?" He asked her.

"Don't rightly know. After my Alf died, I lost track of time. And everything else," she added without a trace of self-pity. "It ain't so bad. Most nights I get a bed, and a bowl of soup." She smiled. "And I get turkey at Thanksgiving and Christmas."

"Don't you have a family?"

"Not no more. I lost my boy, Ernie, in Vietnam. I got a sister, but I ain't seen her in…well, in a lot of years." She lifted her fork to her mouth. Gravy dripped back onto the plate. "You sure you don't want none?"

"Perfectly sure. Now tell me what you saw in that alley." "Alley?"

Please, Dave thought. Don't let her be a head case. I know Ellen Gray was murdered. I feel it in my bones. I need for Wilma to be a real witness. A credible witness, if only to me.

Patience, he thought. Go slowly. "The alley, Wilma? Where the girl was found dead almost a week ago."

A smile lit up Wilma's face. "She was a pretty one. So young." She stared woefully at her now empty plate.

Dave signaled a waitress. "Give her more of whatever she wants." "Whatever I want?" Wilma asked.

"Anything."

She licked her lips. "I been looking real hard at that chocolate pie." "Chocolate pie for the lady," Dave ordered. And, as the waitress walked away,

"Go on. You were saying that she was real pretty."

Tears welled up in the woman's eyes. "She was scratching something out on the trash can. She was dying. I could tell. There weren't nothing I could do except what she asked me to."

"Which was what?" Dave prompted.

"She asked me not to let anyone think that she did herself in." "So why didn't you?"

Wilma's tone was indignant. "I did. I wrote a note." She gave Dave a canny smile. "I figured the cops would think she wrote it, telling them she was done in by that man, so to speak."

"Why not just call the police?"

"Because." The chocolate pie arrived. Wilma helped herself to a large spoonful. "I don't like cops. The only reason I said I'd talk to you was because Loretta said you were okay. Ya see, I took her shoes, stockings, and her coat. Even her underwear. She was dead when I took them," she said defensively. "The poor thing had no use for them no more. The cops, they'd have run me in for stealing. It ain't stealing," she said, defiance in her voice, "when you take what don't have no owner no more."

"You said you saw a man there with her. Can you tell me anything about him?" Wilma scooped the last of the pie into her mouth. She leaned back in her seat.

"Lord, I ain't had a meal like that in a long time." "The man?" Dave urged.

"It was dark, ya see. And it was cold. God bless that poor little thing and her coat. Wilma fingered a garment, a wool coat, that was carelessly slung across the back of her chair. It was a dirty shade of tan, stained and torn in one spot. It now looked as used up and discarded as the woman herself. "It was a man. Just a man."

"Come on, Wilma. Help me. I want to see that whoever hurt her gets punished.

Think. Was he tall, young, old, what?" "I told you, it was dark."

"Was he in a car?"

She brightened. "Yeah. He was in a car. After he stuck the needle in her arm, he drove off in it."

"What kind of car?"

She yawned. "I'm too tired to think. Anyway, I don't know one car from another. They all look the same to me. It was a big one, not one of those little foreign jobs is all I can tell you."

"Had you been drinking?"

She sniffed, then wiped her nose on her sleeve. "It was a cold night. Until I had her coat, my bottle was all I had to keep me warm. What would you know about that?"

"I'd know," he snapped. "My father was a…" Jesus! He'd almost said his father was a lush! But he was, wasn't he? And Wilma was right? What right did he have to condemn? What did he really know about alcohol addiction? Hadn't he, like his mother, ignored his father's dependency on booze? Maybe if they hadn't, he'd still be alive. He took a deep breath and let it out slowly. "Were you drunk that night, Wilma?"

"No more than a half a bottle of cheap wine will get you. You saying I imagined all this? You saying you don't believe me?"

She started to raise herself out of her chair. Dave placed a restraining hand on her shoulder. "Sit down. God knows I want to believe you," he said.

"You won't tell on me for taking her things?"

"No. You didn't mention a purse, Wilma. There had to be a purse."

She shook her head so hard, her hair flew across her face. "No purse. I didn't steal no purse."

"If there was no purse, where did the nail file come from?" A blank look passed across Wilma's face.

Why was there no purse? Dave wondered. He believed Wilma when she said there hadn't been one. He moved behind Wilma's chair and checked the inside lining of the coat. No label there either. There'd also been no label on the dress Ellen wore.

Someone hadn't wanted Ellen Gray to be easily identified.

Dave helped Wilma up out of her chair. "Come on. I'll take you to a downtown hotel a friend of mine runs. I'll pay for a month's rent and see that you get three meals a day. I want you to use that time to get on your feet, Wilma. Will you promise me that you'll try to do that?"

She nodded. A tear slid down here cheek. "No one's cared nothing about me for a long time. I'll try."

Dave sighed. Like Loretta, she'd probably be right back where she started the moment he turned his back.

As he helped her into his car, Dave looked skyward. "It's time I won one, Lord.

We could start with Wilma."

Dave climbed into the car beside his passenger. He smiled. Brad always teased him about asking favors from the Almighty. "You're in the wrong profession to get your wish, Kincaid."

But as Dave so often liked to remind Brad, there was always a first time.

⬭⬤⬭

There was still time to drive back to Briarwood, but Dave decided against it.

First, he wanted to talk to Brad, and then he wanted to see Laura. She always gave him a sense of normalcy in a world that was constantly upside down, and he needed her more than ever, now that he'd seen Trinity again.

Brad greeted him warmly. He glanced around the squad room. "Prentiss is off powdering her nose. I hope you're back to stay, old Buddy."

Dave shook his head. "I just came from talking to Wilma, Loretta's wino friend.

She was half-blotto that night, but I believe she saw enough to establish Ellen Gray's death was murder." He shrugged. "Of course, in court, a smart defense attorney will tear her to shreds. That's why we have to build a case that's strong enough without her."

"We?"

"Yeah, we. I have to go back to Briarwood. I believe the reason for Ellen Gray's murder started there, and that someone from Briarwood either killed her or was behind it. I want to know where she stayed when she came here. She didn't just disappear into thin air until the night she was killed. Check the hotels and rooming houses. I need a path to follow."

"Just like that! Christ, do you know how many hotels and rooming houses there are in this city?"

"Plenty. Get Prentiss to help you." "Have you cleared this with Herring?"

Dave nodded. "I just did. Cheer up. He offered to let me take you back to Briarwood with me. I did you a favor. It's not your kind of town, Brad."

"And Prentiss," Brad yelled after him, "is not my kind of partner."

Dave passed Shirley Prentiss on his way out of the building. She was twenty- four. She was tall, with short dark wavy hair that had a healthy sheen to it that matched the shine in her eyes. She was still eager. Dave envied her that trait. How long since the shine in his own eyes had turned to cynicism? She was pretty, even in the no-nonsense black uniform she wore. She'd be a knockout in civies, no doubt. "How's it going?" he asked her.

"Not so bad," she answered. "Brad puts on a good front, but behind all that he- man stuff is a good cop and a confused and troubled little boy."

Dave raised his eyebrows. "Are we talking about the same Brad Monroe?"

She laughed. "Yes, but if you tell him I had anything nice to say about him, I'll deny it. Seriously, Brad misses you. He told me you've been friends almost from the first moment you teamed up together two years ago."

Interestingly, it seemed like she and Brad had discussed more than just police procedure. Not bad for a guy who claimed to want to get her off his back and off his beat.

Dave was still smiling to himself when he let himself into his apartment.

⚶

Laura arrived home thirty minutes after Dave. He found himself comparing her to Trinity and realized that the beauty of his relationship with Laura was that there was no comparison. In fact, she'd been the first woman in his life who hadn't borne some resemblance to Trinity.

She was twenty-seven, the same age as Margaret Gray. When he'd met her the furthest thing from his mind was a lengthy relationship. He was in awe of her. She knew exactly what she was going to do with her life. No woman he'd met before ever had.

Unlike himself, Laura had led a normal, almost privileged childhood. The youngest of five children, she came from a loving, caring family. It gave them little in common. Somehow, what they'd felt for each other had transcended the differences in their backgrounds and their outlooks.

Their informal lunches had led to intimate dinners, and then, finally, after more than a month, they'd made love. It was a new record for Dave. He usually slept with a girl before their second date. Then everything about his being with Laura in the first place was something of a miracle. For one thing, she'd broken the chain of endless Trinity Gray imitations.

Today, Laura was wary. "You should have told me you were coming back. Are you here to stay?"

"No. In fact I should be on my way back to Briarwood, but I wanted to see you.

To be with you. I've missed you."

"It's only been two days, Dave."

It seemed like forever, like another lifetime. "You don't mind if I stay?"

"Don't be silly. I'll start dinner. What would you like? I can defrost a couple of steaks."

He grabbed her arm as she started for the kitchen. "I'm not hungry." He pulled her to him. For a few brief seconds she resisted, then she gave in to him.

"I've missed you, too, you jerk," she said.

Dave led her to the bedroom. He slid the blouse from her shoulders and unzipped her skirt. She reached behind her and helped him with her bra and slipped out of her panties. She helped him out of his shirt and pants. They fell naked onto the bed.

He kissed her lips, her chin, her shoulders, lingering at her breasts, taking each hardened nipple into his mouth. She squirmed beneath him. He placed her hands on him. She gently fondled his inner thigh. He longed to direct her lips between his legs, but Laura was a conventional lover. She seldom went down on him, although she allowed him to go down on her.

He did so now, lingering at her sex, teasing her with his tongue until she begged him to end it.

When he entered her, Dave felt like he'd come home from a long journey. It was a familiar and warm feeling, one he desperately needed right now. He hated to pull out of her.

Later, sitting around the kitchen table sipping wine and nibbling on cheese and crackers, Dave placed his hand over hers. "Come to Briarwood with me, Laura."

There was an appealing tone in his voice that Laura responded to. "Are you in some kind of trouble?"

Trouble? Hell, he was in so deep, he was drowning. If only he could tell her everything. If only he had the guts. "No. I just thought it would be nice. On second thought, it was a lousy idea. You'd hate Briarwood."

"You could be wrong about that, but I can't just up and leave. We're in the middle of an investigation. It's big time, Dave. The biggest investigation I've ever been involved in." Excitement filled her voice.

"It's okay. Some other time."

Christ, he thought, we sound like polite strangers.

Laura, too, was bothered. "I'd like to come, honest. I can get away this weekend if you're still there. Do you think you will be?"

"I don't know. I don't know how long it will take, or how long Herring will let me hang out there now that it's an official murder case. I'll call you."

"I hope you do. And Dave?" "Yes?"

"I love you, and loving someone means taking the good with the bad. I think I've proven I can do that. If there's something you want to tell me…"

Dave felt warmed not only by her words but by her presence. I'm a lucky son of a bitch, he acknowledged. I won't do anything to spoil the way she feels about me now. He knew he was being selfish. That she deserved the truth. He was sure she could handle the truth. Maybe that was the problem. She could probably handle the truth and deal with it better than he was doing. All that did was make him feel inadequate. For his own sake, he knew that his problem with Trinity was something he had to work out for himself.

He shook his head. "No. There's nothing."

⌘

The first place Dave stopped when he arrived back in Briarwood was the sheriff's office. Bill Lackland greeted him.

"Is the Sheriff back?" Dave asked.

"No," Bill answered. He stuck his fingers in his belt. "Wish he was. Then I could get back to my kids."

"How many do you have?"

"Dozens." When Dave raised his eyebrows, Bill laughed. "I coach at the school." "I thought…"

"I know what you thought." He laughed. "I always have a good time when I'm playing lawman. Truth is, I substitute and fill in when the sheriff's away. My real job is at the school."

"Then I guess there's no use in asking you to help me with the Ellen Gray case." "Ask away. Until the sheriff gets back, I'm your best bet. Besides, I'd like to

help. You still think she was murdered?"

Dave nodded. "We have a witness who saw a man shoot Ellen full of heroin." "Did you get him?"

Dave shook his head. "Not yet."

"Too bad. A man can get lost in the city." "Maybe he didn't come from the city." "What does that mean?"

"He could have come from here. I'd like to take you up on your offer to help. You know these people. No matter what my roots, I'm still an outsider. Can you find out who Ellen saw or talked to in the last few days before she left here? Her mother thinks she was frightened. I want to know of what or whom."

Bill raised his eyebrows. "Frightened? That sounds a little far-fetched. Are you sure Trinity isn't just being melodramatic?"

"Could be, but I have to follow the lead."

Bill scratched his head. "Frightened, you say. Of someone from here?"

Dave nodded. "Any chance of getting a list of all the married men in Briarwood under the age of fifty?"

"What the hell for?"

"Margaret says Ellen was seeing someone who was married. It's a place to start."

Bill whistled. "That's heavy. Is this really necessary? I can think of a few guys who have played around, and maybe still do. That doesn't mean they played around with Ellen Gray. Digging into their personal lives is going to wreak havoc for a lot of decent family men."

"They should have thought about that before they screwed around."

Bill slammed his fist down on his desk. "I don't have to like it, but I'll take care of it."

"Thanks."

Bill sighed. "You might as well start with me. I'm a married man. I got married six months ago."

Dave shrugged. "No one in this town is immune in my book. Not even you. You said you dated Margaret Gray. When?"

"Six years ago. It wasn't serious for either of us." "And Ellen?"

"Was just a kid. Twelve, I think." His tone hardened. "I don't seduce kids.

Anyway, if I'd have thought about going after another of the Gray women it would have been Trinity. You saw her. Even at her age, she's dynamite. I bet every man in this town has had a fantasy about Trinity Gray at one time or another. I wonder why a woman like that stays in Briarwood."

Dave had had the same thought when he'd been up at the St. John house. "What about Steven St. John.?"

"He came through town one day, saw Trinity, and made his claim. Everybody likes him, and with good reason. He's been good for this town."

"How so?"

"The bank was in trouble. Steve optioned stock and sold it all back at cost when the bank recovered."

"What kind of trouble was the bank in?"

"The usual. This is farm country, Kincaid. A lot of men couldn't meet their loans. Some of them got discouraged and gave up. The ones who didn't, Steve helped out. Yes, sir, the day Steve St. John came to town was a good day for all of us."

Dave stared thoughtfully past Bill. "No wonder they call him Saint John.

Anything strange happen right before Ellen left here? Anyone get hurt, or die, commit rape, beat their wife, that kind of thing?"

Bill smiled. "After you was here the last time, I figured you'd ask that, so I ran a check. One drunk and disorderly, several traffic and parking tickets, two kids picked up for smoking pot. Nothing really criminal. If you really want to get trivial, old lady Simkins keeled over with a heart attack, John Biddle busted his leg, and a high school kid named Severn Wokowski died of kidney failure." A cloud passed across Bill's face. "The kid hurt. He was one of my boys. Best quarterback to come down the pike since myself." A cloud passed across his face. "In fact, he reminded me of myself. Except in all honesty, he was better than I ever thought about being because he was more disciplined. He never would have given up his chance at the big time by getting involved in a parking lot brawl."

Dave's recent meeting with Trinity helped him to understand how painful it was to think about what might have been. It hurt. It hurt like hell. Bill missed his chance, Dave thought, and now he's living his life through others. He knew the feeling well.

When some of his friends had gone to law school, a part of him had gone with them.

Dave extended his hand. "I think we're going to work well together, Bill. You'll get me that list and check on Ellen's last few days?"

"Sure thing. What will you be doing?"

"Talking to Ellen's former boyfriend, Chris Briggs."

⚬⚏⚬

Dave parked across from the one and only gas station in town to observe Chris Briggs from a distance. He was twenty, tall and lean, with a pleasant face, not exactly handsome, with unruly blond hair. His parents owned the station. Chris and his father manned it alone, relieving each other every few hours.

Dave pulled away from the curb and parked in front of one of the pumps. Chris leaned in the open window. "Fill it up?"

"Sure." Dave pulled out his badge. "I'd like to talk to you about Ellen Gray." Chris inserted the gas nozzle in the gas tank. "Ellen's dead."

"That's why I'm here. She was murdered, Chris."

Chris lost momentary control of the gas nozzle. Gasoline spurted on the ground and onto his tennis shoes. "Shit," he said. He inserted the nozzle back in place. "There were rumors. In this town there are always rumors. She really was murdered, then?"

"Yes. When did you see her last?"

"The night before she left town." The tank full, Chris replaced the nozzle on the pump. "That'll be thirty five dollars."

Dave handed him a Two twenties. "You two weren't going together anymore.

You don't think it was unusual for her to seek you out?"

"Not really." A car pulled up behind Dave and honked its horn. "Listen," Chris said. "I gotta work. Can we talk later?"

"Where?"

"There's a café. The Brass Kettle. My dad relieves me at three. I'll meet you there."

Dave accepted his change and started his engine. He wondered if Chris Briggs was playing for time. If so, why? He seemed nervous.

He probably wasn't the only one.

Somewhere, there was a married man who had to be more than just a little bit on edge. It stood to reason that in a town this size, someone had to have known the man's identity. Sooner or later Dave intended to know who he was, and his part, if any, in Ellen's death.

⟳⟲

The Brass Kettle functioned as a meeting place for locals a much as it did a restaurant, though the owner, Jethrow Perkins, made a good enough living from such staples as his wife's home-made bread, soup, and pies.

The walls were decorated with old movie posters and wooden shelves with cheap bric-a-brac atop them. The floor was covered with faded linoleum. For all of that, it was bright, cheery, and cozy, and it was meticulously clean.

Dave was waiting at the corner window table when he saw Chris Briggs approaching. With no more than ten tables to the entire place, Dave was easy for Chris to spot.

He slid onto the chair opposite Dave. He looked around the room. "Sorry I couldn't talk earlier. Have you tried Mrs. Perkins' apple pie?"

Dave shook his head. "I was about to. Tell me about you and Ellen."

Chris waved at Jethrow. "Coffee, Jethrow." He turned his attention back to Dave. "Ellen and I dated since high school. I loved Ellen. I loved her a lot. For a while I think she loved me. Then, she told me she'd fallen in love with someone else."

"When was this?"

"About a year ago. I asked her if this man was going to marry her like I wanted to. She said he was already married."

Dave had gotten the impression that Ellen's affair with a married man had started more recently. "Are you sure the man she was involved with about a year ago was married?"

"That's what she said. She had no reason to lie." "So you broke up with Ellen about a year ago?" "The first time."

Dave gave him a questioning look.

"Whoever he was," Chris said, "he only lasted a few months. Afterwards, Ellen came back to me for a while. Then, about two months ago, she broke it off again." Chris refused to look at Dave, an evasive gesture Dave had encountered many times and recognized only too well. Chris was definitely uneasy.

"The same man?" Dave asked.

"I think so. This time she wouldn't say why she was calling it quits."

Chris's coffee and Dave's apple pie arrived at the table. Dave took a bite of his pie. "Damn, this really is good," he said, his mouth full. "Tell me, Chris, I know a little something about small towns. If Ellen was involved with a married man from around here, wouldn't someone have known who he was?"

"Normally." Chris drained his coffee cup. "I often thought she was able to keep it a secret because of who he was."

"Then you know who he is?" "Just a guess."

Dave pushed away his empty plate. "Well, don't keep it to yourself." "I said it was just a guess. I think it was Steven St. John."

Trinity's husband! "Why do you think he was the man?" "The way they were together."

He was guessing and a guess wasn't good enough, but it was worth pursuing, Dave thought. "You said Ellen came to see you before she left town. Seeing as how you'd broken up, that really didn't surprise you?"

"No. We were still friends. She often talked to me when she couldn't talk to anyone else. Margaret was gone so much. Her job as an embassy clerk took her all over the world. She only comes back here about twice a year. Of course, there was Ellen's mother, but they hadn't been close for a while."

"But they'd been close at one time?" Chris shrugged. "I suppose."

Dave rubbed his chin with his forefinger. "I see. Did Ellen say where she was going? Where she was staying? Anything?"

"No. She was agitated. She kept acting like she wanted to tell me something, then she'd change her mind."

"Would you say she was frightened?" "You could say that."

Dave threw some bills and some change on the table. "I'll be talking to you again, Chris. In the meantime, if you think of anything, anything at all, I'm staying at the motel outside of town."

Chris stared down at the checkered tablecloth, then his eyes met Dave's. "Find whoever killed Ellen. I want him to pay for what he did to her."

Dave slapped him on the shoulder. He wanted to feel sorry for him, but knew that was a mistake. "Sure, kid. It's what I do."

Sliding behind the wheel of his car, Dave looked back at the café. Chris was staring blankly out the window.

He's never stopped loving her, Dave thought, and he's hiding something that's eating away at him.

CHAPTER 5

Dave lay on his motel bed staring up at the ceiling. The room was pleasant enough, no different than a thousand others. The motel was a thirty-six room, two-story structure, that had been built less than a year ago, the paint still fresh, the furniture as yet unscarred.

Back in Briarwood he was on dangerous ground again. It had been easier, if not really successful, to put Trinity out of his mind as long as he was on familiar ground, and as long as Laura was around. He rolled over and reached for the phone. He dialed his apartment. It rang three times, then Laura's voice traveled mechanically through the lines.

"No one is home right now," the recording said. "At the sound of the tone, please leave a message."

Dave slammed the receiver down.

Wanting to hear her voice again, if only on tape, he redialed the number. This time he left a message. "Just called to say I wish you were here." He laughed. "Trite and clichéd, I admit, but it's true. I'll call again."

After he hung up, he wished he hadn't left a message. Laura would be bound to try to make something out of it. Ever since Katie, she'd been trying to crawl inside his head, as if by clearing out the cobwebs and washing away the guilt and confusion, she could affect an immediate cure for what ailed him.

He sighed. He wished life were that simple.

Dave called the station and was connected to Brad. "Finding anything?' Dave asked.

"Not yet."

"Why not?"

"Maybe because it's not the only case on the books."

Dave was pushing, and he knew it. "Okay. But you'll let me know."
"You'll be the first," Brad said.

⚬⚬⚬

Bertha Bartlett was seventy-four years old. She'd taught school in Briarwood since she was twenty, refusing to retire and collect her pension until four years ago.

She had a remarkable memory, a keen sense of right and wrong, a genuine interest in humanity, and she'd been the most curious person Dave had ever known. He was relying on the fact that her curiosity was still as keen as he remembered it to be.

He made his way over to her home, the same house she'd lived in for fifty-four of her years. Over a hundred years old, the rock and plaster house which had once housed a general store, was located in what had been the commercial center of town a long time ago. Now it was the only residence or structure, surrounded by vacant ground where store fronts had once existed. The while picket fence that surrounded her home was freshly painted. Her trademark, the garden, was a profusion of color. There wasn't a wedding performed in Briarwood that didn't have at least one bouquet made of Bertha's flowers in it.

She opened the door as Dave walked up the red brick path. She leaned on a cane, her arthritis the only sign of decay in an otherwise healthy body. Her silver hair accentuated her sharp blue eyes.

A few feet away from her, Dave said, "Miss Bartlett, my name is…"

"David Kincaid. I'd have known who you were even if the gossip about you hadn't reached me. How could I not remember you? As a student, you were a constant source of exasperation to me. So bright, and yet to inattentive." She opened her door wider. "Come, sit a spell with me. We'll have tea."

Tea with Miss Bartlett! Back when Dave was in school here, an invitation to tea either meant a tongue lashing or a pat on the back. It was an invitation that struck fear in the hearts of many young men or women, pride in others.

Sitting there, sipping tea from Bertha's fine delicate china, Dave felt sixteen again, she the teacher, he the student. He squirmed in the print covered chair. "Miss Bartlett, I came here because if anybody knows what goes on in this town, I figured it had to be you."

She set her cup down on the polished wooden table by her chair, a pleased smile on her face. "You want to know about Ellen."

"Yes. I saw her in a filthy alley, out of place somehow, beautiful even in death. She's haunted me ever since. I can't get a clear picture of her as she was when she was alive. I've a feeling if I can do that, I can come closer to knowing why she died."

Bertha leaned forward. "You always were a deep one, David." She settled back in her chair. "I liked you when you were my student. I like you even better now. It takes a special kind of man to care this much about a dead girl."

He was both pleased and embarrassed by her praise. "Thank you. Ellen was one of your students?"

"Until her senior year. I retired that year. She was a good student, like you. That is until she was…let me see, I think it was the summer she turned twelve…yes that was the year. Her father died that year."

"She took it badly?"

Bertha wrinkled her brows. "I'm not so sure that was all of it. It was the year that she built a wall around herself."

"Did anyone get past that wall?"

"I did, once or twice, but only briefly. She never told me what was bothering her. There's Chris Briggs. They were close, even then." A sad smile touched her lips. "He would have been good for her. Ellen, unfortunately, was somewhat of a snob, though she tried to control it. She wanted more than a grease monkey for a husband." She paused to laugh, "I think that's what they call them. Chris's roots are strong. He wanted to stay.

Ellen wanted to leave."

"Then you weren't surprised when she did leave here?" "Oh, but I was. She left so abruptly."

At least that much is consistent with what I've heard, Dave thought. "Anyone else break through that wall?"

"Her sister, of course." "And her mother?"

"No. There was restraint there. Sometimes I thought that Ellen resented Trinity. Other times I think she hated her. She lived with Trinity right up until the time she left here. I have the foolish notion that it was to punish her mother."

"Any idea why?"

"It could have had something to do with her father's death. You might ask Margaret. Or Chris."

"I already asked Chris." "I see."

"Miss Bartlett, there are unconfirmed rumors that Ellen had been seeing a married man. Would you know who he is?"

Bertha sighed. "No. But that would explain a lot of things. I could make a few guesses of course."

"Care to give me their names?"

She shook her head. "Not yet. I could be wrong. I wouldn't want to slander anyone."

Dave stood and took her hand. "Thank you for the tea. If you become sure of whom Ellen was seeing, will you tell me?"

She looked up at him. "You take your job and your responsibility so seriously, David. Yes, if you like, I'll be your Miss Marple."

He looked confused.

"Agatha Christie. You do read?"

He felt like he was back in school again. "Sure, I do."

She walked with him down the path to the picket fence. "You wanted a picture of Ellen. I'm not sure I can draw one. She was gentle one minute, aggressive the next. She was sunlight, and she was darkness. She was a troubled young girl trying to find her way. Sadly, it looks like she didn't have time. I understand she was murdered. A terrible thing for anyone to do to another human being. You will find her murderer?"

Dave looked into intelligent, questioning blue eyes. "I don't know. What do you think?"

She smiled. "You'll find whoever did it. I'm sure of it."

෴

Dave heard the phone ringing as he turned the key in the lock of his motel room. He strode into the room and picked up the receiver. He hoped it was Laura returning his call. "Hello."

"Hi. I was just about to hang up. This is Margaret Gray. I was wondering if you'd like to come to dinner tonight."

Dave sat down on the bed and loosened his tie. He was upset because it wasn't Laura. He tried to keep his disappointment out of his voice. "I was going to call you. I wanted to talk to you again."

"Then you can buy dinner." She laughed. "Only kidding. I cook a mean steak.

Can you be here by seven?"

"Listen, Margaret. It's not that I don't appreciate the invitation, but I'm…"

"A cop? And cops don't eat? Come now, it's only dinner. This is a small town with small town etiquette, Detective Kincaid. We're hospitable people. I promise to answer all your questions. So, how about it? Is it dinner, or just the third degree?"

Dave threw himself back on the bed. She had a point. He could use a good meal, and God knows he was tired of the motel room and the limited local cuisine. "All right, but I'm warning you, I can't be bribed, not even with a steak dinner. I really do want to talk to you. About Ellen, of course."

She sighed. "Why else would you want to talk to me?" She sighed again. "See you at seven."

Dave toyed with the idea of picking up a bottle of wine and decided against it. He was going to Margaret Gray's home to question her about her sister. It wasn't a social call.

Tonight, her house had a more lived-in look. The round glass-topped table sitting in an alcove off the kitchen was neatly set with fine bone china and silver flatware. A vase with a single rose served as a center piece.

"Do you mind if we eat right away?" Margaret asked. "I would hate for dinner to spoil."

Dave already felt uncomfortable, sorry he'd let her talk him into coming to dinner. "Sure thing. Can I do anything to help?"

"No. Please, have a seat. I'll bring the food in."

She made several trips to the kitchen, and finally a platter of steaks, baked potatoes, corn and bread filled the table. She made one last trip to the kitchen. She came back into the dining area with a bottle of wine in one hand, two glasses in another. "Wine. Is that permissible? Forgive me if I seem naive, it's just that I used to date Bill Lackland, and he'd often stop by for dinner and we'd have drinks. Then he's only a part-time lawman." She laughed. "Besides, being a lawman in this town is on a parallel with being a big city meter maid." She raised the bottle. "So, what do I do?"

Dave tossed his head back and ran his fingers down his neck. What the hell! "Sit the damn thing down," he said and was immediately sorry for his tone. "Maybe this wasn't such a good idea. Since I'm here, let's enjoy the meal." He inhaled. "Everything smells great."

They ate in relative silence, breaking that silence occasionally for small talk, and Dave's comments on the excellence of the meal. When Dave pushed his plate away, nothing but a small portion of potato left on it, Margaret said, "We can go into the living room. You can bring your wine. Or not," she added with a smile. "As for me, I think I'll finish the bottle, with or without you."

Dave followed her into the living room and took a seat next to the brick fireplace. He fingered his half-empty wine glass that he'd brought with him. He set the glass down, untouched, on a table by the chair.

"I talked to Miss Bartlett today about Ellen." He smiled. "I remembered that she seemed to have a handle on everything that went on in Briarwood. I wanted to get a clearer picture of your sister. Miss Bartlett was helpful to a point, but she suggested I talk to you. She said Ellen changed around the time your father died. She thought you might know why the change was not only drastic, but permanent."

Margaret, who had been standing until now, sat down in a chair opposite Dave, her dress hiked up to her thighs revealing beautiful legs. Dave deliberately kept his eyes above her waist level.

Margaret took a sip of her wine. "Ellen was close to my father. Much more so than I. I think she blamed my mother for his death."

"Any reason to believe that?"

"No. But Ellen was only twelve at the time." "Did you like your sister?"

Margaret gave him a hard look. "I loved my sister." "That's not what I asked."

Margaret poured herself another glass of wine. "You'd have to have been around to know how it was in my house. Ellen was her mother's daughter. Like my mother, she had two sides to her. Sometimes she was sweet and gentle. Other times she was hard and unreachable. We were as close as two sisters with that kind of an age difference can be. I did love her. I would have done anything to see that nobody hurt her if it was in my power to do so. I protected her while she was growing up." Pain filled her voice. "But somebody hurt her anyway, and I wasn't there for her."

This conversation was leading him nowhere, Dave realized. He changed tactics. "Chris thinks that Ellen's secret love affair was with Steven St. John."

"My mother's husband! That's ridiculous. Why on earth would he say that?" "Then you don't think it's true?"

"No! Definitely not."

"Would you have any ideas as to who she may have been seeing then?" She shook her head. "None."

"I bet if you think about it, you can make a good guess. Your sister may have been close-mouthed, but she wasn't Mata Hari, for Christ's sake!"

"You think if I had a clue as to who he was I would protect him! I can't think of anyone in this town I'd go to those lengths for."

"No one?"

"You're goading me. Why? What is it you think I know?" "More than you're telling."

"That's ridiculous, and I resent the implication. Let me give you some good advice. Digging into Ellen's death won't bring her back, but it could hurt a lot of nice people."

That was what Trinity had said. He wondered if they were both protecting the same person. He was still getting nowhere, and from the black look on Margaret's face he wasn't about to.

"I'll be going then," he said. "If you think of something, call me at the motel." Margaret moved ahead of him and opened the front door. "Goodnight,

Detective."

He turned to face her. "Oh, I almost forgot. Thanks for dinner. It was great."

Just before she slammed the door, she said, "You're welcome, I'm sure. I hope you choke on it."

Ⓖⓜⓞ

Dave went back to his motel. He placed a call to Brad. "I need a complete rundown on several people. See what the computers can come up with." He gave him several names. "Call me when you get the information."

He was about to hang up, then he said, "How's it going Brad? With Prentiss, I mean."

"Jesus," Brad said. "Do you know what that broad did?"

Dave was wishing he hadn't asked. "What did she do this time?" "She saved my fucking life."

Dave could hear the excitement in his partner's voice. "She did what?"

"We were on our way to question a suspect in the college murders, when a call came over the car radio about a robbery in progress at a liquor store. We were only a block away, so we responded. Two men were leaving the scene as we pulled up. I got out of the car and had her call in for back-up. One of the bastards started to shoot. I hit the deck. The other one took advantage of the situation and put a gun to my head. I figured I was a dead man. All I could think of was that if you'd been there to cover me, I'd have a chance. Then Prentiss jumped out of the car and told the son of a bitch to freeze. He cocked the hammer of his gun instead. He was going to blow my brains out, Dave. Prentiss didn't hesitate. She dropped him. One shot to the head. Then she turned her gun on the other guy. He took one look at the expression on her face and he gave himself up. I gotta tell you. It was incredible. She was incredible."

Dave remembered the first time he'd shot at someone. He didn't kill the suspect, but there were nights when he couldn't sleep for thinking about what might have happened. "How's she taking it?" Dave asked.

"She's shaken up. The shooting review board will pass judgment in a few days, but it was a righteous shoot, she'll come out clean."

But not untouched, Dave thought.

"She'll need you, Brad. I hope you're there for her."

There was resentment in Brad's voice. "I may be a bastard, but I'm not insensitive. She saved my life. I owe her. Suddenly, it doesn't seem to matter that she's a woman. Today, she was my partner, and she acted like a pro."

Dave smiled to himself. Brad was growing up. "Congratulate her for me, for a job well done, and thank her for me for saving your chauvinistic ass."

Brad laughed. "Done. I'll call you when I get the information on those names you gave me. Anything else?"

"Not right now. You should get a charge out of this, however. There's this old lady, Bertha Bartlett. She was my teacher and everyone else's in town. She's offered to play sleuth for me. What the hell I figured I could use all the help I can get."

Brad laughed. "You know what I think? I think you've had too much small town sun."

After the connection was severed, Dave felt a depressing isolation. Brad's playful remark had hit a nerve. He wished he were back in the city. Back with Brad and Laura.

Dave lay on the bed, his hands behind the pillow. He closed his eyes and went over all he'd learned so far. Ellen Gray had been different things to different people. A real chameleon. Who was the real Ellen Gray? Was she a saint or a sinner? For sure she was nobody's angel.

There were still people he needed to talk to. People who could shed maybe yet a different light on the dead girl. He still had to talk to her friend at the bank, AmySpring.

It was time, he thought, that he met Steven St. John.

CHAPTER 6

AmySpring was two years older than Ellen Gray had been when she died. She was thirty pounds overweight for her five-foot-five inches, and self-conscious about it. Amy's best asset was her smile, which made her almost homely face seem pretty. Dave couldn't help thinking that she and Ellen must have made the proverbial odd couple.

Dave, falling into the same habit as the locals did for using the Brass Kettle as a meeting place, waited for Amy to show up there.

When she entered the café, she nervously looked around the place as if that someone might see her with him. "I can't stay long. I only have an hour for lunch," she said.

"I know," Dave said. "I took the liberty of ordering you a hamburger. Jethrow said it was your favorite meal."

Amy patted her stomach, shooting a resentful look in Jethrow's direction. "And my downfall. I quit smoking, but I just can't seem to give up food."

She intertwined her hands together. She had long stylish fingers, marred by the fact that she chewed her nails. She followed the direction of Dave's eyes, and placed her hands in her lap. "Another bad habit. I didn't always bite them."

Dave lifted his coffee cup. "A recent habit, then?" She flushed. "Yes."

"It wouldn't have anything to do with Ellen, would it?"

Amy sighed. "Chris told me you were sharp." She lowered her eyes. "Ever since I heard Ellen was murdered, I've been trying to think if there was something I could have done to prevent it from happening."

Dave leaned forward. "Like what?"

"Like stopping her from leaving town." Amy bit down on her lip. "Maybe if she'd stayed…" she lifted her head. "Silly, isn't it? Ellen never listened to me. Or anyone else for that matter."

"You were her best friend?" "Yes."

"Tell me about her." "What do you mean?"

"What kind of person she was. How she acted right before she left here. Her affair with a married man. Who was he?"

She sighed again. "Chris said you'd ask me that, too. I don't know, and that's the God's truth. Lord knows I asked her to tell me who he was enough times."

"You knew she was seeing a married man?"

"Yes, but only because about five months before she left here, she became hysterical when she thought she was pregnant. It was right before she and Chris got back together. I mean as lovers. They'd stayed friends. I assumed the baby was Chris's, of course. She began to scream at me. "Not Chris's, she said 'his'. 'His,' who? I asked.

Then I said, whoever it is, make him marry you. It was then that she told me he was already married. She started to laugh. At least I thought she was laughing. Then I realized it was hysteria. A week later she told me it was a false alarm. She was sorry she'd confided in me, I could tell that."

"She never told you his name?"

Amy shook her head. "No. Funny, it seems like a lot of people knew she was seeing a married man, and yet no one knows who he was. Then that would have been in character for Ellen. Either that, or she made the whole thing up."

"Would that have been in character?"

She shook her head. "Maybe. Thinking back to that day when she told me she thought she was pregnant, I'd have to say the man really existed."

"And not confiding in anyone as to his identity?"

"That would have been in character. Ellen was secretive. She was my friend. I knew her about as well as one friend knows another, and yet I realize now that I really didn't know her at all."

"Did she tell you she was leaving?" Dave asked, motioning for a refill of his coffee."

"No. I guess she only told Chris and her mother."

Dave leaned back in his chair. "How did Ellen get along with her mother?"

Amy paused. "That's a hard one. They fought a lot, I know that, but then they were alike in so many ways. Just when I'd think she hated her mother, someone would say something unkind or petty about Trinity, and Ellen would come to her aid like a bear protecting her cub. It was weird."

"How many married men are there at the bank?" Dave asked.

Amy placed her hands on her chin. "Let me see. Three. Jim Bates, but he's fifty- five and bald as an eagle. Carey Bryant, he's the manager. And Felix Gerard."

"If Ellen was seeing any one of them which one would you bet your money on?"

Amy's answer was swift. "I don't know which one she'd pick, but Mr. Bryant would be my choice."

"Why?"

"Because he's good-looking, he's fairly well-off, and his wife is a bitch. Felix is nice, but his wife is an invalid. I don't see him messing around. Then, you never know, do you? Though why Ellen would have given up Chris for either one of them is beyond me." A dreamy faraway look filled her eyes.

People give themselves away with such innocence, Dave thought. Amy was in love with Chris Briggs. He wondered if Ellen had known. He motioned for the bill, and when it came he left a five dollar tip on the table. He picked up the check. "Thanks, Amy. Did Ellen have any other friends I should talk to?"

"None she was close to. She and Beth Woodley used to be friendly, but they drifted apart after Beth married Bill Lackland. Beth and Ellen worked at the bank together when she got married to Bill. Do you think you'll find whoever did it, Detective Kincaid?"

It was a question of the day, Dave realized, certainly number one in the hearts and minds of Briarwood residents. "I'll certainly do my best," he answered.

After Amy left the restaurant, Dave added the names of Craig Bryant and Felix Gerard to that of Steven St. John.

He decided to start with Steven St. John.

⁂

Dave called the St. John home. St. John had just returned from a trip back east. This time a housekeeper answered the door. Trinity was nowhere in sight. The housekeeper led him to a room that was much more formal than the "playroom" Trinity had taken him to. This room was decorated in pastels with tasteful artwork covering the walls.

"Detective Dave Kincaid," she announced, and then left.

St. John had his elbow resting atop an oak-mantled fireplace. Like a picture from a magazine, Dave couldn't help thinking.

St. John moved away from the fireplace and extended his hand to Dave. "Detective Kincaid. I'm Steven St. John."

"Where's Mrs. St. John?" Dave asked.

"Shopping. She said you'd already talked to her about Ellen. She couldn't handle any more questions right now. I think the reality of Ellen's death is just beginning to sink in. I hope her absence isn't a problem."

Dave wondered if Trinity had told her husband that she and Dave shared a past, and immediately doubted it. That wouldn't have been Trinity's style.

Dave took a moment to assess St. John. His features were perfect, literally, as if they'd been carved by a master sculptor. There wasn't a line on his face. He was reportedly forty, eight years younger than Trinity, but could have easily passed for thirty. He could have turned a young girl's head without even trying, Dave thought. A young girl like Ellen.

"No, no problem at all," Dave answered St. John's earlier question. "In fact, I prefer to talk to you alone."

St. John didn't seem at all uneasy, and Dave had the feeling that he was used to answering questions, friendly or hostile. Catching him off-guard was his best bet, Dave decided.

"Ellen's former boyfriend thinks she was having an affair with you," Dave said.

St. John smiled. "I see this isn't going to be one of those casual interviews. You intend to go for the jugular. Good. I like that. It lets me know where I stand. Won't you have a seat?"

"I think I'll stand," Dave said.

St. John moved back to the fireplace and once again rested his elbow on the mantle. "Ellen was seventeen when I married Trinity. A beautiful young woman who wanted everything her mother had."

"Did that include you?"

He laughed. "An adolescent crush that died a natural death when I didn't encourage her. Of course, no matter how gently I tried to rebuff her, it hurt her pride."

This guy makes me sick, Dave thought. It's hard to imagine who loved him more, Trinity, Ellen, or himself. I'll opt for the latter, Dave decided, as he wondered what Trinity had seen in him, besides his youth and good looks. There had to be more than that. Or do I just want to believe it to make our own affair seem more meaningful?

"I understand you helped the town out when it got in a bind. That's very generous. This town never had any real millionaires before that I can recall. Especially the philanthropic kind, Mr. St. John."

"Please, call me Steve. Who says I'm a millionaire, anyway? I do have considerable resources, however, and I like to help my friends. The people in this town are my friends. You aren't suggesting there's anything wrong with helping them out, are you? Surely you don't have anything against success? After all, it's the American way."

Dave had the feeling that St. John was laughing at him. Maybe he did know about him and Trinity. And if he did, so what? Dave didn't like this guy and it had nothing to do with Trinity, he told himself, which of course was bullshit. It had everything to do with Trinity.

"A lot of people think Ellen was frightened when she left here," Dave went on. "Of what?"

"You tell me."

"I can't. And I don't know if I believe it. Ellen had a flair for the dramatic.

Eversince I knew her, she talked about getting away from here. It could have just been her way of leaving without giving lengthy excuses."

"Did she need any? Why not just leave?"

"I told you, Ellen had a flair for the dramatic." St. John removed hiselbow from the mantle. "You don't like me a whole hell of a lot, do you?"

"It's not a requirement of the job."

St. John sighed. "Anything else I can help you with, Detective?"

"Not for now. Though you might tell Trinity I'd like to talk to her again soon." St. John raised his eyebrows. "Trinity?"

Dave flushed, and hated himself for it. "I knew your wife a long time ago. Using her first name is a force of habit."

"I see."

I bet you do, or think you do, Dave thought, and realized he was being unreasonable. He'd come here looking for a reason not to like Steven St. John, and found it easy. Now, the son of a bitch was trying to put him on the defensive. Well, fuck him. It wasn't going to work.

"I'll find my own way out," Dave said. "Give my regards to your wife."

⚬━━━⚬

The desk clerk advised Dave that he had visitors who were staying at the motel for the weekend. "Two," he said with a wink. "Both very lovely. I put them in the room next to yours." He winked again.

Dave ran his fingers through his hair. Jesus, was it the weekend already? "Do these ladies have names?"

"Yes, Sir. Miss Laura Richards and Miss Sheila Prentiss."

Laura! Thank God, she'd come. He frowned. But Sheila? What the hell was she doing here? And with Laura!

He knocked on the door of the room next to his. Laura opened it and flew into his arms. "I'm sorry. I was a bitch when I last saw you. Forgive me?"

Forgive her! Right now he'd forgive her anything. "You came," Dave answered. "Nothing else matters. What's Sheila doing here?"

Laura stepped outside the room and pulled the door behind her. "I'll let her tell you herself. Give me the key to your room, darling. I didn't know what you'd told anyone, if anything about me, so I registered with Sheila to avoid gossip." She smiled. "Of course, I have no intention of staying in anyone's room but yours."

Dave kissed her, a long lingering kiss. "I wouldn't have it any other way. What about her?" He stood at the motel door. "What's she going to do?"

"Stay out of our way. Herring sent her here with the information you requested." "He or Brad could have called it in to me."

"I know, but she's having a rough time. Brad thought she needed to get away.

He talked Herring into letting her bring it to you." "Brad did?"

Laura laughed. "I think he's in love."

Dave gave her a look of disbelief. "Brad is never in love. Just in heat."

"Trust me," she said. "Brad Monroe is a goner." She kissed his cheek. "I'll wait for you in your room."

Dave shook his head as he watched Laura disappear into his room. He tapped on the door of the room that Sheila would now occupy by herself. When she answered, simply, but tastefully dressed in navy slacks and white linen blouse, a strand of pearls around her slender neck, he remembered thinking that she would be a knock-out in civies. She was.

A smile lit up her face. Brad would be damn lucky to have this woman, he thought.

"Please, come in," she said. "I hope you don't mind me bringing your information here. I was raised in a town just like this one. I didn't realize how much I've missed it until now."

"It grows on you," Dave answered, surprised at his own words. Jesus, he thought.

Don't even start thinking about staying.

Sheila reached for a computerized report. Her voice took on a businesslike tone as she began to read from it. "Here goes. Bill Lackland. Born and raised in Briarwood. No arrests, no warrants, four moving violations, mostly speeding. He was a high school football hero who lost his chance at the big time. He married the former Beth Woodley, six months ago. Before that he was married to Carol Brothers. They were divorced eight months ago.

"Quick rebound," Dave said. "Either that or Bill was playing around before his divorce." No wonder, Dave thought, that Bill is concerned about my digging into married men's pasts. "Go on," he urged.

"Trinity St. John," Sheila continued. "Born in Louisiana. Her first husband died in a car accident when Ellen Gray was twelve. She married Steven St. John a year ago. No arrests, no warrants, no violations. Not even a parking ticket. This lady seems pretty pure."

If only you knew, Dave thought.

"Chris Briggs," she went on. "Born and raised in Briarwood. He got into a little bit of trouble with marijuana when he was fifteen. Nothing major. This is interesting, however. He and Ellen Gray were married five months ago. It only lasted a month. The marriage was annulled."

Married! No wonder the poor son of a bitch was nervous, Dave thought. That kind of rejection could create one hell of a motive. He wondered who else knew about the marriage. Trinity? Margaret? Amy?

"Steven St. John," Sheila said, "is really a puzzle. Apparently, he didn't exist until he showed up here a year ago and married Trinity Gray."

"Didn't exist?"

"No. His driver's license and social security card were issued a year ago.

Nothing on him before that. And I mean nothing."

Dave ran his fingers through his hair over and over again. "What does Brad think?"

"Probably the same thing you're thinking."

She was insightful. Dave like that about her. He and Brad had learned to think alike on more than one occasion. "Yeah, of course. St. John could be ex-mob trying to start over again, a fugitive, or he could be under government protection. If that's the case and he's on the witness protection program, we won't get a damn thing on him unless we dig it up for ourselves. They protect their people more than the Russians protect their spies." A frown etched lines in his face. "It makes sense." He ran his fingers through his hair again, causing strands to stand up on end. "I remember thinking that his face looks like it was carved from marble. The son of a bitch has had plastic surgery!" Dave pounded his fist on the small bedside table. "Damn, damn, damn. It's possible we can't touch his past, but if the bastard is mixed up in Ellen Gray's murder, I sure as hell can make his future miserable.Did you find out where Ellen Gray stayed in the city?"

She shook her head. "Not yet. But we did come across something unexpected while we were looking. Margaret Gray stayed in the city three nights before she came back here."

"She did what?"

"Stayed in the city. First, we thought we'd hit pay dirt. At a downtown hotel they had a Ms. Gray registered. No first name. Just Ms. Gray. We showed the clerk Ellen's picture. It wasn't her. Brad got a hold of a copy of Margaret's passport picture on a hunch. It paid off. It was her all right."

"How in the hell did Brad get Margaret's passport picture?"

Sheila laughed. "A favor he was owed, he said to tell you. Though I suspect he used his irresistible charm." She blushed. "Some women fall for it. He also said to tell you that now you owe him two favors. I assume you know what he means."

Dave gave her a pre-occupied smile. The first favor, of course, was sticking Brad with Sheila for a partner. Dave had a hunch that was one favor he wouldn't have to return. Not if Laura was right about Brad and Sheila, that is. "A private joke. Anything else on Margaret Gray?"

"She's worked overseas a lot. She was transferred from the embassy in France to the one in London. There were rumors of an affair with a diplomat. Nothing confirmed. She left the London post on her own volition, but there were uncorroborated rumors there too, about an affair."

"Like sister, like mother, like sister," Dave said.

Sheila glanced down at the long sheet of paper. She frowned. "There's nothing here about Trinity Gray's indiscretions."

"Forget it. Thanks for bringing me the information. Anything else I should know?"

"Bits and pieces. Nothing significant. Not to Brad or myself." She handed him the computerized report. "Look it over for yourself. You know these people. Maybe something will leap out at you."

"I don't know these people. Not anymore. But thanks, I will." He turned to leave. "I'm glad you came. I know how rough a shooting incident can be."

Her expression turned grim. "Did you ever kill anyone?"

"No. Almost. He survived my bullet. When he recovered, my testimony helped send him to death row. Ironic, don't you think?"

"I keep thinking about the man I shot," Sheila said. "I keep seeing his face. I think I always will."

Dave wanted to reach out to her, but resisted the urge to do so. She didn't need his sympathy. She needed to reach inside herself to find the strength to live with the aftermath of killing a man. "You'll be all right," he said. "Take my word for it."

She smiled. "Strangely enough, I believe you. I guess I believe in you." "Believe in yourself. In the final analysis, no one else counts," he said as he left the room.

Laura had left a note on the outside of his motel room telling him that she was in the shower and for him to get a key from the desk clerk.

Moments later, spare key in hand, Dave entered his room. The shower was still running. He knocked on the bathroom door.

The sound of running water ceased. "Is that you, Dave?"

"Were you expecting someone else?"

Her laughter bounced off the tile walls. "Come on in."

Dave smiled. It had been a long time since he and Laura had made love in the shower. Too damn long. He unzipped his trousers, unbuttoned his shirt, stepped out of his shorts and took off his shoes and socks.

He joined her in the steaming shower. Their bodies fused. She ran soapy fingers down his chest and caressed his buttocks. She took his sex in her hands and lathered it. He, in turn, rubbed her body gently with his hands, replacing the sensuous movement with his lips. She arched her back, inviting his mouth to explore her slippery crevices.

He swiftly moved to comply. As their breathing quickened, the steam of the desire for each other increased the natural vapor created by the hot spray.

Dave guided her mouth within inches of his groin. She resisted. "No, please, Dave," she cried. "Take me now."

Dave knew it was wrong to force her, but his need for total fulfillment overrode his judgment. "Just this once," he pleaded.

There was a hurt in her eyes. He pulled her to a standing position. "I'm sorry." He entered her then, his breath ragged. "I love you, Laura," he whispered.

It was hard to tell if it was tears or steam that clouded her eyes. He decided it was tears, and that he'd put them there. Damn!

"I want to believe that," she sobbed. "Sometimes I don't know who you are."

One of Laura's most endearing traits was that she easily forgave. Later, nestled between the sheets of the queen sized bed, their differences put aside, at least for the moment, Laura said, "I discovered there's a lake about twenty miles from here. I'd like to go there."

"When?"

"Tomorrow." "Tomorrow!"

"Yes, tomorrow. I have to leave the next day. Surely you can take one day off from this lousy case to spend with me."

He didn't want to end up fighting with Laura. It was all they seemed to do lately. He knew the lake she referred to. As a boy, he and his father had gone there all the time. His mother hated water. After his father died, Dave hadn't returned to the lake. "Sure. Why not? What do we do about your friend next door?"

"We take her with us." She smiled. "I understand it's a large lake. We could get ourselves temporarily lost. Sheila won't mind."

"You seem to know her rather well."

"We talked a lot on the way here. I like her." She cocked her head on one side. "She has tremendous respect for you. Were you able to help her with the shooting incident?"

"Maybe. In the middle of a dark night, when she's all alone, she'll realize that all she can do is forgive herself. She'll realize that she did what she had to do, and if she had it to do over again, she wouldn't have done it any differently. It was Brad or the other guy. Not being able to forget what she did is the price a good cop pays, and that's a life sentence. For better or for worse, Sheila is a good cop."

Laura gave him a thoughtful look. "You give great advice, Dave. Too bad you never learned to take some of it for yourself."

The lake was bigger and more scenic than Dave remembered. Huge trees bordered the lake's perimeter, with numerous waterfront lush glens cradled by colorful borders of daises and buttercups. Under normal circumstances it would be paradise, Dave thought, but today, there were thoughts running through his head that would give him no peace.

He knew that Laura was irritated by the fact that on the drive here, he and Sheila had discussed the Ellen Gray case non-stop.

A blanket spread out on one of the open glens for Sheila, a boat and fishing gear rented for himself and Laura, Dave tried to push Ellen Gray from his mind.

When Dave and Laura reached the middle of the lake in the small outboard, Dave turned off the engine. "Fishing is better at the banks, but the view is better from here," he said.

Laura stretched. "I wish we could stay here forever." "In the middle of the lake!"

"Why not? Out here it's almost possible to believe there was no Ellen Gray, no Katie to haunt you, no resistance to me."

"I never resisted you."

"Didn't you? You're doing it now. You're talking to me, but your mind is someplace else. What is it about this girl that obsesses you so?"

"Don't be stupid. I'm not obsessed. I'm a cop doing my job, that's all." He handed her a rod. "You want to put your own bait on, or do you want me to do it for you?"

She shuddered. "I never did like worms. Why don't I just watch you? And don't call me stupid."

Dave took the rod from her and baited the hook with a night crawler. "I'm sorry." He made a lame attempt at levity. "Here. You'll probably have beginner's luck and catch a boatful of fish."

For the next hour they fished in near silence. Dave remembered his father telling him that fishing was really meant for thinking. Dave glanced over at Laura. She didn't look happy. We're in trouble, he thought, and I don't seem to be able to do anything about it. It's funny, he thought, and yet not so damn funny. I came back here to find out about Ellen Gray, and instead I seem to be trying to find myself. Laura was his rock, his ladder, his safety net. Maybe that was his real problem. He couldn't spend the rest of his life clinging to her like a drowning man. I can't lose her, a voice from within him cried. while another more pressing voice warned that it wasn't his call.

He voiced his earlier thought out loud. "We're in trouble, aren't we?"

She pulled her line from the water and dropped the rod into the boat. "It doesn't take a real brain to figure that one out."

"What can I do about it?"

She reached out and ran her fingers down his cheek. "That's the horrible part.

Right now, I don't think you're capable of doing anything about it."

Tough to argue the point, he silently conceded. I've been thinking the very same thing, haven't I? He waited for her to continue, knowing she had much more to say.

"You're like a boy scout looking for an old lady to walk across the street," she said. "I think that Ellen Gray is serving that purpose. No one seemed to care about her death at first, so you stepped in to fill that void. It should be over, Dave. She had a family. She wasn't alone like you thought she was."

"Yet no one seems to give a damn that she died so violently, or even why." "You do."

"Is that so wrong?"

She looked away from him, then turned back to face him. "I went to see Katie the day before I came here."

Dave didn't bother to hide his surprise. Laura had gone with him only once to see Katie. She'd hated it. "Why?"

"Driven, like you, I guess. She looked right at me, Dave. There was no vacant stare, no comatose state. She looked right at me and said, "You'll never get him. I've seen to that."

Dave started so hard the boat rocked back and forth. "What?"

"I said she was lucid, Dave, and she was vicious. That's why I came here. I had to see if she was right about us."

Dave was angry. So angry he wanted to lash out. To hurt. "You're a liar. I've sat with Katie. She's a vegetable."

Laura sighed. "She counted on this kind of reaction from you. She knew I'd tell you I'd been to see her. I'm sorry, Dave. Sorry for you. Even sorrier for myself. But I'd rather give you up now than end up as lost as you are." She looked toward shore. "I think I'd like to go back now."

"I didn't mean to call you a liar, Laura."

"I know. But it's me or Katie. I won't ask you to make that choice, even if I thought you were capable of making one. You really ought to call the Victim's Abuse program, Dave."

"I tried that. Katie isn't eligible anymore."

"Not for Katie," Laura added with a sad smile. "For you. You're the victim, not Katie. She likes it that way, and so, I think, do you."

⚬⚬⚬

Dave watched as Laura and Sheila packed Laura's car. Sheila came over to him as they prepare to drive off. "I'll have Brad call you with the information on Carey Bryant and Felix Gerard. You know you're a fool, Dave Kincaid," she said. "Don't let Laura leave here like this."

Dave shrugged. "Don't you think I'd like nothing better than to run over there and beg her to stay? But it would be for me, not for her. She deserves better."

"She loves you."

Sheila extended her hand. Dave shook it.

"Solve this Ellen Gray case soon, Dave, or leave it alone. If you don't, you could lose more than Laura, and she's loss enough."

Dave watched her drive away. The emptiness inside him was unbearable. He was on his own now. There was nothing between him and Trinity except his willpower. So far, that hadn't proved to be very reliable.

CHAPTER 7

Dave walked mindlessly to his motel room. Laura was gone, leaving a void he didn't know how to fill.

He slammed the door to his room behind him with such violence that the sound reverberated through the length of the motel. He leaned against the back of the door, and took note of the message light blinking on his phone. He sighed. He sure as hell didn't feel like talking to anyone right now.

There were two messages, the desk clerk informed him. The first: Sheriff Bromley would like to see him at his earliest convenience. Dave managed a weary smile. So, the good sheriff was back in town. It was about time!

The other message was from Bertha Bartlett. He dialed her number. She answered on the second ring.

"My dear boy," she said. "Thank you for calling. I heard you went up to the lake.

Good. I'm sure you needed the time off."

Dave was immediately annoyed. Jesus! You couldn't make a move in this town without it becoming common knowledge. Yet Ellen had managed to keep an affair with a married man a secret. It didn't figure. Then again, his own affair with Trinity had remained a secret.

"What can I do for you, Miss Bartlett?" Dave said distractedly, his mind still on Laura.

There was a note of satisfaction in the old woman's voice. "It's what I can do for you, my boy, that's important. I don't have it all together yet, but I've been very busy.

People are so used to my being nosy, they automatically answered my questions without a second thought. It gives me a wonderful advantage."

Dave liked Bertha Bartlett, but he wasn't up to dealing with idle chatter. "You have something I can use?"

"I think so. I believe I know why Ellen changed so dramatically in these last few years. I was right about the timing. She did draw into herself right after her father died." Dave could almost hear the wheels turning in her head. "Then there is the way he died," she added thoughtfully. "It happened too fast. It wasn't all it appeared to be, I'll bet my rose garden on it."

"You're talking about Sam Gray?"

Her voice lowered to a hush. Dave pictured her looking over her shoulder. The poor woman had been reading too many mystery novels. "It's too important to discuss on the phone, David. Can you come to my house?"

Dave had had enough drama for one day. "Can I come over in the morning? I was given some information on several Briarwood residents I want to think about, and I have to talk to Carey Bryant and Felix Gerard."

There was momentary silence. "I suppose you do. Yes, of course you do. In the meantime, I'll try to verify what are now mere suspicions. They're strong ones, and well founded," she added firmly.

Dave shook his head. All she had were suspicions. He felt better about putting her off until tomorrow.

After he hung up, he read and re-read the computerized report Sheila had brought with her. He'd have to talk to Chris again. And to Margaret. They'd both lied by not giving him vital information about themselves. Why hadn't Chris told him he was married to Ellen? Why had Margaret given the illusion that she came to Briarwood straight from London? And St. John! The man had a past Dave would give his right arm to know about. Then there was Bill Lackland. It looked like he was playing around with his present wife while he was married to his first. Why hadn't he just admitted it?

Because he was afraid if he confessed to one infidelity, the next stop was to wonder if he'd do it again?

Before he tackled Bill, Chris, or Margaret, Dave decided to talk to Carey Bryant and Felix Gerard first.

Dave made the decision to walk into the bank unannounced and talk to Bryant and Gerard on their home ground, the one place where at least one of them had spent a lot of time with Ellen on a purely business level.

But which one?

Carey Bryant had a private office surrounded by glass so that he could see what was going on inside the bank. That works both ways, Dave thought. The occupant inside the office was just as much on view. It was a fact Dave was keenly aware of as he felt several pairs of eyes focused on him as he shook hands with Carey Bryant.

Bryant was all that AmySpring had prepared Dave for. More pretty than handsome, his blue eyes were framed by incredibly long lashes, wavy blond hair, a pristine nose, and cheek bones a woman would kill for.

A woman's man, Dave thought. Never a man's man. Dave took the seat by the large desk that Bryant indicated.

"I assume you're here about Ellen," Bryant said, easing himself into his desk chair.

"Yes. I suppose by now it's no secret that I'm trying to find the married man Ellen was seeing before she left here."

Bryant smiled. He took a cigarette from a cedar box, offered Dave one, and when he refused, lit his own. "No, it's no secret. It's at a time like this a man wishes he were single."

"Or whenever a man gets himself involved with someone like Ellen Gray," Dave offered. "She seems to have been many things to many people."

"I liked Ellen," Bryant said. "I admit that if she'd encouraged me I might have thought about having an affair with her." He grimaced. "Not without severe penalties, however. My wife is very possessive."

A bitch, Dave remembered Amy saying. "Yeah, but then no man is going to admit to an affair with Ellen now that she was murdered," he said.

"You don't believe me?"

"Right now I'm not taking anyone's word on blind faith." Yours least of all, Dave thought. You're too goddamn smooth. "Mind if I borrow your office to talk to Felix Gerard?" he said out loud.

"Not at all." Bryant moved from behind his desk. "Suspecting me is bad enough.

But Felix! His wife is an invalid. He dotes on her."

"You're assuming I suspect him of having an affair with Ellen. I didn't say that, nor did I imply it."

"Really, Detective? This is a small town. Whomever you talk to is assumed to have been involved with Ellen. Surely you know that."

"That's too bad. If you're innocent, you have nothing to worry about, do you?

Can I see Gerard now?"

"Of course." Bryant opened the door to his office and motioned to Felix. When Felix reached the doorway, Dave said. "That's all, Mr. Bryant. If I need you further, I'll call on you."

Felix Gerard was a mediocre looking man, made to look even more so by the comparison between him and the man who had just left. He looked distinctly disturbed. He wrung his hands together. "Oh, my Lord, I've been dreading this moment ever since I heard you were talking to married men."

"How so, Mr. Gerard? You look a little green. You have something to feel guilty about?"

"I thought a lot of Ellen, Detective. She listened to me when I was depressed about Christine. Christine is my wife. She's an invalid. She'll never get better. Never. Five years ago, the doctor gave her a year, but Christine clings to life."

"That bothers you?"

"Goodness, no! It's the pain she endures that bothers me. Sometimes I wonder not only how she does it, but why. I swear that my feelings for Ellen were silent ones. I never touched her."

"But you wanted to?"

"Yes. I freely admit it. Every day that she was walked through those bank doors.

I didn't do more than fantasize, I swear."

Dave decided to believe him. At least for the moment. Or until, or if, he received damaging information about him from Brad. Then of course, the inquisitive Miss Bartlett might shed a different light on Gerard altogether.

Dave checked his watch. He should go see her, but there was the message from the Sheriff. Besides, he's already gotten away with putting her off until the morning. No sense in changing his plans, or hers.

He drove to the Sheriff's office.

⚭

Clyde Bromley was straight out of a "B" movie. He was everybody's idea of what a small town sheriff should look like.

At age sixty-one, his skin was tanned like rawhide. His uniform fit him like a hand-me-down. When he stood, his keen brown eyes met Dave's. They were the exactly the same height.

Dave smiled and extended his hand. Bromley accepted it.

"You look just like I remember you the night you locked me up," Dave said. "I have to tell you, you scared the hell out of me back then."

"As well I meant to. Have a seat. I understand you've been stirring up a lot of shit in my town. Bill filled me in on this Ellen Gray matter. Murder, you say. You don't think that maybe you're looking in the wrong place? That Ellen met her end at the hands of some city slicker?"

Dave stared past him, an intense look on his face. "I've had moments when I thought that, yes." He grimaced. "The more I learned about Ellen, the more I realized that she was nobody's angel."

Bromley threw back his head and guffawed. "Angel? Ellen? Not likely." He sobered. "She wasn't bad. Just willful at times. Bill tells me you're looking for the married man she was involved with."

Dave leaned forward. "You have any idea who he is?"

Bromley picked up a piece of paper with a list of names on it. "This is the list Bill came up with. I may not know who Ellen was fooling around with, but I sure as heck can take a good guess as to who she wasn't messing with." He passed Dave the list. Lines were drawn through all but four names, Steven St. John, Felix Gerard, Carey Bryant, and Bill Lackland.

"Bill put his name on this list?"

"No. I added it. Bill likes the ladies. I don't happen to think that he had a damn thing to do with Ellen, not the way you mean it, but you wanted likely philanderers. Bill belongs in that category."

"Why not the others on the list?" Dave asked.

"Call it instinct. Call it years of knowing these people. Call it what you want. It would be a waste of time to talk to the others." He shrugged. "But suit yourself."

Dave scanned the list again. He sighed. Maybe he should go back to the city. Maybe he was as obsessed as Laura had accused him of being. Maybe, like the sheriff claimed, the killer could be found back in the city.

"I hear you're putting our Miss Bartlett to use," Bromley said, breaking Dave's preoccupied state.

Dave flushed. "It may have gotten out of hand, Sheriff. She offered to be like some character from an Agatha Christie novel."

"Miss Marple!" Bromley's laughter filled the room. "What a wonderful comparison. Tell me, my son, you never read Agatha Christie?"

Dave flushed again. "No. Well, I may have." His tone was defensive. "I like true-to-life stories, not fictionalized garbage where amateurs make us cops look like jackasses."

Bromley yanked on his pant leg. "Jesus, you're tense. You really ought to loosen up. You'll live longer. About Bertha, you sure have her going. She's nosing into everyone's business. Then, she always does. She's a good woman, though. She never married, and she outlived all her kin, so this town became her family, especially the kids she taught. She was devastated when Severn Wokowski died. His family came here in '57. Hungarian refugees. Bertha befriended them from the start. When Severn died, she was the first to take food and to give the family comfort. She's been there every day since. That's our Bertha." His tone hardened. "Don't mess with her and leave her feeling like a fool, Kincaid. I won't allow that."

Dave's eyes couldn't quite meet Bromley's. He'd almost been guilty of what he was being accused of. He'd go see her right after he left here, he promised himself. He wouldn't wait until morning.

"I won't, you have my word. I talked to her briefly before I left my motel. She said she had some information for me. She insinuated that Sam Gray died under strange circumstances. What do you know about the night he died?"

"The accident happened in Henderson, about fifty miles from here. But, of course, you know where Henderson is. Sam went to a bar there. He had a lot to drink. A few miles outside of town he plowed into a car with four people in it. Three of them died, two right away, one a few hours later. Sam was killed instantly."

"Sam Gray wasn't a lush when I knew him," Dave said.

"He wasn't when he died, either. I'd known Sam since we were kids. He was older than Trinity, of course. He was gone a lot on business. He was a salesman, if you remember. Sometimes, when he came home, Sam and I would go fishing. In all those years I never saw Sam take more than a social drink."

"But he was drinking that night?" "Yes."

"Did you investigate the accident?"

Bromley shook his head. "The Henderson police did that. Maybe Bertha got a hold of the details of the accident somehow. It wasn't common knowledge that he was drinking that night. Strange? No. It was an unfortunate accident. Nothing more."

"What happened?"

Bromley hesitated. "Guess it won't hurt to tell you about it. When Trinity was told about the accident, she came to see me. She asked me if I could stop people from around these parts from finding out that Sam was drunk. Not for her sake, she said, but for her girls'. Ellen was twelve. She adored her father. I contacted the Henderson authorities. Sam's insurance company was going to make immediate restitution to the victims' families. Seeing as how you can't bring back the dead, I didn't see the harm in carrying out Trinity's request under the circumstances."

It was a lousy infraction of the law, Dave thought, but he didn't express his feelings out loud. "Any idea why Sam was drinking that night?"

"Words with Trinity, so she said. I don't know what they argued about.

Whatever it was, Trinity is the one who's had to live with the consequences all these years."

And maybe Ellen, Dave thought.

Dave pulled the computerized report that Sheila had brought to him from inside his jacket. "Take a look at this, Sheriff. It seems you have residents who have some explaining to do."

Bromley reached inside his desk drawer for a pair of glasses. He perched them on the end of his nose. He snorted when he came to the report on Bill Lackland. "Bill's life is an open book." He shrugged when he came to the part about Margaret. "Interesting.

Chances are she had a good reason for giving the illusion she came straight here from London. Why don't you ask her?"

"I intend to."

He frowned when he came to the report about Chris. "Damn fool boy. He put Ellen up on a pedestal. Such an asinine move to try to hide a marriage. He had to know it would come out."

When Bromley came to the information on St. John, he scanned it without a word.

He handed the material back to Dave.

Dave gaped at him. "This information on St. John didn't even get a rise out of you. Do you know who he really is?"

"Yup. He's Steven St. John. I don't need to know anything else unless he's committed, or is thinking of committing a felony here in Briarwood. So far I've seen no evidence of that."

"You're not even curious!"

"Not a bit." Bromley put his feet up on the battered desktop. "I got one more year to go before I retire. I bought me a piece of land in Arkansas that is a fisherman's dream. I'd like to coast until I leave here." He grimaced. "But you ain't gonna let me do that, are you?"

Dave smiled. "No, I'm not. What about Bill? How come if he's so irresponsible you let him fill in your shoes when you leave town?"

Bromley tapped his feet with a pencil. "These shoes ain't so big. Besides, in a town like this he ain't doing any harm."

Dave sighed. "Guess I've been a city cop too long. I can't deal with that kind of logic."

"You learn. If you still want Bill to help you with your investigation, he's willing." Bromley set his feet on the floor. He stood and shook Dave's hand indicating the interview was over.

Dave was almost to the door, when Bromley said. "Don't suppose a big city cop like yourself would like to be sheriff of a town like Briarwood someday?"

Dave gave him a long hard stare, then took the doorknob in his hand, opened the door, and stepped outside.

⌥

Dave checked his watch. Dinnertime. He could take a chance on not ruining Bertha Bartlett's meal or…

"Just the man I want to see," A voice interrupted his thoughts. "I owe you an apology for the other night. I was rude."

He turned to face Margaret Gray. "Could be I provoked you. Let's call it even. I've been wanting to talk to you. Right now, I'm on my way to Miss Bartlett's house. How about I come by tomorrow?"

Margaret wrinkled her nose. "Miss Bartlett! Many is the miserable hour I spent in her classroom. That woman can see right through you!"

"Right. I'll see you tomorrow then. Is the morning okay?"

She pouted. "Surely Miss Bartlett can wait. If I don't talk to you tonight, I may never get up the nerve to say again what I have to say to you now."

Dave had to admit he was intrigued, and Bertha Bartlett wasn't expecting him until the morning. He sighed. "Okay."

She smiled. "Thanks. I don't intend to talk in the middle of the street. I can drive you to my house and bring you back, or you can follow me."

"I'll meet you there."

He watched her walk gracefully to her red sports car and swing her legs onto the front seat. He placed a restraining hand on the door as she was about to shut it. "How did you know where to find me?"

She laughed. "You keep forgetting, Dave, this is a small town. The desk clerk is a friend of mine. He said you had two calls, one from the Sheriff, the other from Miss Bartlett. I came here first, assuming you'd consider the Sheriff's call more important."

He picked up on the way his name easily rolled off her tongue. She didn't seem to be nervous or harboring guilt. Maybe it was just like Bromley said, and she'd have a good reason for letting people think she came straight here from London.

Inside Margaret's house, Dave sensed a new hominess, a more lived-in feeling.

Or maybe it was just that he was getting used to the place. Or maybe it was because Margaret was an attractive woman, and he was still hurting from Laura's rejection of him. Maybe…To hell with maybes!

Margaret disappeared into the kitchen and emerged with two glasses of wine. She extended one of the glasses to him. He shook his head.

She shrugged. "You weren't always this ethical, were you?" "What do you mean?"

She took a deep breath, exhaled, and hesitated. "I know about you and my mother."

"I don't…"

"Don't stop me. I've been waiting to say this ever since I knew you were in town. I was only nine at the time. You were a worldly sixteen, or so I thought at the time, and my mother…well, my mother was just being herself. I don't blame you, but I did resent the fact that my mother treated me like a moron. I watched the two of you one night. I was supposed to be asleep. I opened her bedroom door a crack. It was like nothing I'd ever seen before, let alone thought about. After that, I spied on the two of you whenever I could."

Dave hoped like hell he wasn't blushing. "Does your mother know about this?" "Don't be silly. She had her secrets. You and she were my secret. I developed a

huge crush on you. Then, one day you and your family were gone." She emptied her glass. "Did you know that you and my mother were directly responsible for my having my first sexual experience when I was only ten? No, how could you? He was an inexperienced lout who could have easily clouded my view of sex. I saved myself from that by closing my eyes and pretending it was you."

Dave's palms were moist. He hadn't prepared himself for this. After their last get-together he believed she knew nothing about him and

Trinity. He wondered why she'd waiting until now to bring it up. He had to change the subject, to assume control. Damn Margaret! He'd been wrong about her. She was exactly like Trinity. Or at least she was trying to be. "Okay, so now we've uncovered my past. What about your own? Why did you want not only me, but everyone else to think you came straight here from London? What were you doing in the city for three days?"

She paled. "Good work, Detective. I think I need another drink."

She emerged a moment later with a full glass. "You believe I had something to do with my sister's death, don't you?"

"Convince me that you didn't."

"You're not an easy man to convince. All right. I was in the city. I was there when Ellen died, only I didn't know about her. You have to believe that. Good God, do you know that I was only a mile away from where she was killed? Do you have any idea how that makes me feel now?"

"No, I don't."

"Guilty as hell. If I'd come straight here I would have found out that she was gone. I'd have reported her missing. Maybe you'd have found her. Maybe she'd be alive."

"What were you doing in the city?"

"Waiting. Waiting for a man who promised to meet me there. We all have our vices. Mine is an obsession with titles. The man I was waiting for is a Duke, with an old-world charm that the British hypnotize us gullible Americans with so effectively. His title did the rest. I met him through the Embassy. His mother is a typical English snob who would rather die than let her son marry a common American. He was the reason I quit my job and came back to the States. He was going to tell his mother to go to hell and we were going to be married. We had arranged to meet in the city and fly to Reno.

Instead, I got a cable telling me he wouldn't be coming." She downed her drink in one gulp. "The dowager bitch won."

"Your story can be checked, you know." "Do your worst. I'm telling you the truth."

"What would you have done if your Duke had shown up?"

"Kissed this town goodbye," she responded bitterly. She smiled. "Of course, I may have paraded him around here for a few days just for the hell of it."

"What is it," he wondered out loud, "that seems to make you, and maybe Ellen, want to one-up Trinity all the time?"

"It was always that way. Ever since I can remember."

She moved closer to him. "You were part of the game. Or maybe you started it. But my mother isn't here now, and I'm all grown up. Think about it. You could help me fulfill a girlish fantasy and have yourself a night you'll never forget."

She loosened his tie. Dave backed away. "Give me some slack, Margaret. I have a murder so solve. Your sisters, incidentally, or had you forgotten? I've got enough problems without fighting you off, problems that don't make me anxious to have history repeat itself by crawling into bed with you."

She sidled nearer to him. "It wouldn't be ancient history. It would be new. I'm not my mother. For one thing I don't want to get involved. I told you my nasty little secret." She smiled. "You don't have a title, so you're perfectly safe with me." She tilted her head to one side. "These problems you have? It wouldn't have anything to do with one of those women who left your motel this afternoon would it?"

Dave grabbed her wrist. "Back off, Margaret."

She threw back her head and laughed. "Haven't you noticed that when we're together the sparks seem to fly? Admit it. The idea of making love to me appeals to your baser instincts."

Dave let go of her wrist. "Maybe, but I'm going to walk out of this room and out the front door."

"But not out of my life," she yelled after him. "My mother, Ellen, and now me, will always have a hold on you whether you want us to or not."

He stopped at the door. He raised his hand and pointed his index finger at her. "Not true. If you had anything to do with Ellen's death, in any way, I'll see that you pay for it. You can take that to the bank. Oh, and by the way, you knew, of course, that Chris and Ellen were married. It was annulled."

No one could fake that look of total disbelief, Dave realized. "Married! No! She would have told me. We were close."

"You say all the right words, Margaret, especially where Ellen was concerned.

Why is it that I don't buy your sisterly love act?"

He didn't give her a chance to answer him. He swiftly left.

Outside her front door, Dave shivered. He'd had one bad moment in there. For a few lousy seconds he'd contemplated taking Margaret up on her offer.

It was Laura, he told himself. He missed her, and he wanted to get back at her for walking out on him. It was more than that, he reluctantly admitted. It was Trinity, and the past reaching out like a thousand ugly tentacles to claim him.

⌘

Dave woke with a jolt. He'd dreamed about Bertha Bartlett. She was staring at people through a giant magnifying glass. She was yelling at someone. Telling whoever it was to be careful. In his dream, someone had come behind Bertha and grabbed the glass out of her hand and hit her over the head with it. Dave had tried to shout a warning, but the words never left his mouth.

He dressed in record time, skipping breakfast, even coffee, and drove to Bertha's home.

He briskly walked up the flower lined path to her front door. He felt uneasy. It was that damned dream! There was a feeling of desolation about the place that increased his feeling of doom.

He knocked on the door. There was no answer. He tried again. Still no answer.

He frowned. Bertha would never ignore or forget an appointment.

It was possible she was working in the rear yard. He walked around the house.

His uneasiness intensified as he was met with silence when he called out her name.

He knew before he found her lying behind a neatly pruned hedge that bordered a rock garden that he would find her dead. He'd known it when he'd awakened from his dream.

She lay face down, one knee twisted outward. Blood caked the back of her head, matting her silver hair. He stared down at her, feeling responsible. It could have been an accident, he told himself. It had to be, he justified, squishing his sense of guilt. Why hadn't he come here last night? Why on earth would anyone want to hurt this harmless old lady? Had she really known, or found out something that someone couldn't afford for her to tell?

He slowly walked to the back door. It was unlocked. The house smelled of lavender and last night's dinner. The kitchen table was cluttered with dirty dishes. So few dishes, he couldn't help thinking. A plate, a glass, a cup, a knife, fork and spoon. It must be hell living alone.

Get used to it, a voice inside clamored. This is what life without Laura will be like.

The old lady must have died right after dinner. She didn't strike him as the kind to let dirty dishes sit for long. Why was she in the rock garden in the first place? Then again, why not? Her yard was her pride and joy.

Dave moved to the phone on the counter. He called the sheriff's office. When Bromley came on the line, Dave said, "You'd better got out to Miss Bartlett's place.

She's dead."

CHAPTER 8

Clyde Bromley stared down at Bertha, his shoulders slumped. Regret filled his line-etched face. He looked over at Dave. "Did you touch anything?"

"No."

"Good." He sighed. "You know what I'd like to do? I'd like to call this an accident, but we both know I can't do that until I'm sure that's exactly what it was."

Dave didn't try to hide his surprise. "I guess I thought you'd want to wash this one. Why don't you? Something I said?"

Bromley turned on him, an angry flush spreading from his face to his neck. "Maybe, but don't take all the goddamned credit. I just don't buy coincidences, not when two days after you have Bertha bird-dogging for you, she turns up dead. That's one hell of a coincidence in my book. He slammed his fist into the palm of his hand. "Goddamn you, Kincaid, you know it's possible you got her killed."

Dave was surprised at Bromley's vehemence. "If you believe that, Sheriff, then you believe that someone from Briarwood had something to do with her death. If you believe that, it follows that you believe Miss Bartlett died because she knew something so damaging to someone that whoever it was had to kill her to keep it quiet."

"I thought that was what I just said." Bromley looked back down at Bertha's body and shook his head again. "I'll make a call to Henderson. We ain't got a sophisticated crime unit here."

"Would you consider letting me call my Captain?" Dave asked. "We have a top- notch crime team and lab."

Bromley looked away from Bertha's body. "Yeah, I bet you do. Okay. Why the hell not? I owe Bertha that much. The town owes her." He sighed. "Why couldn't you stay in the city and leave us alone? Thanks to you, I have a town full of jittery people, family men wondering when you're going to come knocking on their doors upsetting their apple cart, and now one of the pillars of this community is dead. Coincidence? I hope so. For your sake I hope so."

"That sounds like a threat, Sheriff."

Bromley raised his fist, then lowered it. "So it did. Could be I wish it carried more weight. No question in my mind that we'd all be a lot better off if you hadn't come nosing around here with your allegations of murder."

"Better? You think that protecting a murderer would make this town a better place? Come off it, Sheriff. Aren't you the son of a bitch who wants to drive away from here a year from now with your feet up on the end of a pier, with a fishing pole in your hand? Whose town will it be then?"

Bromley gave him a hard look. "That's one for you, Kincaid. I'll call the County Coroner. You call your crime people." He looked back down at Bertha. "Someone should stay here until they show up."

"I'll stay. I'd like to go through Miss Bartlett's things after they get through here. Yesterday, you told me Miss Bartlett had been talking to a lot of people about Ellen. She may have stumbled onto something. She seemed convinced she had information that would help me with my investigation. Maybe she made notes," Dave said hopefully, "or kept a diary. When I was in school, I remember Miss Bartlett always made notes to herself to use in class." Dave kicked at the dirt creating a cloud of dust. "I wish I'd taken her more seriously when she called me yesterday. After I left you last night, I was going to come over here and talk to her."

"What stopped you?"

"Margaret Gray. She was waiting for me outside your office." Dave stopped short. "You don't suppose she was trying to keep me occupied?" Dave flushed, thinking about last night, and how close he'd come to sleeping with Margaret Gray.

"Could be, but that would mean collusion. You'll want to check it out, of course."

"Of course," Dave replied, thinking that he wasn't looking forward to the task.

No man wanted to think he was duped. Especially if that man was a cop. "It's okay with you if I go through Miss Bartlett's things?"

"You got a job to do. I don't have to like it." Bromley abruptly changed the subject. "Your people released Ellen's body. Her funeral is tomorrow. You going?"

Dave nodded. "Who is liable to be there?"

"Ask me who won't be, the list will be shorter. Let me know if you find anything of interest inside the house."

"You don't want to help me?"

"No. Underneath this badge is an old-fashioned man, Kincaid. I still believe in people's right to privacy. That may make me a lousy law man, I know, but I sleep real good at night." He shrugged. "Bertha ain't in any position to argue with you, that's for sure. Just make sure you bring anything you feel is important to my office."

"No problem. One more thing. No matter what the investigation into Miss Bartlett's death reveals, I want to treat it as an accident. If this was murder, I'd like whoever killed Miss Bartlett to think they got away with it. It will make him or her less wary."

Bromley nodded in agreement. He was halfway down the flagstone path that led to the front of the house when Dave said, "I don't like the way it came about any more than you do, but I'm glad you're with me on this case now, Sheriff. I can use your help."

Bromley gave him a long cold stare, started to say something, changed his mind, and continued on down the walkway.

Dave used the phone on Bertha's kitchen. He contacted Captain Herring who immediately dispatched a crime lab crew. Then Dave spoke to Brad. He told him about Bertha.

"You think she was murdered?" Brad asked.

"I don't want it to turn out that way. If it's murder, I have to take some responsibility. I was using the old lady."

Brad gave a short laugh. "You don't have enough to feel guilty about? Sorry, Dave. That was thoughtless. I heard about Laura. You don't need me beating up on you." There was a brief and awkward silence. "She moved in with Sheila," Brad said.

All Dave could think about was that Laura hadn't wasted any time in clearing out of his apartment and out of his life. He tried to keep the hurt from his voice and didn't succeed. "Nothing's forever, Brad."

"I sure thought you two were."

"I didn't call to talk about Laura," Dave said, bringing personal talk to an abrupt end. "You got anything on Bryant and Gerard yet?"

Dave heard the shuffling of papers. "Yeah. St. John came along just in the nick of time to save Bryant's bacon. The bank was not the only thing in trouble; there's also a possibility he was manipulating funds."

"That's interesting," Dave said. "That's damned interesting. He isn't from Briarwood. Where did he come from?"

More shuffling of papers. "New York. He moved to Briarwood ten years ago. Started as a loan officer and worked his way up…fast. He has no arrests, no warrants."

"What's the story on Gerard?"

"He's squeaky clean. He moved to Briarwood five years ago from a Chicago suburb, hoping the climate would help his wife's condition. Same story. No arrests, no warrants."

Dave sighed. "I think I knew he'd be clean. Why don't we concentrate our efforts on St. John? I've a feeling if we can come up with his true identity, we'll be halfway to a solution to this damn case. Can you see your way clear to using your unfailing charms on Glenda in research? I want the names of any key witnesses in any major trial dating back two, three years ago. Then I want a profile on anyone she digs up who fits St. John's general description."

"That's a tall order. Herring might not go for it."

"If I wanted Herring to know, I wouldn't be asking you to flex your handsome muscles. What I need requires not only gentle and subtle persuasion, but a lot of overtime."

Brad laughed. "Oh, I see. You're lucky. Glenda isn't exactly dog meat. I guess I can handle it, but that's favor number three, Dave. You're building quite a tab."

"I'm good for it. Call me when you get anything."

Dave severed the connection. He looked around Bertha's kitchen. Where in the hell should he start? If Miss Bartlett's death wasn't an accident, whoever killed her would have considered that she might have made notes, just as he had. If so, there'd be nothing to find. What the hell, Dave thought, you know her death wasn't an accident.

You don't need a crime lab crew to tell you that. Her head was at the wrong angle, the wound on her head too brutal for a fall. Like Bromley, you don't believe in coincidence.

Dave ran his fingers through his hair. He closed his eyes. Try to think like Miss Bartlett, he counseled himself. Where would she hide anything she thought was important? This is useless, he told himself, wishing Sheriff Bromley had stayed around to help. What do I know about Miss Bartlett's habits or thought process? My memories of her are eighteen years old!

"Fuck it," he said out loud. "You're going to have to do it the hard way. Inch by inch."

⟨ﷺ⟩

Knowing better than to touch anything until the crime lab crew arrived, Dave aimlessly wondered around Bertha's home. The living room, or parlor, as Bertha would have preferred to call it, was designed for comfort, the only modern piece of furniture a nineteen-inch television set. Dave started to turn it on to pass the time, then changed his mind. He glanced at his watch. It was twelve minutes past nine. It was an hour-and-a- half to a two hour drive from the city, depending on traffic. He'd called Herring a half- an-hour ago. Even if the crime lab crew had left right away, they wouldn't be here until eleven-fifteen at the earliest.

Dave moved down the hallway of the one-story dwelling. There were three closed doors. He reached inside his jacket for a handkerchief and placed it around the doorknob of the first room. It was cold inside, and it had an unlived-in feeling. It was obviously a guest room. The second closed door, when opened, revealed a sewing room. Neatness was the major theme here. Everything was in its place.

The last door he opened led to Bertha's bedroom. A huge walnut bed dominated the room, a small nightstand on one side of it, with a lamp atop it. There was a chest at the end of the bed. It was the walls that captured Dave's immediate attention. They were covered with pictures of her students, class group pictures for the most part, methodically, and he imagined lovingly, arranged by year. He wondered why here, and not in the living room for all to see. She must have wanted them to be the last thing she looked at before she fell asleep. He searched for one of himself. An amazed look passed over his face when he actually found it. It was a clear picture taken when he was fifteen.

He moved around the room until he came to the latest of the pictures. He was able to identify Ellen Gray in a group shot taken in her last year of high school.

Dave clenched his fists. Bertha Bartlett had been one of those rare individuals who really cared about people, and some son of a bitch had snuffed out her life like it was nothing. Worse, this hadn't even been a clever murder like Ellen's. If Dave hadn't had his "gut feeling" about Ellen's death, he knew that she would still be listed in the files as an accidental overdose. On the downside, Miss Bartlett might still be alive if he hadn't been so insistent on calling Ellen's death, murder.

He was about to close the door to the bedroom when he spied a paperback book sitting on the nightstand. He picked it up. It was titled, MURDER IN THE VICARAGE, by Agatha Christie. He read the inside cover. It was a Miss Marple mystery.

Dave carried the book to a rocker that was located in the corner of the room. He sat down. He looked at the book again. He shook his head. It's not your kind of reading, Dave, a voice inside murmured, while another urged him to read it. Bromley had said Miss Bartlett was like this Miss Marple character. Maybe if he read the book…What the hell! He had time to kill.

A non-fiction and sports reader, Dave had a hard time getting into the Agatha Christie who-dun-it, but he had to admit, the author's Miss Marple character was Miss Bartlett, but with one important difference. The fictional Miss Marple survived, according to the promo on the inside cover.

He looked at his watch again. Christ, it was after eleven! He heard the sound of a van approaching. They'd made good time. Dave placed the book back where he'd found it and went to greet the crime lab crew, most of whom he knew, at least by sight.

"Let me know when it's okay to touch anything," he said. "I'd like to search the place."

The crew was fast and methodical, operating with a precision that came from years of experience. They took pictures, they dusted for prints, and they measured. They examined the area around Bertha's body. They missed nothing. Dave felt a measure of pride. These guys were good, and they were from his own precinct.

Gil Mason managed his crime team with care and an iron hand. The operation concluded, he approached Dave. "We're going to head back to the city. You want a written report or a brief verbal?"

"Both," Dave responded. "What's the immediate word?"

"I understand the Sheriff is calling for an autopsy. That's good. I'm not a coroner, but she didn't die from a fall. The head wound is all wrong. Somebody smashed her on the head with this rock." He held up a smooth shiny blood-stained rock. "I'll take it back to the lab." He sighed. "There are so many prints in the house it will take forever to identify them. Will the local law be cooperative with us?"

Dave nodded. "You're here, aren't you? Believe me, that's cooperation.

Anything else?"

"Footprints. As many as there are fingerprints. A lot of them were put here in the last twenty-four hours. What did the old lady do? Have open house?"

Dave managed a grin. "Miss Bartlett was very sociable. Everybody liked her.

She had a lot of visitors, especially in the last twenty-four hours, according to the sheriff."

"Better she would have been a hermit," Gil wryly observed.

Dave couldn't agree more. "Okay to look around now?" he asked. Gil nodded. "Sure, we're done. What are you looking for?"

What was he looking for? "I won't know until I find it."

"That's what's so great about my job. I don't have to live with a case like you guys do. Especially you."

"What is that supposed to mean?"

"You got a rep, Dave. Some cops take off their guns and badges and leave a case in the squad room. That's not your style." He slapped Dave on the back. "That's what makes you such a good cop. Best of luck to you."

"Thanks. I've got a feeling I'm going to need it."

After the van left, Dave wandered back into the house. He opened drawers, careful not to mess anything up. Not that it mattered anymore, but there was that look on Bromley's face when Dave said he was going to go through Miss Bartlett's belongings. Dave searched closets, he looked under beds, he even looked in the toilet tanks. All he found was old diaries in the chest at the end of her bed. This year's diary was missing.

That in itself was significant.

Had Miss Bartlett made notes other than those in her diary? Miss Marple would have, he was sure. The more Dave thought about it, the surer he became that some form of notes had been made. Had her killer already found them? The sewing room? He went through everything in the room again. He shook every piece of material twice, and methodically emptied each drawer of the sewing chest, carefully sifting through the contents. Nothing!

Where would she hide anything, if indeed she had hid anything. Maybe what he was looking for and couldn't find had been in plain sight, and whoever killed her had merely picked it up and carried it off.

He needed to get out of here. To think. He was about to leave when he was drawn to the bookcase in the living room. Books! There was a whole row of Agatha Christie novels and other more literary works. He took them one by one and turned them upside down and shook them. All that fell out were a few book marks and some recipes.

Dave sighed. It was no use.

He was halfway down the walkway when it struck him. There was one very obvious place he hadn't looked. The book by Miss Bartlett's bed! His belabored reading hadn't taken him past chapter six. He strode back inside the house and made his way to Bertha's bedroom. He picked up the book and flipped the pages. A few pages before the end, he found a folded piece of paper tucked neatly inside. Dave held his breath. It could be another damn recipe! He opened up the sheet of paper.

Exhaling sharply, he slapped the paper. He had found what he was looking for. Bertha's notes were written in bold print.

THINGS TO DO AND PEOPLE TO SEE

TRINITY – SO MANY QUESTIONS! WHERE DO I START? MARGARET – I HARDLY KNOW HER ANYMORE. CAN'T SAY I EVER

LIKED HER MUCH – TOO CRAFTY.

CHRIS – I THINK HE HOLDS THE KEY TO ELLEN'S MURDER, BUT HE MAY NOT KNOW IT!

STEVEN ST. JOHN – I KNOW HIM LEAST OF ANY OF THEM. UNLIKE THE OTHERS, HE'LL BE WARY OF ME.

CAREY BRYANT – COCKY. HE WON'T GIVE MUCH AWAY. (NEVER LIKED HIM MUCH EITHER.)

FELIX GERARD – COULD IT BE THAT STILL WATERS RUN DEEP HERE?

BILL LACKLAND – A FOOL AND A PHILANDERER.

BETH LACKLAND – SHE AND ELLEN WERE FRIENDS, BUT ELLEN DIDN'T ATTEND HER WEDDING. WHY?

SHERIFF BROMLEY – DEAR CLYDE. ALL HE THINKS ABOUT THESE DAYS IS RETIREMENT. HE CAN HELP DAVE IF HE WILL. I MUST SEE THAT HE DOES.

DOCTOR CHRISTIAN – HE'LL TRY TO USE PATIENT CONFIDENTIALITY. I'LL HAVE TO OUTSMART HIM.

BUY MORE CANNING JARS AND BLUE THREAD. NO TIME! There was a neat line drawn through this entry. THIS CAN WAIT.

WOKOWSKI'S – TAKE SOME HOMEMADE JELLY TO THEM, AND TRY NOT TO UPSET THEM WITH ELLEN'S DEATH. THEY'VE BEEN THROUGH SO MUCH, AND THEY LIKED ELLEN.

ASK THEM ALL HERE TO SEE ME ON THE PRETEXT I HAVE PRESERVES TO GIVE THEM. THEY ALL LIKE MY PRESERVES. IT'LL MAKE THEM LESS SUSPICIOUS. YES, I'LL ASK THEM ALL HERE, EXCEPT CLYDE, ST. JOHN, AND THE DOCTOR. I'LL HAVE TO GO TO THEIR OFFICES AND TO THE ST. JOHN FARM.

THOUGHTS

ELLEN: COMPLEX AND SECRETIVE. NOT EASY TO KNOW, BUT EASY TO LIKE OR NOT TO LIKE, DEPENDING ON WHO YOU WERE.

ELLEN AND ST. JOHN? ELLEN AND BILL? ELLEN AND CAREY?

ELLEN AND CHRIS.

HOW DID "HE" REALLY DIE? DID ELLEN KNOW? IS THAT WHAT SCARED HER? OR WAS IT SOMETHING ELSE?

DAVID AND PAUL KINCAID. LIKE FATHER LIKE SON? DAVID AND TRINITY. SHOULD I TELL HIM I KNOW? WHO IS ELLEN'S FATHER?

STEVEN ST. JOHN CAME HERE FROM OUT OF NOWHERE. HE NEVER DID REALLY SAY WHERE HE WAS FROM. WHY DID HE COME TO BRIARWOOD? WHY DID HE MARRY TRINITY?

WHO WAS ELLEN GOING TO SEE IN THE CITY? I THINK I KNOW. MUST TELL DAVID.

TIRED NOW. DAVID AND I WILL TALK TOMORROW. I'M SURE HE CAN MAKE SENSE OF IT. HE ALWAYS WAS A GOOD BOY. I'M SURE HE'S GOOD AT HIS JOB. UNFORTUNATELY, BECAUSE OF HIS PAST AND HIS CONNECTION TO BRIARWOOD, HE HAS TO BE MORE THAN JUST GOOD, HE HAS TO BE OBJECTIVE.

Dave's attention kept straying to one particular notation. DAVID AND TRINITY. SHOULD I TELL HIM I KNOW. It could only mean that Miss Bartlett knew about his affair with Trinity eighteen years ago. Had she always known, or had his coming back here triggered old suspicions? And what did she mean, LIKE FATHER LIKE SON?

Dave placed Bertha's notes in his jacket pocket. He remembered that he was supposed to tell the Sheriff about anything he found. Could he get away with reading the highlights of Miss Bartlett's notes to him over the phone? Why drag up an eighteen- year-old affair that had nothing to do with Ellen or Miss Bartlett's death?

Dave sighed. The man in him wanted to keep his secret from Bromley. The cop in him knew he couldn't.

⌘

Ellen's funeral was tomorrow. It would be a good place to question Chris about why he kept his marriage to Ellen a secret, Dave decided, and maybe a few of the other key suspects as well. He thought about Miss Bartlett's notes. What could Chris know that he didn't know he knew? Something Ellen told him that had gone over his head?

Dave drove from Bertha's house to the service station. A man in his late fifties, his hair gray and balding, was pumping gas into an old beat-up truck loaded with fodder. Dave waited until he was through.

When the truck drove off, Dave produced his badge. "You must be Chris's father. What time will he be in?"

The man wiped his brow with a dubious looking rag. "Good question. He never showed up for work this morning. His bed wasn't slept in last night, neither."

A warning bell went off in Dave's head. Miss Bartlett had thought that Chris knew something. "Has he done this before?" Dave asked.

"Once. Right after he and Ellen got back together again. Wished they'd stayed together. Maybe, then, Ellen would still be alive."

Dave had no doubt about it. "Has Chris always lived at home, Mr. Briggs?" "Yup."

"I assume you're worried."

Briggs used the rag on his brow again. "Course I'm worried. So is the wife. On one hand, he's old enough to stay gone the night, but on the other hand, it ain't like him."

"You said he did it once before."

"Ellen was alive then. We had no reason to doubt they were together. Besides, I called Trinity. Ellen was gone, too. Made sense to all of us that they was together someplace. Sure enough, they were."

"When did you see Chris last, and where was he?"

"Yesterday, here at the station. He worked till five when I relieved him. He said something about going to see Miss Bartlett."

"You never saw him or heard from him after that?"

"No, I didn't. I called Miss Bartlett around eight, but she didn't answer her phone. I heard about her passing away. I guess that's why she didn't answer her phone. Accident, so the sheriff says. Too bad. She was a nice lady."

"She was a real nice lady," Dave agreed. "Your son may have been one of the last people to see her before she died."

Sid Briggs rubbed his balding head. "Is that so? Miss Bartlett will be missed.

She had nothing but friends in this town."

She had one enemy, Dave thought. The person who killed her.

It was obvious that Chris's father knew nothing of real importance. "Thanks.

You will have Chris get in touch with me when you hear from him?" "Sure will."

From the gas station Dave made his way to the Sheriff's office. Bromley came from behind his desk and showed Dave into a small room and closed the door. "We can talk better in here," Bromley explained. "Tilda is good people, but she can't keep her jaws from flapping. What did you find?'

Dave pulled Bertha's notes from his pocket, wishing there was some way to erase her observations about him and Trinity. He knew the moment when Bromley got to that particular notation from the look on the older man's face. "You and Trinity?" Bromley said, disbelief in his voice. "Is this Bertha's fantasy, or is there any truth to it?"

Dave sighed. "It's true. It's not relevant to Ellen or Bertha's death, however.

Hell, Sheriff, I was only sixteen at the time."

"I know how damn old you were," Bromley exploded. "I just can't figure it. Half the men in this town were scheming how to get into Trinity's drawers, and she chose a high school boy! Jesus, Kincaid. They have a name for that, even here. It's called statutory rape."

Dave's tone hardened. "I wasn't an unwilling participant. Anyway, do you want to press charges after all this time, or do you want to solve a couple of murders?"

Bromley sighed. "Bertha's death was murder, then?"

"I don't have a written report, but I talked to the head of the crime lab crew. He thinks it was murder. So do I. So do you, for that matter."

"I admit I was afraid it might be. Is this all you found?"

"I found a stack of old diaries dating back to last year. I didn't read them," he said defensively. "This year's diary is missing. I think whoever killed her, took it."

"Anything else?"

"Yeah. I think there was another page or pages to her notes. I believe Miss Bartlett made comments about her visits to the people on her list. She may have been working on it when her killer showed up at the house."

"Makes sense. Too bad you didn't make it over to her house last night, Kincaid." "At least I wasn't fishing," Dave bristled. "I was working. My visit to

Margaret's house was police business."

"Sure it was. I'm sorry I brought it up."

Dave had the feeling he wasn't at all sorry. "Yeah, well, if I could change things I would. By the way, Chris Briggs is missing."

Bromley shot forward. "The hell you say. Since when?"

"Since he went to see Miss Bartlett. Makes you think, doesn't it?" "Sure does. What are you going to do about it?"

"Nothing right now, just hope like hell he shows up, if not before, at Ellen's funeral tomorrow. I have to know if any of the people on Miss

Bartlett's list had alibis for the nights both she and Ellen were killed. Can you handle that for me, Sheriff?" Or will you? Dave thought.

There was no resistance. "I can do that. Can I keep Bertha's notes?" "If I can get a copy of them."

Bromley started to call Tilda in, then checked himself. "She'll read every damn word. I'll make you a copy myself."

A few moments later he returned with a photocopy of Bertha's notes. "What are you going to do now, Kincaid?"

"For starters, I'm going back to my motel. There may be messages for me from the city."

Dave felt weariness spread through his bones as he drove back to the motel. He could sure use a nap.

There would be no immediate sleep for him. This first thing Dave noticed when he entered his room was that it wasn't empty.

Trinity was waiting for him.

CHAPTER 9

Dave slowly closed the door behind him. His heart pounded so furiously, he though surely she must be able to hear it. His breathing was so shallow, he felt light- headed. He silently damned her for still having the power to affect him like this. He had expected that a second encounter with her would naturally be easier on him. He was annoyed and unnerved because it wasn't.

He tossed his jacket on the bed, loosened his tie, and tried to affect an air of nonchalance, but when he opened his mouth to speak, his voice seemed high-pitched to his ears. "What are you doing here?" He cleared his throat.

Trinity rose from the chair she'd been occupying. She wore a sapphire-blue silk jumpsuit that hugged her like a second skin. She looked even lovelier than the last time he'd seen her. She took a few steps toward Dave, then paused when he held up his hands to ward her off. "Don't worry, I wasn't going to touch you," she said. "I came to ask you to leave Briarwood. Two people have died. I don't want anything to happen to you."

In a precariously weak moment, Dave almost told her the truth about Miss Bartlett. He restrained himself with great effort. He could trust no one. Least of all Trinity. "Miss Bartlett's death was an accident. She stumbled and hit her head on a rock."

Trinity moved toward the bed and sat on the edge. Her hands gripped the mattress. The look of relief on her face made Dave want to run to her.

"Then it really was an accident?" Trinity whispered. "Thank God! When I heard Bertha Bartlett was dead, I thought…"

Dave forced himself to keep his distance. She looked so vulnerable. But she's not vulnerable, Dave reminded himself. Or if she is, she's not nearly as vulnerable as you are at this moment. "That it was murder?" he responded. "I'm curious, Trinity.

What made you jump to that particular conclusion?"

She got up from the bed "Silly, wasn't it? Of course, it was an accident. I overreacted. It's Ellen. We're burying her tomorrow, and that makes her death suddenly seem so final, more real." She shook her head. "Then death is final, isn't it?" She passed her hand across her brow. "Forgive me, I seem to be falling apart."

Dave grabbed her by the wrist, ignoring her painful cry. "Not silly. Not silly at all. You know something you're not telling me. Who did you think killed Miss Bartlett? Your husband?"

Trinity pulled herself free of him. "I don't have to listen to this."

"You're right, you don't. Then you didn't have to come here either, and yet you did. What do you really know about your husband, Trinity? Where did he come from? Where is his family? What exactly does he do when he's away on his consulting trips?"

"You have all the answers," she hissed. "You tell me."

"Okay. I'll give it a try. Let's see, he never talks about where he's from, he has no living relatives, and he doesn't like to bore you with the details of his business trips. How am I doing so far?"

The look on her face told him he'd hit home. "Steven didn't kill Ellen," she said. "Maybe. Who are you trying to convince? Me, or yourself?"

She retrieved her purse from the small table by the window. "I came here because I was afraid for you. It seems I had no reason to be. I'd better be going."

He grabbed her wrist again, but more gently this time. "I want to find whoever killed Ellen. I think you could help me if you wanted to."

"No.!"

"Just what is it you're scared of?"

"Nothing. I really must be going. It was foolish of me to come here. The clerk let me into your room. I bribed him, but I have no assurance he'll keep his mouth shut. By this time tomorrow, we could be the main topic of backyard gossip."

He suddenly realized how much she'd risked by coming here. When this case was over, he'd be leaving, but Trinity would be staying behind to face the wagging tongues and contemptuous looks, just as she always had. "Why didn't you ever leave Briarwood?" He asked.

"No reason to. Most people who leave are running away from here. I was already running away from something when I came to Briarwood."

"What was that?"

A look of determination passed over her face. "Nothing I feel like talking about."

She had her hand on the doorknob. Dave struggled with himself. Was he up to confronting her on personal issues? His answer came quickly. He knew if he didn't do it now, he might not get this chance again. "Sit down, Trinity. I have to talk to you."

She responded to the urgency in his voice. She gave him an inquiring look, hesitated, and sat back down in the chair by the window. She sat on the edge of the seat prepared to take flight at a moment's notice.

Dave was wishing he'd let her leave. His palms were moist, his mouth, dry. He turned away from her so as not to have to look at her. He took a deep breath and exhaled.

"Miss Bartlett knew about us, Trinity. Maybe she always knew, or maybe the idea came to her when I came back here. We'll never know now. She compared me to my father. What did she mean?" Dave whirled around to face Trinity.

Consternation filled her lovely face. Her hands trembled. Tears filled her eyes. Her trembling increased. She refused to look at him, staring past him as she rocked back and forth in her chair, chanting, "Oh, my God," over and over again.

It was the most ominous sound Dave had ever heard.

When she stopped, the silence in the room was deafening. Dave slowly lowered himself to the bed. He felt like someone had thrown ice water in his face. "Wow! I wouldn't be much of a detective if I didn't know what that reaction means. You and my father were…"

Pain filled her dark eyes. "It wasn't what you're thinking. I loved him, Davie, but it was one-sided. Your father was a good and decent man. He cared for your mother. He would have never hurt her, or you. You were only six-years-old at the time."

Six! He'd been about six when his father started drinking heavily. Now, Dave knew the reason why. He wondered if his mother had known about his father and Trinity. "What was I?" he yelled. "A consolation prize, or just a way to get even with my father for rejecting you?"

Tears formed mini rivers down her cheeks. "It wasn't like that. You were so much like him, that at first, I just liked having you around. Later, when I began to care very deeply for you, I knew I had to let you go before I destroyed you, like I almost destroyed him."

An agonized moan escaped Dave's lips. "You're a piece of work, Trinity. First, you screw up my life, and now you're shattering the image of a father I believed in. It was the only real thing I had left of him. Did he make love to you?" Dave challenged.

"Please, Davie. Don't do this," she begged. "It was a long time ago."

"Did he make love to you?" Dave shouted, mindless of the fact that the motel walls weren't designed for privacy.

She stood up. "Yes, damn you," she screamed. "He did. Once. I savored that moment for years. No one else ever made me feel like that until you came into my life." She sank back down in the chair. "I didn't think anyone knew. Not about him, nor about you."

"Well, it's no secret now, Trinity. Not about us, anyway. Bromley knows." Dave hesitated. "So does Margaret."

"You told her!"

"What do you take me for? Of course, I didn't tell her. She told me. She's always known. She used to watch us make love."

Trinity turned as white as the sheet on the bed, and for a moment it looked like she might pass out, but she quickly recovered, the quiver in her chin the only outward sign of her distress. She stood. "It's been quite a day. For you, too, I imagine. I really am going to leave now. Sooner or later, Davie, like it or not, we're going to have to deal with what's going on between us."

"Us? Is there really an us?" he asked.

She gave him a sad smile. "You know there is. It isn't what either of us expected or wanted, but it's a reality we can't ignore."

She was right and Dave hated her for being right. He felt a need to strike back. "One more thing before you leave. Margaret came on to me. What do you think I should do about it?"

Trinity spun around and slapped him. "You stay away from Margaret, Davie.

You think I screwed up your life? Margaret will trash it. She's my daughter, and I love her, but I'm not blind to her faults, nor do I run from the fact that I may be responsible to some degree for what she is. Margaret doesn't care whose bed she leaves her shoes under. Iif she knows about us, her interest in you could be a way of getting even with me for cheating on her father. You, too, for that matter."

She responded to the accusation written on his face with, "Don't even think about it, Davie. Margaret was born two years after your father told me he didn't ever want to see me again. He never changed his mind on that score, though I never gave up hoping he would."

Dave rubbed his cheek where she'd slapped him. It felt like it was on fire. He stared at the door for what seemed like an eternity after Trinity stormed out of his room. For a brief moment he'd wanted to kill her. When he felt like he could move, he fell down on the bed, kicked off his shoes, and threw them across the room. He got a sense of satisfaction when one of them hit and toppled a glass lamp to the floor and it broke into several jagged pieces.

⌾⦚⦚⦚⌾

It was raining. A perfect day for a funeral. The chapel was filled to capacity.

Many of the mourners had to stand against the wall in the rear of the room.

Steve St. John, Trinity, and Margaret sat together in the front row. Chris Briggs had yet to make an appearance. Dave, sitting in the last row, continued to look for him and hope that he'd show up.

After the service, Dave declined the Sheriff's offer to ride with him to the cemetery, with the explanation, "I may not stay around that long. I'd better take my own car."

The line of cars that followed the hearse to the cemetery was a long one. For someone who made few friends, today's turnout was impressive. Murder had a way of pulling in a crowd, Dave thought.

At graveside, Dave avoided looking directly at Trinity. Today, mother and daughter were putting on a good show of togetherness, but none performed that act as well as St. John himself. With one arm around Trinity, the other around Margaret, he presented an ideal picture of a loving husband and dutiful step-father.

Dave knew he was being unreasonable. Aside from his suspicions about St. John's involvement in Ellen's death, his resentment of him was purely personal.

Moments into the graveside service, Dave spied a movement from behind an oak tree about a hundred yards away from the masses. It had to be Christ. Who else would sneak his way into the cemetery? Everyone else who was here was happy to have their presence duly noted.

Dave slipped away from the crowds and stealthily made his way over to the trees.

Chris was about to bolt, when Dave grabbed his arm. "Hold on there, Chris. I've been waiting for you. I was sure you wouldn't be able to resist one last chance to say goodbye to Ellen."

Chris was belligerent, almost aggressive. "You want to arrest me?" "Should I?"

"You think I killed Ellen." "Did you?"

"No.!" The word was torn from his throat.

"Then you have nothing to fear. Come on. My car is parked nearby."

Chris measured his chances to run, then, albeit reluctantly, he responded to the kindly, yet firm tone of Dave's voice, and the pressure Dave still exerted on his arm.

Dave led him to his car and pushed Chris inside. "Okay, Chris," Dave said. "Let's talk. Why didn't you tell me you and Ellen were married?"

Chris glances nervously at the crowd gathered around Ellen's grave. "Can we get out of here?"

"Sure. Where to?"

"My house. My parents are probably worried about me." Dave nodded back at the crowd. "They're over there."

"I know, I saw them, but I'd rather wait for them at the house. Even if I'm not guilty of anything, I'm beginning to feel like it."

Dave started his engine and placed his car into gear. "Why?"

"I keep thinking I could have prevented what happened to Ellen." "How?"

Chris shrugged. "I don't know."

"Take it from me, some things are beyond our control." Dave eased his car out onto the road. "We can talk on the way to your house. Tell me about you and Ellen, and where you've been for the last twenty-four hours."

"Miss Bartlett told you about my marrying Ellen, didn't she?"

"No. Marriage is a matter of public record. What made you think Miss Bartlett told me?"

"She asked me over to her house to pick up some preserves for my mother. I told her I was busy, but she insisted. I should have known that it was only an excuse to ask me a bunch of questions. We had tea." He grimaced. "I hate tea. She asked me about the night Ellen and I got married. Neither of us came home that night. Miss Bartlett didn't really know anything, but I panicked and I gave myself away. It was almost a relief to talk to someone about it. There were even moments when I wanted to call you and tell you about it, but I was afraid of how it would look. Miss Bartlett asked me a lot of other questions, like what had Ellen told me the night she left. I told her, just as I told you, that Ellen was scared. She asked me of whom. I told her I didn't know."

"But you do know, don't you, Chris?" Dave asked quietly. "Sometimes I think so."

"Who was it?"

"The married man she was in love with." "Who was that?"

"I told you, I think it was St. John."

Dave pulled up in front of Chris's house. The street was all but deserted. Most of the residents were still at the cemetery. "I'm not buying it, Chris. If what you say is true, the man she was having an affair with could have killed her, I suppose, but people rarely kill to hide an affair, not in this day and age. There had to be more to it than that. I think it had something to do with drugs. After all, it was a drug overdose that killed her. You were picked up for smoking pot. Did you ever try anything stronger?"

Chris gave him a long calculating look. He wonders how much I know, Dave thought. He doesn't know that this is all of it!

"We tried coke once." "Who is we?"

"Me, Ellen, and Severn." "Severn?"

"The kid that died recently. I liked him, so did Ellen. Severn was shy around girls. After he became a football hero, the girls started to chase after him. It embarrassed him. He'd always been a loner."

"Did Ellen chase after him?"

"No," Chris protested. "Ellen and Severn were friends. Some of the kids made fun of Severn because his parents are old-fashioned and speak broken English. Ellen used to stick up for him. She tried to fix him up with AmySpring. She's as shy with guys as Severn was around girls. Ellen thought they were perfect for each other. Severn wasn't interested. Football consumed his life, he didn't have time for anything else.

Coach Lackland was grooming him for the pro's and Severn would have made it, too, if he hadn't gotten sick."

Ellen, defender of the underdog. It was yet another side to her that hadn't been revealed, Dave thought. "So, the three of you experimented with drugs. How long ago, and how long did you use?"

"Just once, I swear it. It was about a year ago. Ellen got real sick when we tried it, and I was just plain scared. Severn was afraid it would mess up his chances at being a pro, and that Bill Lackland would cut him off."

"Cut him off of what? Was he subsiding him financially?"

Chris shrugged. "I guess so. I know that he was real good to Severn. But we really did quit after that. We made a pact never to use the stuff again."

"Why didn't you tell me about doing drugs before, Chris?" "I didn't think it was important."

"Everything you can remember about Ellen is important, Chris," Dave scolded. "Where did you get the stuff?"

"At school. This guy used to hang around the grounds." He gave Dave a belligerent look. "The city isn't the only place you can get dope, you know."

"Yes, I know. You have the guy's name?"

Chris shook his head. "Never knew it. He wasn't from around here. Then, one day he quit showing up at the school."

"Okay, let's say I believe you, for now. This guy, who may or may not be St. John, that Ellen was afraid of, why would he hurt her?"

Chris stared down at the floor of the car. "I think she was blackmailing him."

Dave strummed his fingers on the dashboard. "Was Ellen the kind of person who'd resort to blackmail?"

"Not in the beginning. At the end, she was…she was different." "Different, how?"

"Distant. Harder. She didn't seem to care about anything anymore." "Where did you spend last night, Chris?"

"In Henderson. I figured that Miss Bartlett would tell you about marrying Ellen, and that you'd think I killed her because she had it annulled. I was scared."

"Why did you keep your marriage to Ellen a secret?"

"Ellen's idea. Everything we ever did was her idea. It was her idea to get married in the first place. Not that I was against it. One day, out of the blue, she breezes back into my life and says, "Let's get married." It was all I ever wanted to do, so I said yes, of course." Chris stared into space. A smile played around his lips. "That was the most wonderful night of my life. She said we should keep our marriage a secret until we could have a big church wedding so as not to make our folks mad at us. So, I went back home to live with my folks and she went back to the St. John farm. We only made love one more time before she told me she wanted an annulment. I think I hated her in that moment, but I got over it," he hastily added. "I loved her too much not to. Can you understand that?"

Dave nodded, silently acknowledging that the Gray women had that effect on the men in their lives.

"Right after the annulment, she told me it was over between us," Chris went on. "Did you hate her for that?" Dave asked.

"No. I saw it coming. I'd prepared myself for it." He smiled sheepishly. "I even had a speech ready. Ellen didn't even let me finish it. You sure Miss Bartlett didn't tell you about us?" he insisted.

"What time did you see Miss Bartlett?" Dave asked. "A little after five-o-clock."

"You may have been one of the last people to see her alive, Chris. Miss Bartlett died of a fall later that same day."

Chris paled. "Dead! She can't be dead."

"Well she is." Dave decided to take a chance on Chris. "You could be next. I talked to the coroner earlier today, and to the crime lab. Miss Bartlett was murdered around six-thirty or seven the day you talked to her. I found some notes she made. Miss Bartlett thought you knew something, but might not realize it."

Chris placed his hand on the car door. "I can't stay around here. Can you get me away to some place safe? If you do, I promise you I'll tell you everything I know."

Dave gave him a shrewd look. "All right. I'll come inside with you while you get some things together."

"No, please. I want to talk to my parents, and I'd like to do it alone. I can't just disappear. Not again. I saw the look on my mother's face back at the funeral. She's worried about me." He shrugged. "It's the penalty I pay for being an only child." He glanced down at his watch. "I'll come to your motel in about two hours."

Dave shook his head. "Not a chance. We'll both wait here in the car until your parents come home."

Chris sighed. "You don't trust me. Can't say I blame you. You have my word. I won't try anything."

"Not good enough, Chris. We'll wait together."

The Briggs couple arrived home ten minutes later. Dave watched as Chris disappeared into the house. After fifteen minutes passed, Dave began to get nervous. He climbed out of his car and strode over to the Briggs's home. He knocked on the door.

Chris's father opened it.

"I want to see Chris," Dave said. "Now."

A bewildered look passed over the older man's face. A woman appeared at his side. "What is it, Sid?"

Dave's father opened the door wider. "This is the detective from the city, Martha.

He wants to see Chris."

The woman pushed herself forward. "He's in his room. Packing. What did you say to him that makes him think he has to leave?" She sniffed. "He was so upset he didn't even come to Ellen's funeral. After all he and Ellen meant to each other, do you know how that's going to look to everyone? He's scared, I tell you. I've never seen him like this."

"I'm trying to protect him, Mrs. Briggs. Now where is Chris's room?" Chris's father indicated a hallway. "First room on the right."

Dave threw open the door to Chris's room. It was empty. Drawers stood open, their contents spilling from them. The window was open. Dave leaned out. There was an alley in the rear of the house. "When did he come to his room?" Dave asked.

"About ten minutes ago," Chris's father said.

Dave cursed under his breath. Chris had a good head start, and he knew the countryside well. He could hide out until dark and disappear again. He had to let Bromley know. Maybe they'd get lucky and pick him up. "Stupid fool," he said out loud, and to Chris's parents, "Where would he go?"

Sid Briggs shook his head. "I don't know. If I did, I'd tell you. My wife is right.

Chris is really bothered about something." "Chris's friends? Can you give me a list?"

Sid Briggs nodded, left the room, and returned with a folded piece of paper.

As Dave prepared to leave, Martha Briggs blocked his way and pounded on his chest with her fists. "I hate you. It's your fault my boy is gone."

Sid Briggs pulled her off of Dave. "Calm down, Martha. It's not his fault. He's just doing his job."

Dave wasn't so sure. Chris had run before. Why hadn't he seen this move coming? He should have come inside with Chris. Too late for recriminations, he knew. The best he could hope for now was that Chris didn't do something foolish.

⌘

Dave stopped by the sheriff's office. Clyde Bromley was in. He took one look at Dave's expression and ushered him into the same little room as before. "What is it?" he asked. "You look like you just lost your best friend."

"Worse than that," Dave responded, and went to tell him about Chris. Dave made no attempt to whitewash his poor judgment. When he finished telling the whole story, Dave handed him the list of Chris's friends to check up on, and waited for Bromley to come down on him hard.

Bromley, Dave conceded, was full of surprises. Dave had expected harsh criticism and condemnation of his actions. Instead, Bromley leaned forward in his chair and said, "I've been rough on you, Kincaid, but not nearly as rough as you're being on yourself."

"I fucked up! At best I lost a material witness. Then again, I just may have let a killer walk away."

"You want me to put an APB out on Chris?" Dave nodded.

"You want me to issue a murder warrant?" When Dave didn't immediately answer, he said, "That's what I thought. You don't believe that Chris Briggs killed Ellen Gray and Bertha anymore than I do, and I know the boy better than you do. I do think, however, after everything else you've told me, that Chris needs to be brought in for his own protection."

Dave nodded. "I agree. Chris admitted to trying coke. Do you have much of a problem with drugs around here, Sheriff?"

"Abuse ain't just a big city problem, Kincaid, but we've been pretty lucky. We did pick up a fella about a year ago, name of Jack Pembroke. He was hanging around the high school peddling misery. We got an anonymous tip. I always figured it was from one of the parents. We caught the guy with uppers, downers, and some nickel and dime bags of heroin and coke on him. He was put on trial over at the county seat. He's doing ten years. Myself, Bill and a couple of the other deputies gave a talk at the school on drug abuse right after Pembroke's arrest. We had a great turn-out. Ain't had any trouble since. Not that I know about," he added wryly. "Not unless you count Ellen Gray."

Dave stood and shook the Sheriff's gnarled hand. "Thanks for your time. I think I'll stake out the St. John farm. Chris may go there. Any objections?"

"Nope. I could say I think you're wasting your time, but you wouldn't listen. No more than I would when I was your age." He sighed. "Matter of fact, I was about your age when I took this job. Lordy, that was a lot of years ago. Ain't never been an idiot since who wanted my job. I been checking alibis like you asked," He went on, "but it's hard to establish alibis for the night Bertha died without telling folks why I want to know. Unless someone was seen there, it's going to be damned near impossible to prove they were. Wish her place wasn't so remote." He got a wistful look on his face. "Bertha would have figured a way. I'll miss that old lady. The town will miss her." He sighed. "I'll get you a preliminary report by late tomorrow, if that's soon enough."

"Tomorrow will be fine."

Dave stood and shook the sheriff's hand. "Thanks for not raking me over the coals."

"No need," Bromley said. "You're doing a fine job of that all by yourself. Where you headin' now?"

"I think I'll take a drive. I need to think."

Bromley knowingly nodded. "I've taken a few of those same drives myself."

⌇⌇⌇

Dave found himself back at the cemetery. The crowd was gone. All that remained was a mound of new dirt and a host of flower arrangements and wreaths.

Dave left his car and strode toward the now deserted gravesite. He stared down at the fresh dirt. He placed his hands in front of him, clasped them together, and conducted a silent conversation with Ellen Gray.

You hold the key, Ellen. You, and maybe you alone, know why you ended up under six feet of dirt. Dave shook his head. No. Whoever killed you knows, and maybe Chris knows, and I think that if Trinity doesn't know, she suspects something. Why did you leave here in such a hurry? Who did you go to the city to see? Who were you having an affair with? So many questions, Ellen, and damn few answers.

Dave's shoulders slumped. I wish I'd known you. Funny, I came here to find out the truth about you, and all I seem to do is uncover things that affect me, not paint the picture of you I came here looking for. I still just have this fuzzy sketch of you. You were no angel, but I can't help feeling that if I'd known you, I would have found something there to admire, like the way you stood up for an immigrant's son. How much like Trinity were you? Now there's a woman for you. I loved your mother. It's possible I still do. I wouldn't have minded if you'd been my daughter. I admit it would have taken some getting used to. What am I saying? You'd still be dead, and I would never have had the chance to hold you, or to get to know you. Trinity had an affair with my father. If I'd known that was going to surface, I never would have come back here. Did you find out about their affair? Is that what Trinity and Sam argued about the night he died? Did you overhear them arguing? Is that what set you against Trinity? A short mirthless laugh escaped him. My own father! I have to tell you, that came out of left field. I've tried to picture the two of them together, but all that does is drive me crazy.

Christ, what a mess!

Dave kicked at the dirt. One thing's for sure. I'm not fit to run this investigation.

But I can't leave. There are still so many questions. If I don't get some answers now, uncertainty will haunt me for the rest of my life. Trinity was right about that.

Dave stared at the mound of dirt, willing the same kind of telepathic message he'd received at the city morgue. None came.

"I'll find whoever killed you," he said out loud. "I won't attempt to do it alone anymore. I'll get help."

"She can't hear you," a voice behind him said. "But I accept your offer on her behalf."

Dave whirled around. Margaret was the last person he wanted to see right now. "You shouldn't creep up on people," he said.

"Creep? I didn't creep up on you. My God, you were so wrapped up in yourself, I think I could have been accompanied by a brass band and you wouldn't have heard me coming."

Dave brushed his way past her. He wondered how long she had been standing there.

⁙

Dave called the city. He talked first to Herring, and then to Brad.

"Are you getting in to deep, Kincaid?" Herring asked. "You sound a little frayed at the edges."

"Just the edges?" Dave attempted a joke. "Yeah, I guess I'm getting a little too close to people I shouldn't, but I don't want to be taken off the case," he hastily added. "Just let me have Brad for a few days."

"Okay. A few days. Then, I think we should let the locals have the case. "If that happens, the case will get closed fast. Not solved. Just closed." "We only do what we can, Kincaid. Think about it."

Brad took his temporary assignment cheerfully. "I can use the break. I'll drive down in the morning. You okay, Dave?"

"Sure. I just need an objective viewpoint."

Dave severed the connection before Brad could pursue the subject further.

Dave had the motel coffee shop make him up a thermos of coffee for his vigil outside the St. John farm. It was quiet, the only sounds were those of the night, an owl hooting, crickets chirping, a gentle breeze swishing through the trees.

It was seven minutes after midnight when the shrill screech of a siren cut through the night air. Seconds later a blue and while ambulance sped up the driveway of the St. John home.

Dave jumped out of his car and chased the ambulance up the driveway.

Two attendants leaped out of the van carrying a stretcher. They ran inside the house through the front door that the white-faced housekeeper held open for them.

"What happened?" Dave demanded of the housekeeper as the attendants ran up the stairs.

"It's Mrs. St. John," the woman blurted out. "She took a bunch of pills." Dave glanced up at upper floor of the house. "Pills? When?"

"I don't know. She went up to her room at nine is all I know. She said she had a headache."

"Where was her husband?"

"In his study. Mr. St. John never goes to bed till after midnight. He just found now found her, with an empty bottle of pills by her side. She was unconscious."

Just then the attendants came down the stairs. Trinity was strapped to the stretcher. Dave had seen enough death and near death to know that she was in serious condition. St. John was right behind the attendants.

"What happened?" Dave asked him.

St. John pushed him out of the way. "My wife tried to kill herself. She may have even succeeded. Now get out of my way."

Dave glanced over at the attendants. One of them shook his head. "Too soon to tell," he said. "She swallowed some powerful stuff."

"Why would she want to kill herself?" Dave asked.

St. John gave him a cold stare. "Maybe it's because you pushed too hard. I understand she came to see you yesterday. Just what in the hell did you say to her?"

Dave made no effort to defend himself. Defending himself would only incriminate Trinity.

Besides, there were more important things to consider right now. Such as, would Trinity survive the attempt on her own life?

CHAPTER 10

It was a night filled with blurred dreams and haunted premonitions. Bertha Bartlett was once again a feature player in Dave's dreams. The magnifying glass was in her hand as before; as she waved it at a distant figure. "Be careful," she warned, "they'll kill you if they can." The distant figure turned, joined by another. As the two figures came nearer, Dave could see the first figure's face. It was bloodied and battered, his clothes torn. He was holding a young woman's hand. The man was Chris, and the young woman was Ellen. Chris smiled over at Miss Bartlett. "Don't be concerned," he said. "Ellen and I are together now, Miss Bartlett. See?"

Dave sat straight up in bed. Sweat poured down his face and drenched his upper torso. He glanced over at the clock by the bed. It was 5:12 a.m. He reached for the phone book, found the number he wanted and dialed it. Clyde Bromley answered on the third ring.

Dave identified himself. "Jesus, Kincaid," Bromley barked, "First you get me out of bed after midnight to tell me about Trinity, and now you call me at the crack of dawn. What is it now?"

Dave suddenly felt foolish. Bromley knew nothing about his dreams and their comic book inaccuracy. "It's Chris. I think he's dead, or if he isn't, he's in terrible danger."

"You called me because you thought there was something I could do about it?" "Not exactly," Dave answered, wishing he'd never called Bromley. "Have you heard anything on Chris?"

"If I had, you'd be the first to know. Come by the office and we'll talk. I'll be in at eight." Bromley severed the connection.

Dave replaced the receiver. He rubbed his tired sleep swollen eyes. He hadn't gotten back to the motel until after three this morning. He'd followed the ambulance to the small hospital in Briarwood. Trinity was in a coma, and, because the facilities in Briarwood were limited, a decision had been made to transport her to Henderson. The prognosis for recovery was a guarded one.

When the ambulance drove off on its journey to Henderson, Dave felt helpless and left out. Watching St. John climb into the ambulance with Trinity, Dave envied him his right to be there.

After his dream, sleep was impossible. It was almost three hours until he could see Bromley. Several more than that before Brad would arrive.

He turned on the television set. A nineteen-fifties movie flashed onto the screen. It was a gangster movie. A thug was beating up on a defenseless old man. It reminded Dave of his dream. He turned the TV off in disgust.

He knew there was no point in dwelling on his dream. Like all the others, it gave him no clue how to prevent a tragedy borne by wheels already in motion. One thing he was sure. A tragedy had either struck or was going to.

⌇

Dave's meeting with Clyde Bromley was a brief one. Bromley handed Dave a handwritten report. "Hope you can read it," he said. "I wrote it myself rather than have

Tilda type it. The poor woman is about to bust a gut trying to find out what's going on around here. I hope it helps you. Sure didn't do much for me. Seems like no one on your list of likely suspects has much of an alibi for Ellen's death. It also seems to me that any one of them could have made it to the city and back in less than four hours, giving them more than enough time to get the job done." Bromley stretched. "Then again, I'm not ruling out the possibility your murderer was one of them city slickers."

"Nice try, Sheriff," Dave said, "so how do you explain Miss Bartlett's murder?" "An accomplice?"

Dave nodded. "Maybe. Any word on Chris?"

"Nope. Ain't found his car yet, neither. What is this nonsense about his being dead?"

"If I told you it was a dream, would you believe me?" Bromley gave him a strange look. "Nope."

"That's the problem," Dave said. "No one ever does until it's too late. I'd better be getting back to my motel. My partner is coming in from the city."

Bromley leaned back in his chair. "Another one of you? Was this one raised here, too?"

Dave grinned. "Not hardly. Brad was raised in the Bronx. No reflection on you and the help you're giving me, sheriff, but I need Brad. He knows how I think. That is, when I'm thinking straight, which I'm not right now, so I asked him to come here."

"Another city slicker," Dave heard Bromley muttering as he left. "Another goddamn city slicker!"

෧ᛊᛊᛊᛊᖯ

When Dave returned to his motel, Brad was checking in. The clerk had given Brad a room that connected to Dave's. Brad tossed the motel key up in the air. "So this is where you were raised. Beats the Bronx."

After Brad unloaded his bag, he and Dave met in Dave's room. Brad sprawled out on Dave's bed. "Okay, bring me up to date and tell me what you want me to do."

Dave told him about Miss Bartlett and the people he'd questioned so far. He saved Chris's disappearance until last.

"You lost a suspect? No wonder you called for backup. You never pulled a boner like that before."

"I never came back home before. It's a long story, Brad, and I haven't told you all of it, but I didn't leave out anything that's pertinent to the case. The rest is personal."

Brad raised an eyebrow. "Sounds heavy." "It is."

Brad gave him a thoughtful look. "Have it your way." He reached inside his jacket and pulled out an envelope. "I promised to wine and dine Glenda in style to get you this information. I also gave her fifty bucks. She only came up with one possible. It's all in there."

Dave took the envelope from Brad. The man's name noted inside was Christopher Burnett. He'd been a key witness in a murder trial a year-and-a-half ago. The accused had been a powerful congressman, the witness his right-hand man, with enough inside knowledge to bring down a lot of high-powered people. The FBI became involved in the case. The congressman went berserk on the stand and was declared mentally incompetent, but not before he threatened to have revenge on Burnett for giving testimony against him. The congressman was committed to a mental institution, and then escaped a week later. Christopher Burnett had gone underground, presumably with the help of the authorities.

There was a physical description of Burnett that could have fit St. John as he'd been before plastic surgery. He was about the same height, had the same color eyes, and the same build as Burnett. Burnett would be thirty-five now. There was a picture of him included with the report.

Dave fingered the photograph. "I remember this case. Burnett was kept under wraps throughout the entire trial. No photographers were allowed within a hundred yards of him." He shook his head. "Somehow, it doesn't feel right. I had St. John figured for mob connections. There were no other likely matches?"

Brad laughed. "Not unless you count a sixty-year old Mafia accountant and a mobster's girlfriend a match."

Dave frowned. "Could I have been that wrong about St. John? I don't think so.

He's still number one on my list of suspects." "What else have you got?" Brad asked. "Some notes Bertha Bartlett made." "Can I see them?"

Dave hesitated. Bertha's notes contained questions about him and Trinity, and Dave's father. He'd reluctantly shared them with Bromley. He was even more reluctant to share them with Brad. "I said there were personal aspects to this case. Miss Bartlett made note of those personal aspects. I'd rather not discuss them. Okay with you?"

"Sure. But if you need a friendly ear…"

"I'll think about it." Dave handed him a copy of Bertha's notes and waited for Brad to study them.

Moments later, Brad looked up from his reading. "Do you place any credibility on what she wrote?"

Dave nodded. "To some degree, I do."

"Then, let's attack her notations one by one. Trinity, that's the girl's mother, isn't it? So many questions, the old lady wrote. Anything there?"

"Possibly. Trinity tried to kill herself last night. She's still in a coma."

Brad sat up. "Really? That's something you forgot to mention?" At the warning look on Dave's face he caved "Okay, we'll bypass that, for now. Margaret? What do you think?"

"I think Miss Bartlett was right. She is crafty."

"Chris? Do you really think he holds the key to Ellen's murder?" "I think it's a possibility."

"St. John." Brad smiled. "I know how you feel about him. Bryant, Gerard, and Lackland. Possibilities?"

"All except Gerard. I don't think he's the dark horse Miss Bartlett intimidated he might be."

"Who's Wokowski?" Brad asked.

"Parents of a high school kid who died recently. No connection to Ellen. He died of natural causes. Miss Bartlett made daily visits to comfort the kid's parents. It was the kind of person she was. I figure they got on her list from force of habit, just like the canning jars and thread she crossed out after she made her list of things to do."

Brad threw Bertha's notes down on the bed. "The rest of this? The stuff about you. I'd like to help."

Dave smiled. "Thanks. Some other time. I think it's enough to say that what Miss Bartlett referred to is the reason I can't handle this investigation by myself anymore. Let's split up our suspects. I never got a chance to talk to Bill's wife, nor to Mrs. Gerard and Mrs. Carey. Bill's wife used to be Ellen's friend. I'll take them. You take Bill, St.

John, Margaret, Bryant, and Felix."

Dave told Brad about Margaret preventing him from going to see Bertha the night she was killed by asking him over to her place. "It may not mean anything," Dave said. "Then again, it might. I'll talk to her again after you do."

He pulled out Bromley's report. "The sheriff prepared a list of alibis or lack of one, in this case. Bill claims to have been home, but his wife is pregnant and she was having problems. She was in the hospital fighting a threatened miscarriage. Bill went to see his wife in the hospital at seven, left there at seven-thirty. No one saw him after that. Carey claims to have been at the bank. Says he stayed late to go over the books and fell asleep at his desk. That's the worst alibi I ever heard, but it's stupid enough to be true.

Gerard also claims to have been home, but his wife is an invalid and takes heavy doses of pain medication. He could have been gone for hours and she'd never have known it. St. John was out of town, so he says, four-hundred miles from where Ellen died. He, too, could have driven there and back. Margaret, as you know was in the city, close enough to have killed Ellen. But Wilma saw a man on the scene, not a woman.'

"Wilma is also a drunk, Dave. Not the most reliable of witnesses."

Dave grimaced. "Yeah, I know. But she's all we've got. As for Chris," he continued, "he was visiting a friend in Henderson. He claims to have had car trouble. He didn't get home until sometime after 3 a.m. His parent can't swear to an exact time; they're heavy sleepers. So there you have it. Any one of them could have killed EllenGray."

"Motive?"

Dave shook his head. "Nothing. Not unless you believe Chris's theory about blackmail."

Brad got up from the bed. "I'll get right to work. I noticed you didn't mention an alibi for Trinity Gray."

"She doesn't have one. She was home alone. It was the housekeeper's night off.

She didn't kill her own daughter!"

"Right. Sorry I mentioned it. Tell you what? Let's get a bottle or two, later on, and tie on a good one. You can tell me your problems and I'll tell you mine. We haven't done that in a while, Dave. I think it's time."

Dave smiled. He felt warmer, more secure now that Brad was here. "I'm glad you could come," he said. "I needed a friend."

Dave's first stop was to see Beth Lackland. It was possible, he conceded, that she was very pretty under normal circumstances, but a problem pregnancy, and an overdue delivery date, had caused her face to swell up like a watermelon. Her eyes were puffy, resembling two tiny peepholes, and she was as uncomfortable with herself as any human being he'd ever seen.

She ushered him into a small but clean and uncluttered living room. She sat sideways on a straight-backed chair in an effort to accommodate her bulk and assume a position of some comfort. Her efforts were fruitless. "Excuse me," she said. "No matter how or where I sit, I not only look awkward, I feel like a beached whale. I used to think I wanted a big family, but after this, I think Bill and I should adopt." She wiped sweat from her brow with the back of her hand. "I don't want to appear uncooperative, but can you make this quick? I don't feel so good."

"Of course. You know, of course, that Ellen was murdered?" "Yes. Is my husband a suspect? "

"Everyone is a suspect who knew Ellen well, Mrs. Lackland. I primarily came here to talk to you about your friendship with Ellen. You were friends?"

Beth shifted in the chair. She drew in her breath and held her stomach. Dave was visibly alarmed. "Are you okay?"

"Yes. The baby just kicked me, that's all. I got to know Ellen through my friendship with her sister. Margaret and I are the same age. Ellen was mature beyond her years. When Margaret got her job as an embassy clerk and was away so much, Ellen and I remained friends. We both liked classical music. It gave us something in common."

"She didn't come to your wedding. Why?" "How did you know that?"

"Miss Bartlett. She made mention of it the day before she died."

"Ellen didn't come to my wedding, that's true, but Bill and I didn't have a big wedding. Look at me, Detective! My baby is due in less than a month. Simple arithmetic will tell you that I was pregnant when Bill and I got married."

"Friends attend small wedding ceremonies. Especially those," Dave emphasized. "So why didn't Ellen attend yours."

Beth shrugged. The gesture caused another reaction from her unborn child. "Oh, God, I wish this baby would get itself born. I think this awful pregnancy is punishment. I was seeing Bill before he and his first wife were divorced. I was one of the reasons for their breaking up." She sighed. "What the hell, you'll probably find out one way or another. I wasn't the only one Bill was playing around with. Of course I didn't know it back then. I found that out when I told Ellen that Bill and I were getting married. Choice of music wasn't all we had in common, it seemed. We also had Bill, and amazingly enough I didn't know about Ellen. My marrying him caused a nasty end to what had been a nice friendship. A lot of things were said on both sides that couldn't be forgotten. Ellen was bitter and resentful, and with reason. I ended up with Bill and she didn't."

It was like coming to the end of a tunnel and finding only a dim light, Dave thought. Somehow, finding out that Bill Lackland was the married man in Ellen's life was anti-climatic. Or maybe I just wanted it to be St. John for personal reasons, he acknowledged.

"Did Bill see Ellen after you and he got married?"

"Yes. We fought about it. Then Bill stopped seeing her. Or so he said." "You don't believe him?"

She sighed. "I guess I do, but not because I think he loved me more. Bill really wants this child. He longs for a son. He never had any children with his first wife. I told him that if he didn't stop seeing Ellen, he'd never see this baby." She shifted uncomfortably. "Bill will be furious when he finds out I told you about Ellen, but quite frankly I'm glad it's finally out in the open."

"You know this puts your husband at the top of my list of suspects, don't you, Mrs. Lackland?"

She nodded. "I know, but I'm not afraid. Bill may have slept with Ellen, but he didn't kill her. He had no reason to. Who else but me would really care about their affair, and I already knew about it."

"I'll keep it in mind, Mrs. Lackland." Dave glanced at her swollen belly. He felt sorry for her. She'd won the battle with Ellen over Bill, but she'd lost the war.

⌘

There was no point in bothering Gerard and Bryant's wife, Davedecided. The mystery of Ellen's married man was now solved. The next step, of course, was to talk to Bill himself, but Bill was on Brad's list to talk to today. Dave toyed with the idea of getting to Brad before he interviewed Bill. He quickly discounted that idea in favor of the value of getting Brad's first impression of Bill.

Dave's questioning of Bill Lackland could keep.

What wouldn't keep, Dave knew, was Trinity. He had to know how she was doing. He decided to risk the unpleasantness that would surely come if St. John was at the Henderson hospital.

Luck was with him in one respect, but not in another. St. John had just left. Trinity was in intensive care, still in a coma. Dave's badge did nothing to gain him access to Trinity.

A dour-faced nurse in a crisp white uniform, was very firm. "Family only."

Dave knew when authority could be usurped and when it couldn't. He gave a resigned shrug. "Give me a prognosis at least."

She was a woman of few words. "Guarded," she said, and immediately looked down at her patient charts, instantly dismissing him.

"Can I talk to her doctor?"

"If he was in, you could. He won't be back until tonight." "What if Mrs. St. John goes into a crisis situation?"

She looked up. "We can handle it."

"Problems, Detective?" A voice behind him asked.

Margaret! She was like a bad cold that wouldn't go away. Dave turned around to face her. "Red tape. They won't tell me anything because I'm not family. How is she?"

"Guarded, just like the woman says. Steve blames you for what happened, Dave.

Does he have grounds to?"

Dave thought about his last conversation with Trinity. Bringing up her affair with his father had been hard on both of them. "I don't know. Trinity came to see me the day she overdosed. We talked about things neither of us were comfortable with. I told her that you knew about us, for one thing."

"And I always thought you were such a nice guy! I guess she had to know sooner or later. I should have told her myself, instead of treating her so badly all these years.

Finding out I knew could have triggered an attempt on her life I suppose, but I doubt it. My mother is a strong woman. The strongest woman I ever knew. Ellen and I spent our whole lives trying to measure up to her, just as you guessed we did. Now, Ellen is gone, and it's just me and my mother. If she dies, there'll be no one left to blame everything on when I screw up. I don't know if I'm up to that."

He should tackle her, he knew, about her part, if any, in making sure she was occupied when Miss Bartlett was killed. But now was not the time. Sarcasm crept into Dave's voice. "You'll manage. I have to get back to Briarwood. If Trinity comes out of her coma, tell her I was here. It might mean something to her.'

"It will mean a lot. I know it would to me. Why don't you like me, Dave? What did I ever do to you?"

"Nothing. Nothing at all." Except remind me of my weaknesses, Dave silently thought.

Brad was waiting for Dave back at the motel. Sitting on a small table by the window in Dave's room were two bottles of Scotch, a bottle of soda, a bag of potato chips and pretzels, and two cartons of dip. There was also a large box containing a pizza.

Brad grinned. "All that's missing is women. Got any ideas?"

Dave shook his head and smiled. "In this town?" He looked over at the mini feast. "You're doing this for me. Don't think I don't appreciate it."

"Don't mention it. Besides, it'll be good for both of us." He grinned. "We'd better eat this pizza before it gets any colder, then we can get shit-faced and drown our sorrows."

Dave tossed his jacket in the direction of his bed. It missed its target. Dave shrugged and left his jacked lying on the floor in a heap. "What possible sorrows could you have?"

"Same as you. Woman trouble."

Dave raised an eyebrow in disbelief. "I don't believe it. Who is she?" Brad sobered. "Prentiss."

"I thought you got over your problems of working with a woman, Brad."

"I did. She makes a great partner. Not as good as you, of course," he hastily added, "but she's damn good."

"Then what's the problem/"

"I got to like her. I got to like her a lot. I took her out to dinner and the theater. I spent a bundle. She seemed to like me as much as I liked her, so it was a reasonable assumption that we'd end up in bed." Brad grimaced. "She set me straight in one hell of a hurry. She made it damn clear that she didn't mind sharing a beat with me, or dinner, but that was as far as it was going to go. Sheila doesn't intend to mess with this cop, or any other cop, for that matter. She wants a "normal" relationship, with a "normal" man. Someone who won't end up with a bullet instead of a paycheck. She said that one hazardous career in a relationship was enough, and she wasn't about to give up hers."

Then Laura had been right about Brad and Sheila, Dave thought. Laura! So much had been going on around here he'd managed to put her out of his mind. It was painful to think about her now. "Let's eat the pizza, compare notes on the Gray case, and then drink till we drop."

Brad gleefully rubbed his hands together. "What are we waiting for?" Dave proceeded to tell Brad about his visit to Beth Lackland.

"Makes my day kind of redundant, doesn't it?" Brad said.

"Not necessarily. I don't think that Ellen was killed because of an affair, but it does make Bill Lackland a prime suspect nonetheless." He shook his head. "Maybe the Sheriff is right. He holds on to the theory that someone from the city killed Ellen." Dave frowned. "Except why did someone murder Bertha Bartlett? Her murder is the one thing that ties Ellen's death to someone in this town. But for that, I might just buy the fact it really was someone from the city. It sure as hell would make my life a lot simpler." He ran his fingers through his hair. "Someone was feeding Ellen heroin days before she died. This is a small town. You don't just go to your medicine chest and haul out a supply of dope you kept around just in case you might need it to kill someone. Whoever killed her had to have access to the stuff, or connections with someone who did. Chris tried coke. Maybe he lied to me, and he tried heroin too."

"You don't sound too convinced."

"You're right, I'm not. First thing tomorrow I'll ask Bromley if there was any way Bill could have got a hold of the stuff in his duties as a part-time deputy. Or, if he can think of anyone else who may have access to the stuff. Bromley threw out the possibility of collusion. Could be he was right. I've been guilty of thinking of him as a small-time law man with small-time ideas. Could be he's smarter than all of us. How did it go with Bill?"

Brad nodded. "Fine. I told him the same thing I did all the others. I told them I was following up on Ellen Gray's murder at your request and asked them if they had anything to add that might help us out."

"What was your impression of Bill and the others?"

"Lackland is not a happy man. He wallows in the fact that life dealt him a bum hand. He carries a nasty chip on his shoulder, and hopes it doesn't show, but it does. Gerard is a wimp. I don't think he'd have the guts to kill anyone. Bryant is intelligent, and he's shrewd. But murder? You're going to need more than you've got so far where he's concerned if you're going to involve him in this. St. John? He's cool as ice and hard to read. He doesn't care much for you."

"The feeling is mutual."

"So I gathered. It's not like you to let personalities get in the way of an investigation, Dave."

Dave ignored the silent question. "Do you think St. John is capable of murder?" "Sure. Anyone is. You know that. Even Gerard under the right circumstances,

but I'd still rule him out. What about the women? I know that Trinity Gray is still in a coma, but I never did connect with Margaret Gray."

"Then you have a treat in store, Brad. You two should get along famously." Dave laughed. "I'd really like tickets to that, I'll tell you."

"You trying to tell me something?"

Dave laughed again. "I wouldn't want to spoil what could be a class encounter. "Dave licked the tomato sauce off his fingers, throwing an unfinished slice of pizza back in the box. "Now, what was that about getting drunk?"

Two hours later, neither Dave nor Brad was feeling any pain. Once before, about a year ago, they'd tied one on of about the magnitude of tonight's session. That particular night was the time that their role as partners fused into an honest friendship. It had been after the brutal slaying of a prostitute. They'd both lived with violence, but this killing was about as gruesome as it ever got. The woman's hacked up body was strewn from one end of her apartment to the other. The place looked like a blood bath. Brad had been the one to find her severed head. He'd gotten sick and was ashamed of his reaction. Getting drunk after that seemed like the only logical thing to do.

Dave learned a lot about Brad that night. Drinking made him dwell on his past and his roots, just like he was doing now. Brad was sprawled out on the bed. Dave was stretched out in one chair with his feet up on another.

"You seen that TV show 'Bronx Zoo'?" Brad's words were slightly slurred. "There's a good reason for calling the Bronx a zoo. Did I ever tell you we were one of the few white Anglo Saxon families in the neighborhood?" And, when Dave nodded. "So, I did. There were days I wished I was black, Italian, or Puerto Rican, so I'd fit in. I swore that no matter what it took, I was going to get out of there and never look back.

As a boy, I decided that I had only two choices. I could be a cop, or I could be a hood." He laughed. "The odds were better that I'd be a hood, but I beat them." He raised his glass, spilling some of its contents onto the bed. "To me, and to being a cop. That in itself was a revelation. I thought it would get me away from low-life, but as a New York City cop, I was just exchanging one kind of contact with low-life for another. When I wrangled a transfer away from New York, and ended up working with you, I thought it would be different, but all big cities are alike. Only you were different."

Brad hiccupped. "My family still lives in New York. I can't even make myself visit them."

Dave had heard all this before. He admired Brad for making it out of what bordered on a ghetto environment. He'd always suspected that Brad's prowess with women was compensation for his upbringing, his way of always coming out on top. Now, it seemed, Sheila Prentiss had put a chink in Brad's armor. No one understands Brad as well as I do, Dave thought. Most people think he's arrogant and self-assured. Like me, he's vulnerable. We both put up barriers, hoping no one will break them down. Laura got past mine, and now Sheila has gotten past Brad's.

"What was it like to grow up in a town like this, Dave?"

"I never gave it much thought. I guess I took it for granted." "Yeah, you would. Like you took Laura for granted."

Dave was surprised at the animosity in Brad's voice. It must be Sheila, Dave thought. He voiced his thoughts out loud. "What made Sheila so special, Brad? Other than the fact she turned you down, that is."

Brad laughed. He reached for the almost empty bottle by the bed. "Enough for one more. You want to split it?"

Dave shook his head.

Brad killed the bottle. "Sheila's the one who got away. She's the first woman who ever said no to me."

Dave laughed. "It had to happen sometime. You'll get a kick out of this. Laura thinks you're in love with Sheila."

"Love! I like her, I told you that, and I admire the hell out of her, and I wanted to sleep with her. But love? Not this guy!" He stared into his glass. "I may have come close once, but not with Sheila. And you," Brad said. "Tell me about Trinity St. John. I mean about you and her. About the notes made by the old lady. David and Trinity, the old lady wrote."

Maybe it's the booze, Dave thought, or maybe it's because Trinity and me aren't a secret any more, or maybe I just need to tell someone how it really was. Whatever the reasons, and later he would try to justify his reasons, Dave found himself telling Brad about himself and Trinity. When he finished, his voice was full of emotion. "You haven't met her yet, but when you do, you'll get some idea of why it happened. She lights up a room like sunlight on a dreary day. When I'm in the same room with her my hormones explode. Breathing is an effort, and I want to rip off her clothes and ravage her until she begs for mercy."

"Watch out, buddy, I thought this woman was in the past, but you're talking present. Are you in love with Trinity St. John?"

"I keep asking myself that. I only know that I can't put her out of my mind. I guess I never did."

Brad whistled. "If it ain't love, it's awesome." Brad shifted on the bed. "Where does this leave Laura? Is this thing you have for Trinity St. John the reason you and Laura split up?"

Dave drained his glass and looked woefully into his emptiness. "Laura left me, not the other way around. I think she sensed something, but I don't think she knew it was another woman. I miss her. With Laura, it was like I was someone else, the kind of person I wanted to be, not who I really am. Meeting Trinity again made me realize that Laura gave me space. Trinity crowds me. I love Laura. I hate my life without her, but I can't stop thinking about Trinity." Dave kicked the chair out from under his feet. "I sound like a fucking head case. What if she dies, Brad? I'll never know if we could have made it, or if we should have tried. Damn, I'm fucked up, and this case isn't helping any. I can't get a handle on Ellen Gray, and it's driving me nuts."

"Is it so important that you do?"

"I thought so when I first came here. Now, nothing is very clear. See why I needed you?"

Brad slid his feet to the floor. "Well, one good thing. You haven't had time to brood about Katie lately."

Dave laughed, a mirthless sound. "Now there's a whole other story. I think now that Katie was just an excuse to make myself miserable, because it allowed me to forget Trinity." Amazement crept into his voice. "After all these years, Trinity's always been there."

"You're drunk, Dave," Brad said. "We're both drunk. Let's call it a night." "Sure, but I'm still fucked up. I don't think sobriety is going to change that." "We're all fucked up. We all hurt people we don't mean or want to." He stared

past Dave, started to say something, then thought better of it. "I'd better go to my room while I can still walk." He placed his hand on Dave's shoulder. "You're like a brother to me. I want you to know that. I want to…"

Whatever he was going to say was interrupted by the sound of the phone ringing.

Dave staggered to answer it. He placed his hand over the receiver and looked back at Brad. "It's Chris Briggs!"

⚬⚬⚬

"Chris," Dave yelled into the phone, struggling to clear his head, wishing he hadn't chosen tonight to indulge in liquor. "I ought to lock you up for pulling a stunt like that. Where in the hell are you?"

"I'm in Duncan."

Duncan! Fuck the booze! Why can't I think where Duncan is? Then it came to Dave. Duncan was the next largest town to Henderson, about a hundred miles from Briarwood."

"How did you get there?"

"I hitched a ride. I'm sorry for taking off, Detective. I didn't know what else to do. You said I could be the next one to be killed." Agony filled his voice. "And I don't know why."

Dave glanced over at Brad. He indicated the glass coffee pot on the bathroom wall. He placed his hand over the receiver. "Make me a cup of coffee, will you, Brad?" Of all the times to get drunk! He removed his hand from the receiver. "We need to talk, Chris. Will you come back here?"

Chris hesitated. "I suppose so. I've been thinking about what you said. That I knew something. I don't know anything. I swear it."

Dave cursed. Excitement was beginning to clear his head. Chris was in a talkative mood, but he was a hundred miles away. All Dave could do right now was let him get whatever was on his mind off his chest, and hope he was still this talkative in the morning. "Think, man. You were one of the last people to see Ellen before she left Briarwood. You said she was scared. What did she say that made you think she was frightened?"

"She was upset about Severn. She said she didn't want to die young like he did. I told her it wasn't going to happen, that she was healthy, and Severn was sick. She gave me a funny look and said that health was no guarantee of mortality. When I asked her what she meant, she said that better I shouldn't know, or they might get me, too." Chris paused. "I think I helped to kill her."

"How so?"

"I didn't take her seriously. I should have."

Dave accepted the coffee in a cone-shaped paper cup that Brad handed to him. He responded to Brad's questioning look with a shrug. "Don't blame yourself, Chris. I want you to think real hard. You said that Ellen said 'they' might get you. A figure of speech, or do you think she meant more than one person?"

There was silence on the other end of the line. "I don't know. If I come in, Detective, can you protect me?"

"Yes. I'll come and get you myself. Where are you staying?" There was more silence.

"You can trust me, Chris. I think you know that."

"I'm at a motel called The Travelers Inn. It's just off the highway."

Dave snapped his fingers to get Brad's attention and placed his hand over the receiver again. "Pen and paper," he said. "Over there, in the top drawer of the dresser."

Dave took the sheet of paper and ball point pen from Brad. "What room number?" he asked Chris.

"It's a cabin. Number 15."

Dave wrote down the name of the motel and Chris's cabin number and placed it on the stand by the bed. "Okay, Chris. I want you to stay put. Lock your door and don't answer it, and don't talk to anyone else until I get there. Do you understand the importance of what I'm saying to you?"

"Yes."

"Good. I can help you. Brad, my partner from the city is here to help me out. I'll get him to take you back to the city with him. Nobody will look for you there. You'll be safe, I promise."

"Why can't you take me?"

"I have to stay here, but you can trust Brad, just like you can trust me." "All right. I'll see you in the morning, then?"

"Count on it."

Dave turned his attention to Brad. "He's scared and he's talkative, blabbering about some football jock who died recently."

"You don't think we should pick him up tonight?" Brad asked.

"Sure! Just what the kid needs to give him confidence! Two drunken cops picking him up! Besides, leaving here at night will create too much interest in what I'm doing.'

"What if he decides to run again?"

"Call it instinct," Dave answered, thinking he was starting to sound like Bromley, "but I don't think Chris will run. For one thing, he has no one to run to other than to me. He knew that when he decided to call me just now."

The dream was much the same. Bertha Bartlett and the magnifying glass, trying to warn someone, the words unable to leave her lips. She looked down at the blurred image of a man lying on his back, horror filling her face.

The blurred image took on shape. It was Chris.

Dave awoke with a jolt. He flipped on the beside lamp and looked at his watch. Four-thirty-five a.m. Five hours since he'd talked to Chris. He tumbled out of bed and threw on his pants, shirt, shoes, socks and jacket. He started to pick up the phone to tell Brad where he was going, then changed his mind. Let the poor bastard sleep it off.

The night was still and quiet when Dave leaped into his car and steered it toward the highway.

Just once, he prayed, let my dream be a warning I can do something about.

CHAPTER 11

Dave had the road to himself. He accelerated and glanced down at the speedometer. Eighty-five miles per hour. Thank God it was a straight road between Briarwood and Duncan.

The motel sign was visible from the highway. Dave steered his car toward the exit road. It was 6:14 a.m. The sun was beginning to come up.

The motel consisted of a one-story building that housed ten units and fifteen outlying cabins. Only three cars sat in front of the long one-story building. Dave glided his car past the building and slowed to five miles an hour looking for cabin number fifteen. Only four more cars were parked in the area reserved for cabins. Number fifteen was located in a recessed corner of the u-shaped property line, several feet from a neighboring cabin. A towering elm tree shaded it from the afternoon sun.

Under normal circumstances, Dave might have considered the surroundings almost picturesque, but at this moment, all he could think about was that the seclusion of Chris's cabin presented more of a danger than a sanctuary.

Dave got out of his car and walked up to the door of cabin fifteen, looking from right to left out of sheer habit. Also, from sheer habit, his hand strayed to the gun in his shoulder holster. He knocked on the cabin door. "Chris, it's me, Dave Kincaid. Open up."

There was no response.

Dave waited a full minute before he knocked on the door again. This time, he pounded forcefully. There was still no response.

His apprehension was enhanced by a rising of the hairs on the back of his neck. It was the same uneasy feeling he'd experienced when he'd gone to Bertha's house the day he'd found her lying dead there.

Dave stepped away from the cabin and made his way to the office that was located at the front of the motel. It was dark inside. There was a note on the door.

OFFICE AND SWITCHBOARD OPEN AT 7 am. IN CASE OF EMERGENCY, SEE MANAGER IN CABIN ELEVEN.

Dave cursed. He couldn't wait until seven. He walked back to the cabins and located number eleven. It was the biggest and the best of the wooden structures, showing signs of permanent residency. Potted plants lined the cobbled walkway. Lounge chairs were situated on one side of the front door, a bright red kettle-style barbeque on the other.

Dave knocked on the cabin door. A not too happy voice yelled out, "What is it?" "Police business," Dave yelled back.

The door to cabin eleven shot open. A small man in his late fifties stood in the entranceway. He hastily tied a sash around his knee-length robe. The smell of freshly brewed coffee assailed Dave's nostrils. He realized how badly he needed a cup. "Police?" the man inquired. "What's the problem?" Then, more suspiciously, "Let me see your badge."

Dave impatiently showed the man his badge. "I have to get inside cabin fifteen. I have reason to believe the man inside may be in some kind of trouble."

The man peered at Dave. "Trouble? What kind of trouble?" "He could be hurt."

The man frowned. He hesitated, but something in Dave's expression suppressed any argument he might have been thinking of making. "Wait here a minute. I'll get the key." He glanced down at his bare legs and feet. "I was getting ready to take a shower. I have to open up the office in less than forty-five minutes." His tone was accusing and resentful.

"The key?" Dave prodded.

"Okay. Keep your shirt on, officer. I'll go get it."

A moment later the man returned with a key. "You're lucky. I keep spares in here." He gripped the key tightly. "Don't you need a warrant or something?"

"I can get one," Dave said. "Or you can make it easier on both of us if you'll just cooperate."

The man grunted. "Okay. Follow me," he said, his tone belligerent.

The man pounded on Chris's cabin door. When he was satisfied there was going to be no answer, he inserted the key in the lock and opened the door.

The interior of the cabin was small, the furnishings old and worn.

Faded pictures adorned the walls. Dave took all this in before he allowed his attention to focus on the man lying on the bed, one arm dangling over the edge. On the floor beside him was a rubber strap, a hypodermic needle, and a small empty plastic bag, plus seven others filled with a white powdery substance. Dave opened one up, stuck his little finger inside and tested a small amount with the tip of his tongue. It was heroin. In Chris's now rigid clenched fist was a crumpled piece of paper.

The manger stared at Chris. "Is he…?" "Yes. Call the local police."

"Aren't you…?"

"No. Call them," Dave ordered, his tone harsh.

After the man left, Dave pried the piece of paper form Chris's fingers. Rigor mortis, though it had begun, was slight. Chris hadn't been dead for too long.

The paper was cheap motel stock with the motel letterhead at the top of the page.

Dave read the handwritten note.

I'M SORRY ABOUT ELLEN AND BERTHA. THEY GAVE ME NO CHOICE. I BURNED BERTHA'S DIARY AND NOTES. SHE GUESSED THE TRUTH. I COULDN'T LET HER TELL ANYONE, AND I'D NEVER SURVIVE PRISON.

CHRIS.

The manager returned. "I called them. They'll be here any minute." "Did you see or hear anyone near this cabin in the last few hours? A car?

Anything?" Dave asked him.

"No." The man looked puzzled. "Why? Do you think someone was here with him doing drugs? This is a nice motel," he said piously. "We don't encourage those kind of goings on."

Dave ignored the question, and made note of the man's holier than thou attitude. "Do you record all the calls made from rooms? Local, too?"

The man nodded, peering at Chris's lifeless form. "Completed calls, we do. Do you want me to check?"

"That would be nice," Dave responded with sarcasm. "That would be damn nice."

The man returned a few minutes later. "Three calls," he said. "None of them local. All of them were made to Briarwood." He handed Dave the numbers. Two of them Dave knew. One was his motel. That would have been the call Chris made to him. The other was Clyde Bromley's home number. The third number, Dave didn't recognize.

Dave shook his head. It was like finding Ellen all over again. This latest supposed suicide left the same empty feeling inside of him as he'd felt then.

It was much later that same day. Dave was in Clyde Bromley's office. Bromley handed Dave the note Chris had left behind.

"The Duncan police turned it over to me since Chris was a Briarwood boy. I had the nasty job of telling Sid and Martha about Chris," Bromley said.

"Then you have no doubts about it being suicide?" Dave asked.

Bromley came from behind his desk. "Chris's parents swear its Chris's handwriting, and if that ain't enough, Kincaid, who else but you, me, and whoever killed Bertha, knew about the missing diary? Who else knew she was murdered?"

Dave thought about the last time he'd seen Chris. "Chris knew Miss Bartlett was murdered. I told him."

Bromley pounded on his desk. "I thought we were playing it close to the chest.

Who the hell else did you tell? Trinity?"

"No one. I thought Chris needed to know. I had good reason to think he might be the next victim."

"He was, Kincaid. And he was the last. It's over. At least it can be, if you'll just let it be. Hell, you don't think I hate the way it turned out? I've known Chris since the day he was born. When I put out the A.P.B. on him, I really believed it was to protect him, not to pick him up for murder. Never would have thought that he could hurt anyone, but the fact remains that he did, and the only way to let the wounds heal, is for you to close the books on Ellen and Bertha. I'd like to think that Chris wanted it that way, and that's why he did what he did."

Dave sighed. It was tempting to take Bromley's advice. "Just between you and me, you don't really think that Chris killed Ellen and Miss Bartlett, do you, Sheriff?'

Bromley reached for a cigar from a wooden box on his desk. He lit it, and took a deep drag. Aromatic smoke filled the air. Bromley coughed. "I gave these damn things up once. Never should have started again." He stared thoughtfully at Dave. "Don't matter much what I think, Kincaid, it's you that has to give it up. Everything points to the fact that Chris took his own life. The Duncan police found one set of prints on the needle and the bags of heroin. Chris's. No one was seen even close to his cabin." He leaned back in his chair. "I'm a tired old man, and I'm smart enough to know when I'm licked. How about you?"

Dave vehemently shook his head. "Not yet. Oh, I admit it looks like everything has been wrapped up in a nice neat little package, but I'm not buying it."

Bromley's expression was both puzzled and full of grudging admiration. "Goddamn, you're just a stubborn son of a bitch. Don't you ever give up? Ain't you ever been wrong?"

Dave shook his head again. "I never give up until the last card is played, and this deck is just starting to get warm. I can feel murder just like an arthritic feels rain in the air." He reached inside his jacket and pulled out a small notebook. "Chris called three

 Briarwood numbers before he died. One was to me. One was to you." He pointed to the third number. "You know who this number belongs to?"

Bromley placed his glasses on the end of his nose and peered at Dave's open notebook. "Sure. It's Sid and Martha Briggs' number. They told me he'd phoned them when I called on them. He phoned them because he didn't want them to worry about him. Something you could have done incidentally, Kincaid, but then you're not a father, are you? What would you know about a parent's anguish?"

"It occurred to me to call them and tell them where Chris was, but I wasn't about to tell anyone. Not even them. Could they have told anyone where Chris was?"

"At two-o-clock in the morning!"

"It's possible. Improbable, but possible. Someone knew where to find him, that's for sure. What about the call to you, Sheriff. Why did he call you?"

Bromley stiffened. "I don't like the nature of the question, but I'll gladly answer it. Chris wanted to know if you could be trusted."

"What did you tell him?"

"I told him, yes. I also told him to get his butt back here, pronto."
"Is that all Chris wanted?"

Bromley nodded.

"Doesn't it strike you as odd, Sheriff, that a man about to kill himself is concerned about whether he can trust the man he's just asked to keep him alive? And then there's the call to his parents. He didn't want them to worry, and yet not much later he supposedly kills himself?" Dave frowned. "Then there's the note. Something about it bothers me. Like Chris, in a last desperate moment was trying to tell us something, and I don't mean to confess to murders I don't think he committed."

Bromley moved back behind his desk. "It's irregular, I grant you that, but Chris was in a strange state of mind. I can't pretend to know what he was thinking. Neither can you. He didn't have the market cornered on wanting to kill himself, Kincaid. Are you forgetting about Trinity?"

Dave raised himself out of the desk-side chair he occupied. "I thought you didn't believe in coincidence, Sheriff. Two murders, and two suicide attempts, one of them successful! You're buying it? Just like that?"

Bromley touched the file on his desk. The file was labeled, ELLEN GRAY. He opened his top desk drawer and pulled out a rubber stamp and ink pad. He inked the stamp and pressed down on the buff-colored pad. Big red letters pronounced: CASE CLOSED.

"Does that answer your question?" Bromley asked, his expression grim and determined.

Dave's face turned an angry shade of red. "It sure as hell does. You're willing to call it two murders. I make it three."

"Can you prove it?"

"Maybe not," Dave responded angrily, "but I'm sure as hell going to try."

Dave pounded on Brad's motel door. Brad opened it and said, "Come in. I heard about Briggs. Tough break. I know you believed in him. Think about it, Dave. What in the hell did you really know about Briggs? Just because some bored, nosy old lady who had nothing better to do than pry into other people's business saw him as a victim, is no reason to take her word for gospel. Look how the old woman lived! She lived her life through others. All those pictures on her bedroom wall!"

Dave's tone was distracted. "You think I should walk away from this case, don't you?"

Brad nodded. "There isn't a case anymore, Dave." "You and Bromley! Maybe you two should team up."

Brad's jaw tightened. "Low blow, Dave. You want to pursue this fucking case?

Okay. I'll buy in. Satisfied?"

Through Brad's eyes Dave suddenly saw himself as others were seeing him, stubborn and unyielding. And, with what justification? A nagging little voice inside was telling him not to walk away just yet? But who else really cared about the truth? How many people was he hurting with his dogged persistence? "Forget it, Brad," Dave said. "You're probably right. It's over. Go on back to the city."

"What about you?"

"A few loose ends to tie up. Personal ones. I'll try to square the extra few days with Herring."

"You mean it? You'll really walk away from here?" "You don't sound like you believe me."

Brad smiled at him, but behind the smile was concern. "Only because I know you too well."

An hour later Brad's car was packed and ready to go. "Sure you won't go back with me?" Brad asked Dave.

Dave shook his head. "Positive."

Dave watched Brad drive away. I'm back where I started, he thought. Back with a case everyone wants to trash. No matter what he'd told Brad, Dave knew, deep inside, that Chris hadn't killed Ellen or Bertha. All that left him was the same giant question mark. Who had?

Dave had left the door to his room open. The sound of the phone ringing interrupted his jumbled thoughts. It was Bromley. His voice was gruff, just short of unfriendly. "Just thought you might want to know. Trinity came out of her coma. She's going to be okay."

Dave hugged the receiver to his chest. "Thank God," he whispered. And more audibly, "Thanks, Sheriff. I owe you one."

Dave's first instinct was to rush to the hospital, but he had no right. Not unless Trinity asked to see him. She has to, he thought. She must. I can't leave here until I've seen her again. Too much has been left unsaid.

He couldn't leave without one last try at finding out who really killed Ellen Gray. He reached into the drawer by the beside stand for his copy of Bertha's notes.

Brad might try to discount them, but Dave couldn't afford to. His eyes were drawn to the one name on the list he'd ignored. Chris had mentioned Ellen's concern about Severn Wokowski's tragic death. Had Wokowski's parents got onto Bertha's list of people to see from force of habit, as he'd first thought, or was their presence there deliberate and meaningful?

Dave made his own list of people to see. WOKOWSKI'S PARENTS, BILL, MARGARET.

And of course, one way or another, he had to see Trinity. The phone in the room rang again. It was Sheila Prentiss.

"Hi," she said. "I have some information I thought you might find interesting and helpful."

"I thought Herring pulled you off the Ellen Gray case when he let Brad come to Briarwood."

"He did, but I've been working on it in my own time." She sounded nervous, embarrassed. "I know it's none of my business, but I'd like to see you and Laura get back together again, and as long as you're there, and she's here…she still loves you, Dave."

"Did she tell you that?"

"She didn't have to, it's obvious. I suppose Brad told you that she moved in with me?"

"Yes."

"I want to help."

Dave sighed. Sheila meant well. "Haven't you heard? There is no more Ellen Gray case. Her former boyfriend admitted to killing her before he checked out with an overdose. Appropriate, don't you think, considering that's the way Ellen got it?" Bitterness filled his voice.

"Then you'll be coming back?" There was little conviction in Sheila's voice.

And at Dave's silence. "I guess I already knew the answer to that. You'd better take this information from me, then."

"About who?"

"Bryant, Gerard, and," she hesitated, "Ellen Gray. It was a fluke really. I was working another case, checking out motels and boarding houses, when I came across the name Trinity Ambrose on a register. Trinity isn't your average run of the mill name, so I checked further. Ambrose was Ellen Gray's mother's maiden name. Ellen Gray used an alias when she came here. That's why she was so hard to track down."

Excitement filled Dave's voice. "Did you talk to anyone who saw Ellen?" "One of the clerks. He remembered her, because, in his words, 'she was a

knockout.' She registered for a week, but only stayed one night, then checked out. She told the clerk that her plans had changed. He saw her leaving with a young guy, tall with blond hair. He couldn't tell much more. He only caught a glimpse of the guy."

Dave's heart sank. Chris was tall with blond hair. "What about Gerard and Bryant?"

"It seems redundant now. Bryant worked as an accountant for a large corporation before he moved to Briarwood, one of those corporations within a corporation. There were hints of underworld connections."

"Proof or conjecture?"

There was no mistaking the disappointment in her voice. "Nothing concrete, so I guess you'd say conjecture. Bryant was arrested when his supervisors reported him for misuse of funds, but nothing was ever proven, and none of the charges stuck. Get this, the guy who turned him in was the one who got the axe."

"Which could mean that Bryant was innocent," Dave offered. "Or guilty with connections," she replied.

"Couldbe. Howcome this information just surfaced?"

"Sloppy research, I guess. Besides, this isn't the only case we're handling. There is a whole list of others with higher priority."

"So I keep being told. What about Gerard?"

"His wife is an invalid, as you know, but what you didn't know, and I just found out, was that his medical insurance ran out about a year ago. His wife's medical expenses are staggering, but Gerard always pays them. On time, and in cash."

"I'll check into it. Thanks, Sheila. I appreciate it." "Any time. About Laura…"

Dave sobered. "I haven't given up on her, but I have to get my house in order before I can ask her to share it. I need time."

"I'll keep my fingers crossed for both of you."

"You do that," Dave said. "I need all the help I can get."

⌇⌇⌇

Dave was on the way out the door when a car drove up in front of his room. It was Brad.

Dave's partner climbed out of his car, a determined look on his face. He threw up his hands. "You're not fooling anyone, Dave, you're still investigating Ellen Gray's murder. We're partners, Dave, and we're friends. So, if you're staying, then so the fuck am I."

"The hell you are! Herring will suspend your ass."

Brad shrugged. "So he'll suspend me. You, too, probably. We both know that there are too few really good cops. If he yanks our badges, we'll figure a way to get them back."

"Why are you doing this, Brad?"

"I told you, we're partners." He grinned sheepishly. "I cannot tell a lie. There's more. On my way out of town, I was stopped by a very attractive young woman who identified herself as Margaret Gray. She knew who I was. Some grape vine you got here. We got to talking. She invited me to dinner. I remembered you insinuating she and I were two of a kind. Hell, I couldn't resist! Here was a chance to find out what in the hell you were talking about, and help you out at the same time. You were going to question her again, weren't you? Why not let me do it for you?"

Dave shook his head, looked skyward, and said, "You're a crazy son of a bitch, but I love you for it. So, you want to take on Margaret Gray? You two really deserve each other." He laughed. "Well, why the hell not?

⌘

Bill Lackland didn't look surprised when Dave appeared at the high school football stadium. He was sitting in the bleachers, overseeing a practice session.

Bill continued to look at the field, not at Dave. "I guess I knew you wouldn't leave town without wanting to see me. Too bad about Chris. Who would have guessed it?"

Dave took a seat on the bench beside Bill. "Who indeed? He didn't kill Ellen, Bill."

Bill tore his gaze away from the field beyond. "What?"

"I said he didn't do it. I may have a hard time proving it, but I'm going to try." "You think it was me?"

"No. I think the reason for Ellen's murder began with you, Bill, but it didn't end with you."

Bill stared past Dave. "Beth told you about me and Ellen."

Dave nodded. "Why did you lie to me? You had to know I'd find out sooner or later."

"Two reasons. One, I really thought I might get away with keeping our affair a secret. Two, I found it hard to talk about Ellen. I still do. I loved her. I loved her right up until the day she died."

Dave registered surprise. "But you married Beth Woodley."

"Beth was pregnant." Bill stood. He shook his fist and yelled at one of the players. "Tackle goddamn it, don't ask him to dance." He turned back to Dave. "My first marriage was far from perfect. I played around some. I was already seeing Beth when I started to see Ellen. It was funny, I'd known her all her life, practically watched her grow up, but one day she was just a girl, someone's kid sister, then suddenly, overnight, it seemed, she was this beautiful, exciting woman. It was casual at first, for both of us, but then I fell hard. I asked Carol for a divorce so I could marry Ellen, though I never mentioned her by name. Carol didn't object. We hadn't cared about each other for a long time. Beth didn't know about Ellen, but Ellen knew about Beth. I went to see Beth for what I meant to be the last time, intending to tell her about Ellen. I chickened out. Worse, I slept with Beth. That was the night she got pregnant, and it was the night it was all over for me and Ellen."

"But you saw Ellen after you married Beth?"

"Yes. I couldn't help myself." His face lit up. "You should have seen her. She was something. Angel one moment, hellcat, another. I would have left Beth, but you know the rest. Beth said she told you about threatening to take away my kid."

"Tell me about Wokowski," Dave asked. Bill frowned. "Wokowski?"

Bill almost got away with an attempt at puzzled nonchalance, Dave thought, but not quite. There was a momentary trace of fear in his eyes that gave him away. "Yeah, Wokowski. What did he really die from?"

"Kidney failure. I told you that, already." "Sudden?"

"Yes. What are you getting at, Kincaid?"

"If I knew that, I'd have all the answers." Dave rose from the bench. He stretched. "I'll get the answers. Like I said, Bill, the trail starts with you. All I have to do is follow it."

⌒⫘⌒

The Wokowskis were a nice older couple who had sacrificed everything for their only child. Now that Severn was gone, they had nothing worthwhile left, and their eyes reflected it.

No wonder Miss Bartlett had felt responsible for these people, Dave thought, and once again he cursed whoever had ended her life. If Miss Bartlett hadn't been able to give these people hope, she'd at least let them know someone cared, and cared deeply.

It took very little time for Dave to see why Miss Bartlett had been so concerned about upsetting the Wokowskis. Their emotions were fragile, the pain they still felt clearly written in their prematurely aged faced.

Dave sat in their small but comfortable living room. There were those who might have called the faded couch and chairs shabby, but Dave was more charitable. He considered the cheap furnishings a refreshing lack of ostentation and a disregard for outward material trimmings.

Olga Wokowski handed Dave a cup of steaming hot chocolate. "My own recipe," she said. "From the old country. I make the chocolate myself." She wrung her hands together. She was nervous, for reasons she soon verbalized. "In my country, when a policeman comes to your door, often you are never seen again." Her English, though quite good, was spoken with a heavy accent.

She glanced at her husband, Carlof. He came to her side and placed his arms around her reassuringly. "My wife, she is right. Nineteen years we have been here, and we still cannot forget how it was in our homeland." He threw his chest out with pride. "We are now American citizens." Like his wife, his accent was strong.

"Severn was born American citizen," Olga Wokowski proudly proclaimed.

Just the sound of their son's name caused tears to spring to the woman's eyes and a distressed look passed across her husband's face.

"You came to see us about Chris?" Carlof Wokowski said. "We feel his mama and his papa's pain. He was a good boy like my Severn. If he did what they say, he must have suffered a moment of terrible madness. Chris, he loves Ellen. My wife and me we like her, too. She was kind to my son when others were cruel."

"I didn't come here about Chris," Dave replied. "I came about your son." "My Severn?" Carlof Wokowski asked.

"And Miss Bartlett," Dave went on. "Miss Bartlett was murdered." "Miss Bartlett take a fall," Carlof protested.

"A story the Sheriff and I made up so we could catch whoever killed her. She came to see you the day she died, didn't she?"

Carlof looked at his wife and hugged her closer. "Why you ask?" "Why are you so reluctant to answer?"

Carlof sighed. He led his wife to a chair, placed her in it, and stood behind her. "Since our boy died, all we have done is try to forget the tragedy of his death and remember instead the wonderful years we had him." His wife raised her hand and he took it in his and squeezed it. "We had no children for so many years, then God gave us Severn. Birthing him was God's will, and so was taking him away. We'd come to accept that."

Dave noted the use of the past tense. "Miss Bartlett said something to disturb that acceptance?" Dave prompted.

Olga took over the conversation. "Miss Bartlett, she like our boy. When he died, she help us to make all the arrangements. She came every day since Severn died. The last time she came, she asked questioned that puzzled us, made us to wonder if it was only God's hand that took Severn from us."

"Drugs," Dave said. "Did Miss Bartlett mention drugs?"

Olga nodded. She squeezed her husband's hand once more. "She did. But she was wrong. We thought much of Miss Bartlett, but like we told her, Severn don't take drugs."

Dave, of course, knew better. Their son had tried drugs at least once, and who knows how many more times? He wouldn't necessarily have told Chris everything. Maybe he'd kept on using after Chris and Ellen swore off, or Chris had lied about how long he and Ellen had been users. Anything was possible, and the only ones who knew the truth were dead.

A sad but proud smile lit up Olga's face. "Severn always wanted to be a great American athlete. Mr. Lackland, he see Severn's promise. He helped him. Soon, Severn became so good at the football that we, like Severn, began to believe his dream really could come true. He was going to buy us a fancy house. He worked hard. He became strong. So very strong. Then, one day he got this infection. We thought it was a cold, but it got worse, so bad his kidneys got sick, too. We couldn't afford machine to do work his kidneys had stopped doing." Tears that had merely filled her eyes now streamed down her cheeks. "Mr. Lackland, he says, never mind, he had the money.

Imagine! He took a loan from the bank in his own name! For my son! He says we could pay back whenever we could. And it wasn't only Mr. Lackland. Many more people wanted to help. It was a wonderful thing. Then my son died. It all happened so quick." Sobs wracked her body.

Dave leaned forward in his chair. Right now he hated his job. "Mrs. Wokowski, I have to ask again, are you sure your son wasn't using drugs?"

She vehemently shook her head. "No. All Severn took was the vitamins Mr. Lackland say he need to stay strong. Severn, he try so hard to please Mr. Lackland, because he know that Mr. Lackland believe in him. Mr. Lackland was very strict with Severn's diet. No sweets, no junk food, not even his mama's rhubarb pie."

"Then what killed him?" Dave said softly, more to himself than to the Wokowski's. Miss Bartlett's notes! The notation: HOW DID HE DIE? Dave cursed himself for being so incredibly stupid. Bertha hadn't been talking about Sam Gray.

She'd been talking about Severn Wokowski!

Dave stood up to leave. Another name on Miss Bartlett's list came to mind. "Was Doctor Christian your son's doctor?"

"Yes," Olga replied. A frightened look clouded her face. "Severn didn't do anything wrong."

"I'm sure you're right," Dave said kindly. With rancor, he added, "I think your son's only crime was letting someone turn his dream into a nightmare."

⟐

Doctor Christian was that rare kind of medical man that only a small town like Briarwood boasted. He still made house calls.

He was away on one when Dave stopped by his office, which was actually the front half of the home he shared with his wife.

A large amiable woman, Clara Christian, greeted Dave with a warm smile. "My husband is over at the Revstoke's place. He should be back soon. Would you care to wait?"

Dave was about to say no, when a car pulled up.

"That's him now," she said. "Come on in."

187

The doctor was stout like his wife, and just as pleasant. "You're the city detective, aren't you?" he asked. "Which of them are you here about? Ellen, Bertha or Chris?"

"I could be in need of medical help," Dave said.

The doctor led Dave into a small cozy room that doubled as his office and his study. He smiled. "You look perfectly healthy to me."

Dave liked him. Maybe it was because his kind was a dying breed in a world of specialists. "Okay, I'll come to the point. I came to see you about Severn Wokowski."

The doctor frowned. "Severn? Not about one of the others?"

Dave sat back in the chair beside the doctor's desk. "Only in a roundabout way.

Did you treat Severn?"

The doctor nodded. "He caught a cold that turned into a virus. I gave him several different antibiotics, but nothing helped, he just got worse. Then, his kidneys started to shut down, one at a time. I wanted to send him to Duncan or to Henderson. I'm just a small town doctor. His condition was beyond my medical capabilities."

"You didn't send him to Duncan or Henderson?" "No. Have you met the boy's parents?"

Dave nodded.

"Then you must know what I was up against. They're good people, poor but proud. They had no medical insurance. I treated the boy for practically nothing, because…well…" He shrugged. "That's the way we do things here. I liked the boy. He would have put Briarwood on the map. This town isn't what it used to be. We could have used the boost. According to Bill, Severn was Joe Namath and Joe Montana rolled into one. Severn needed dialysis. I told his parents that. They worried about how to pay for it. When word got out about how sick Severn really was, money started pouring into my office for his care."

He shook his head. "Severn died before we could get him the help he needed. Maybe he'd have died anyway. He was very ill."

"Are you so sure the Wokowski kid had a virus, Doctor?"

Christian reached for his pipe, lit it and blew smoke into the air. "What are you trying to say?"

"Before Chris Briggs died, he told me that he, Ellen, and Severn, tried drugs.

Only once, according to Chris. Let's say, just for arguments sake, that Severn Wokowski went further. What kind of drug would cause the symptoms he displayed before he died?"

Christian placed his pipe in an ashtray. He stood. "Go home, Detective Kincaid. Two very nice people suffered a loss that no one ever really gets over. They were proud of their son. So was this town. I won't help you to smear Severn Wokowski's memory with insinuations. If you try it, you won't find a friendly soul in this town."

"Then I'll have to find out what I need without your help, Doctor."

"Tell me," Christian asked as Dave turned to leave. "Why are you doing this?

What could Severn's death possibly have to do with Ellen Gray's murder?"

"Maybe nothing," Dave answered. "Then again, maybe it has everything to do with it."

⚬⚬⚬

Dave placed a call to the city's Coroner's office, to Sid Carter, specifically. He was hoping that Sid might shed some light on what kind of drug usage would have caused Severn Wokowski's sudden and fatal symptoms.

Sid was out sick. He was expected back tomorrow, the next day at the latest. Ted Archer was filling in for Sid. Dave could have talked to him, but he preferred Sid's input. Sid was a strange duck, but one of the best men in his field, and Dave was one of the few cops Sid got along with and opened up to.

Loose ends. Too many loose ends, Dave thought. Too many brick walls. Too many people wanting it to be over. To hell with Chris and what his parents were going through, he couldn't help thinking angrily.

He called the motel from a pay phone to check for messages. There was only one.

It was from Trinity. She had called him from the hospital. She wanted to see him.

CHAPTER 12

Trinity was resting against raised pillows when Dave entered her hospital room.

She was wearing a scoop-necked blue gown trimmed with lace. Pale from her ordeal, she looked, if it was possible he thought, more beautiful than he'd ever seen her. And so very vulnerable. He swallowed a lump in his throat.

There were several flower arrangements in the room. I never sent her flowers, Dave anguished. Then, how could I? Once again he regretted that his claim on her, if any, had yet to be established, even for something as simple as his right to send her flowers.

He admitted now that she'd recovered, that he'd never dared to let himself believe that she might not survive the attempt on her own life. It she'd died, he'd have spent the rest of his life wondering about their future.

He still might, he acknowledged, because her being alive and well, was no guarantee of anything as far as they were concerned.

She smiled at him, indicating a chair by the bed. "Thanks for coming."

He wanted to take her hand in his and wondered if he dared. He decided to take the risk.

Physical contact caused sensations within him that he now expected, but still found hard to deal with. "How could I not come?" he responded. "I was here once before, but you were still in a coma. They wouldn't let me see you."

"I know. Margaret told me. There are so many things I want to say to you.

Where do I begin?"

"You could start with why you tried to kill yourself."

She looked away from him. "I don't know that I really did. Oh, I know I took the pills, and that no one shoved them down my throat. I was miserable after I left you at your motel. I came home and started to drink, non-stop. Then, I took one pill and another, until I didn't know how many I'd taken. I don't believe I wanted to die, just to stop the hurt. Everything was crowding in on me. Ellen. My marriage to Steve. My brief affair with your father. The look on your face when I told you about it. Us. I've had time to think, lying here waiting for you to show up. Before, you were a boy, and I didn't dare to admit I could be in love with you. It seemed obscene, and technically statutory rape. You're a man now, Dave, and I freely admit, I loved you then, and I love you now. It's just easier to say it to you." She smiled. "See, I even managed not to call you Davie."

Dave was flabbergasted. He'd waited years to hear her say she loved him.

Dreamed of this moment. Now that it was here, he was terrified. Terrified of feelings he couldn't categorize, terrified to start something that could end the same way it had years ago. He couldn't let it happen that way again.

She noted his silence. "You don't have to say anything. Besides," she went on, "I wanted to talk to you about more than about us. I heard about Chris. Tell me, Davie, Dave," she corrected, "Is it true? Did he really kill Ellen?"

She wasn't just making conversation, Dave realized, she really wanted to know, and she deserved the truth, he decided. At least the truth the way he believed it. "I don't think so. His suicide and even the note he left were just too pat, and too damned convenient."

She sighed. "I was afraid of that. Then whoever killed her is still out there." Fear entered her voice. 'I'm scared, Dave. What if he kills again?"

"Who is left to cause a threat?" "Me," she whispered.

"Your husband?"

She bit down on her lip. "He wants to send me away from here for a while. He says I need to get away from Briarwood and from the stress of everything that's happened here lately. I think he wants to get me away from you."

"Because of what we meant to each other?"

"Or, maybe more than that." She gripped his hand. "Take me out of here. Take me somewhere where no one can find me. Keep me there until you find out who killed Ellen. Please."

Dave thought about his last conversation with Chris. "Chris trusted me to keep him safe, and look what happened to him. I don't know if I'm ready to be responsible for another human being, or even if I want to be."

"It's what you do! Please," she whispered. "I don't know who else to turn to. You once said that I could help you find Ellen's killer if I wanted to. I want to now."

She was pushing, but he couldn't turn her down, because there was no one else.

Where could he take her? Not to his apartment. If Steven St. John was involved in Ellen's death, it was the first place he'd think to look for her. And who would keep an eye on Trinity if he took that risk? He couldn't leave Briarwood just yet. He thought about Sheila. No, that wouldn't work. Laura had moved in with her. It was unthinkable to have the two women in his life in the same apartment. Brad? No. He needed him here. An image of the lake where he'd taken Laura came to mind. There were cabins there. It was off season. It should be easy to rent one.

"What about your husband? He isn't going to be too happy when he finds out I've hidden you away."

"Steve is away on business. He won't be back until the day after tomorrow."

Dave knew that what she was asking was crazy, but… "Give me a few hours to set it up," he said.

Trinity smiled through her tears. "Thank, you."

"Don't thank me yet, Trinity. I used to be a good cop. Maybe I still have it in me to be one again. Katie got in the way for a while, then Brad and I found Ellen in that alley, and the merry-go-round just wouldn't stop. I came here about murder, but you and I became more important. I got careless. I quit thinking about my job, because I couldn't stop thinking about you." That hasn't changed, he thought. I'm just going to have to be a cop and a man. Laura had said he couldn't be both. Maybe she was right.

"I have to get back on track," he said, "but with you…" "I won't get in your way, I promise."

He knew that she would. "This could spell disaster for both of us. You know that?"

She nodded. She gripped his hand tighter. "Kiss me, Dave," she said. "I need reassurance."

A kiss. A simple kiss. Dave knew there was no such thing where he and Trinity were concerned. He took a deep breath, thinking that he'd wanted to do nothing else but kiss her from the first moment he'd seen her again.

He leaned over and touched her lips gently with his own. She pulled him closer. Her tongue found his. He responded. He wanted her so badly he felt like ripping off her gown and climbing into bed with her. He wanted to touch her, to feel her beneath him, to be inside of her.

He wrenched himself free of her, his breathing ragged. "Later," he said, and swiftly left the room.

Outside her room, in the corridor, Dave wiped the sweat from his brow. If he was smart, he'd never see her again.

He knew he had to see her. She was still a part of him, and he either had to exorcise her or have her for his own.

Dave stopped off at the lake and rented a cabin. Since resort, rather than small town mentality reigned here, he felt reasonably sure he could get away with anonymity.

His next stop was the bank. Bryant was out, but Felix Gerard was in his cubicle- like office.

Felix leaped to his feet as Dave entered the cubicle. His hands shook, though he tried to hide the fact by placing them behind his back. "Detective," he said, "I thought you'd be gone by now."

"Well you thought wrong. Sit down, Gerard. I just have a question or two, then I'll get out of your hair."

"Questions? What about? Chris killed Ellen. What can I say, except that I'm sorry it turned out to be him. He loved her too much it seems. Surely, in your line of work, crimes of passion aren't that unusual."

"You loved her, too, Gerard, and you didn't kill her, did you?" At his downcast expression, Dave responded with. "Don't worry. Your secret is safe with me, for the time being, anyway. I'm here because I hate loose ends Gerard, and you're a loose end. I have it on good authority that you pay your wife's staggering medical bills without one red cent from health insurance. You want to tell me how you manage to do that? I checked. Your salary here at the bank is forty-eight thousand dollars a year, yet last year you paid over fifty thousand dollars in medical bills. In cash."

"Savings?" Gerard offered hopefully. Dave shook his head.

"I don't know how it can be of concern to you, but I got a loan from the bank." "With what as collateral? Your house in mortgaged to the hilt. I checked that, too. You have no equity left to borrow against."

Gerard's shoulder slumped. "Carey. Carey lent it to me. All of it. He gave it to me on a signature loan."

Dave gave him a thoughtful stare. "But cash? What took so long for you to come out with the truth?"

"I have my pride, Detective. I don't particularly like Carey, but he was the only one who would help me."

Dave stood. "If that's all there is to it, you have nothing to worry about." As he started to leave. "Oh, and by the way, before you get to feeling too comfortable, I don't think Chris killed Ellen. So I'm going to be around for a while. You might want to tell Bryant that, and that I'd like to talk to him."

❦

Dave touched base with Brad. He told him about his talk with Bill and Gerard, and Sheila's call. "Somebody paid Gerard a lot of money for something. My guess is it was his silence, and that Bryant is the one who paid the tab. If Sheila is right, Bryant has a lot to hide. I haven't made contact with the son of a bitch yet, but he has a lot of explaining to do." Dave looked agitated.

"Let me talk to him, Dave, Brad said. "You seem distracted. I can talk to Bryant and Margaret. Bryant first. He seems more important."

"Thanks, Brad. I'll take you up on that. I do have something I need to take care of."

"Want to tell me what?"

"It's personal." He shrugged. "Oh, what the hell! I'm going to be with the one person in this town who knows St. John better than anyone else."

Brad grimaced. "Fuck. I knew it. It's Trinity St. John. Don't you think you might be playing with fire?"

"Think? Hell, I know I am."

"Try to keep your mind on business." He smiled. "On second thought, maybe you could use the diversion."

Oh his way to the hospital to pick up Trinity, Dave pondered the inevitable. When St. John returned and found out that his wife had been spirited away from the hospital, all hell was going to break loose.

Trinity had the car passenger window rolled all the way down. Wind whipped through her black hair. Her grey eyes sparkled. She looked happy.

Dave thought about the scene back at the hospital. Trinity wasn't supposed to be checked out until St. John returned. There'd been a ruckus. The duty nurse had called in Trinity's doctor who'd forbidden her to leave the hospital.

That was all it took. Grey eyes flashing, she'd admonished all of them, nurse and doctor alike. "Am I well enough to leave?"

The doctor had hedged. "Physically, you're stable, but we'd like to keep you for observation."

"I asked if I was well enough to leave, not if you're afraid I might try to kill myself again. I won't incidentally. Let me rephrase my question. If I leave now, am I in any physical jeopardy?"

"No, but…"

"That's all I wanted to know."

He'd given in. "You'll have to sign a waiver of responsibility." "Then get me one," she'd demanded.

Dave smiled to himself. Any chance of quietly leaving the hospital after that was out of the question.

"We're almost there," Dave told her.

She smiled at him. "I know. I live around here, remember?"

The cabin was in a tree shaded glen. It consisted of a living room-bedroom combination, kitchenette and bath. A natural rock fireplace covered the length of one wall. It was furnished simply but adequately.

Trinity unpacked the groceries they'd purchased while Dave went to gather wood for a fire.

Trinity prepared a simple meal of cold ham, canned vegetables, and French bread.

As yet they hadn't discussed the case or anything personal.

After their meal they sipped wine before the fireside. It was a dangerously intimate atmosphere. Isn't that what you wanted? Dave asked himself. Isn't that why you chose this place? As if aware of the danger, they sat on opposite ends of the king- size couch. She was the one who brought up the subject of Ellen and she and Dave.

"It's time for the truth, Davie. Sorry, I mean Dave. All of it. I really was afraid to go home. I didn't just say that to get you alone." Her eyes lit up. "Now that we're here, I'm not ashamed to admit that I'm glad we are alone."

She was at ease for the first time since he'd come back to Briarwood. Dave wished that he were just as relaxed. His insides felt like someone had walked all over them, his head ached, and he was sweating profusely. He knew in his heart that before he left the cabin he was going to make love to her, and the very thought of it scared the hell out of him. Which was why he was glad of the distance that separated them right now.

"You're afraid of St. John?" He asked. "Yes."

"You think he had something to do with Ellen's death, don't you? Are you going to tell me why?"

"I'm going to tell you all I know, just as I promised. I realize now that I should have done it from the start." She bit down on her lip. "Maybe if I had of, Chris would be…"

"Don't blame yourself. I speak from experience. I tried to take my share of the blame, too, but it never changes anything."

She held out her glass. Dave refilled it with wine. "I'll start at the beginning," she said. "I mean the real beginning. Ellen was a very special child, intelligent, intuitive, and loving. She adored Sam, and she and I had a wonderful relationship until he died.

Sam and I argued the night he was killed. It was a horrible senseless argument that never should have happened. He'd just come back from a sales trip. I found lipstick on one of his shirts. It was so silly, because you see, I hadn't ever been in love with Sam, only deeply fond of him. He'd always been a womanizer when he was out on the road. I knew that when I married him. Here, in his hometown, he was a perfect husband and a perfect father. I don't know why I wanted to start something that night. It's a question I've asked myself over and over again. I guess my pride got in the way. I confronted him about the stains on his shirt. He flew into a rage, accusing me of having numerous affairs of my own. It wasn't true. There was only you, and…and there was your father. He demanded to know who Margaret's father was. Of course, Sam was her father, but he refused to believe it. He said he knew about me and Paul. It was impossible! No one knew. Then, he started in on Ellen. I became hysterical. I didn't think about what I was saying. I was angry. I can still hear myself saying, "All right, you bastard, what is it you want to hear? You want to think I cheat on you so your own escapades seem purer?

Well, let me oblige you. Ellen is not your daughter. Furthermore, I loved the man who fathered her, which is more than I can say about the way I feel about you."

Dave spilled wine from his glass but didn't seem to notice. "What are you saying, Trinity? I thought…"

"Let me finish," she pleaded. "I remember those ugly words as if I'd spoken them yesterday. I crushed him. I stood there and watched the life flow out of him. Sam may have quit breathing in the accident, but I killed him right there, in that one rash moment, just as if I'd put a gun to his head and pulled the trigger." Tears filled her eyes as she relived the moment. "I wasn't even telling him the truth."

Dave frowned. "I don't understand."

"I told him you were Ellen's father. It wasn't the truth." She turned away from him. "Then it wasn't a lie, either. I don't know who Ellen's father was, you or Sam. My diaphragm, it turned out, was defective." A sob crept into her voice. "So much for modern technology."

Dave was still reacting to the fact that he might have fathered a child. Don't think about it, a voice of reason warned. He struggled to keep his voice even and authoritative. "Ellen overheard you and Sam fighting?"

"Yes."

"Did she hear all of it?"

Trinity nodded. "Every miserable, rotten word. In time, we might have worked it out, she and I, but Sam died that same night. She blamed me for his death. She was right to, of course."

Dave was stunned, unable to think like a cop at this moment, thinking instead with the heart and mind of just a man. For one crazy off-balanced moment he saw Laura in his mind's eye. She'd been wrong. He could be both cop and man. Ellen could have been his, just as he'd dreaded when he'd first found out who she was. It had been simpler thinking of her as Sam's daughter. He made a fist, resisting the urge to slam it up against the wall. He stared blinding at Trinity. He'd wanted honesty from her. Well, now he had it.

As if she read his mind, she went on, "I didn't tell you that to hurt you. I had a very good reason."

Dave could hardly wait to hear it.

"Don't look at me like that," she pleaded. "I suppose you have a right to, just as Ellen had a right to resent me for what I'd done. After Sam died, she withdrew. When Sam was alive, she laughed all the time. Then, the laughter stopped. Margaret took my place in her life. Ellen no longer confided in me. Not up until the night she left Briarwood. I knew then how frightened she was. She must have been desperate to come to me."

"What was she so frightened of?"

"I told you the truth when I said I didn't know. I mean, not really. She was rambling, almost incoherent, which certainly wasn't like her. She went on about Severn Wokowski. I knew she was upset when he died, but that night she was morose, edgy, almost hysterical."

It coincided with what Chris had said, Dave thought. "Just what did she say? Try to remember, Trinity. It's important."

"She said that he died for nothing. He died, she said, all because he wanted to be the greatest quarterback this country had ever seen. It made absolutely no sense to me.

She said she had to get away from Briarwood because she was a threat to someone, but when I tried to push her, she withdrew and wouldn't tell me who it was. She said I was better off not knowing. I knew she was having an affair with a married man. Chris told me about it when he came to see me one day, hoping to gain my help in getting Ellen back. That's why I'm sure he didn't kill her. He loved her so very much." She stared past him. "Though, I often wondered why. Ellen treated him badly."

Dave sighed. "I don't think she was killed because of an affair. Bill doesn't have the guts."

"Bill?"

"Lackland. She was having an affair with him. He's admitted it."
"That can't be! I always thought it was Carey Bryant she was seeing."
"Why Bryant?"

"When I saw she was going to leave no matter what I said, I asked her if she needed money. She gave me a strange smile. "No. I got a loan," she said. "I asked her from whom. She said the bank had given her one. You have no collateral, I told her.

You don't even own a car."

"I'll get one, she said," Trinity continued. "I do have collateral." She gave me that strange smile again. "With Carey I have lots of collateral," she told me.

"I assumed she meant her affair with Carey, but now I don't know what to think.

Are you sure it was Bill she was seeing?"

Dave nodded. "Is it possible that she was having an affair with both of them?

You have an advantage over me, I never knew her," he said, unable to keep the bitterness out of his voice. "Would that have been in character for her?"

Trinity shook her head, oblivious to the accusation in his voice. She spoke in a hushed tone, almost more to herself than to Dave. "My God, that would make her…No, I don't think so. I admit I lost touch with her. But two affairs?" She blanched. "Was I that bad of an example? Surely, she didn't want to get back at me that desperately. Did she pay for my mistakes with her life?"

"Quit it! I don't think Ellen was killed because of something you and I did eighteen years ago. If I'm sure of nothing else, I'm sure of that. St. John? Why have you been afraid of him since you heard that Ellen was murdered?"

She stood and moved toward the fireplace. "After Ellen left I began to worry. I decided to get Steve's help. I went to his study. The door was open. I was about to knock, when I heard his voice. He was talking to someone on the phone. His words chilled me. I don't know who he was talking to, but I overheard him saying, the girl knows something. She can get in our way. Whoever was on the other end of the line said something, then Steve answered, 'I don't know where. Probably, the city. She has to be stopped before she screws everything up.' It was then, I knew," Trinity added, "that I couldn't trust Steve."

"Did you know where she was going? Or what she knew that St. John referred to?"

"I don't know what she knew that could hurt anybody, not enough to kill her for, but I know where she was going. I was the one who suggested she go to the city. I gave her your name, Dave. I told her to call you. I told her if she was in trouble she could count on you."

"Did she know who I was? That I could have been her father?"

"I think she may have guessed. I told you, she was bright. She was supposed to call me after she'd spoken with you. I never got that call."

"Neither did I," Dave said. "I wonder why."

Trinity moved away from the fireplace. She knelt at his feet. "Who killed her,

Dave?"

Dave's voice was grim. "I'm not sure, but the pieces are starting to fit. I'm getting close, which means that someone is probably getting damned nervous."

He ran his fingers through her hair. "I'd better be getting back. Will you be all right here by yourself?"

"Don't leave me, Dave. Not tonight. Whoever it was will still be there tomorrow. If he thinks Chris's suicide ended it, he won't be anxious."

What she was saying, he realized, was that if St. John had killed Ellen, there was time. St. John wouldn't be back until the day after tomorrow.

Trinity began to unbutton Dave's shirt. A fire raged within him that had been burning since he'd brought her to the cabin. He struggled to keep control. He stayed her nimble fingers. "Wait," he said. "I want you. I want you badly, but I have to know how it was with you and him." Dave knew that no matter what she said, he'd still want her, and he'd end up making love to her. It had gone too far to stop it, but he had to know about his father.

She removed his fingers from his shirt. "Oh, Davie, it was so very long ago.

Dave," she corrected herself, then gave him a defiant look. "Sorry, but you'll always be Davie to me."

He didn't mind anymore. "It's okay. Tell me about my father."

"Sam was away a lot, which meant I had to fend for myself most of the time. Not that I didn't get offers of help," she said bitterly. "From men, of course, most of them married, all of them more interested in my body than my problems. One day my car broke down outside of town on the old back road that goes by Miss Bartlett's place. It was a hot muggy day. There was little traffic on the road that day. I figured I was in for a long hike. Then, your father came driving by. He couldn't fix my car, so he gave me a ride home. Like I said, it was a hot day. We were drenched from the heat. He seemed different than all the others. I asked him in for a cold drink. I handed him the glass. Our hands touched. It was an electrifying moment. I'll spare you the details, but we ended up in bed together. Paul was a wreck afterward. He hated himself, and me, for what had happened. For me, the impossible had happened. I'd just met him, and yet I was madly in love for the first time in my life."

"Then you really never loved Sam?"

"Sam was my savior. I told you I was running away when I came to Briarwood. My father had been molesting me since I was thirteen. Sam found me huddled in a New Orleans side street one day. I was only fifteen. I'd run there to escape my father. I told Sam everything. He wanted me to go to the police, but I was too ashamed. He took me home instead and told my father that he was going to marry me and take me away and that if my father tried to stop him, he'd turn him in. Sam brought me here and slowly began to teach me that sex wasn't bad or dirty, that it was wonderful. I will always be in his debt for that, but I never loved him or lied to him and said I did. How could I have loved him? I didn't know the meaning of the word until that day with your father, and later with you."

She'd said she was fifteen when Sam brought her here! "Back up! You were only fifteen when Sam married you?"

"Yes. We lied about my age because of what people around here might say. Oh, I know what you're thinking, but you were still only sixteen when we were lovers. My being three years younger than you thought didn't change that."

Dave thought back to the first time he and Trinity had made love. Sam must have been one hell of a teacher! "Who came after my father?" Dave asked.

"No one. Your father created a hunger inside me that was never satisfied until you and I…until we made love. Paul wouldn't see me again. If we'd pass in the street, he'd act like I was a stranger."

So that was how Bertha Bartlett had come to suspect Trinity and Paul Kincaid of having an affair. It was not what they said or did, but what they didn't, that had set her to wondering.

Dave's respect for his father came rushing back to him. Paul Kincaid had had the courage to walk away from Trinity, which was more than his son had been able to do.

Dave intuitively felt that his father had loved her, which is why he'd begun to drink. Dave couldn't blame Trinity. Man, woman, and passion were explosive ingredients as hard to control as time itself.

"Why Steven St. John?"

She shrugged. "Why not? Maybe it was because he wasn't from Briarwood." "Are you saying you never loved him, either?"

"Would you say that because you're here with me, you never loved Laura?" She knew about Laura. "Damn you, Trinity. It's not the same thing." "Why isn't it? You don't think it's possible to love more than one man or woman? Look at us. We're here. We're going to make love, aren't we? Yet I'm married, and that girl still means something to you. If we make love, will that mean I must leave Steve, or that you won't ever see her again?"

Dave's tone was sober, almost cruel. "Laura didn't kill anyone. We haven't established that your husband hasn't yet"

Trinity moved away from him. "Maybe you should leave."

Dave was by her side in a split second. He grabbed her shoulders. "No, you don't. You've managed to turn me inside out since the moment I came back here. You've been inside my head until I couldn't think straight. I want you. I want you now."

He pulled her roughly to him. His mouth pressed down on her lips. His tongue found hers. He ripped the blouse from her, pulled down her bra straps and unhooked the clasp. He hiked up her skirt and felt her tender flesh. In turn, Trinity stripped him of his shirt, undid his pants zipper and took him in her hands. He groaned and tore the skirt from her and then her panties. Naked, their flesh met. Eighteen years of dreaming of this moment made Dave anxious to be inside of her. He lowered her to the floor and entered her.

He rolled away from her. His breath came in quick gasps, "Christ," he said. "I'm sorry. I wanted you so much I couldn't wait."

She smiled. "I didn't mind. Not all the eagerness was yours."

Dave padded naked to the wooden bar top that separated the kitchen from the cabin's main room. "More wine?"

She nodded. "What I really want is more of you."

Dave placed the bottle down on the counter. "What the hell! The wine can wait."

He came back to her side. She lay unabashed on her back, her legs up off the floor, exposing herself to him. He took a deep breath. "You still have a great body."

"You mean for an older woman?"

"Knock it off, Trinity. I'm not sixteen anymore." "I'm still older."

"I don't care. No more than I did back then."

She smiled. "I believe you. I just wanted to hear you say it."

Dave lowered himself down beside her. The fire had dwindled to embers, but neither of them noticed. He kissed her lips, then, trailed his tongue downward. He lingered at her full breasts, taking each hardened nipple in his mouth, teasing her with intermittent tongue and teeth motions. His mouth traveled down to her naval, barely lingering there before he buried his head in her softness, his tongue searching. He turned his body around, his tongue still tantalizing, so that she could take him into her mouth, and when she did, a moan escaped him. Anxious to make the excruciating blissful agony last, he held back, and when that no longer became feasible, he rolled over and pulled her on top of him. As they rocked back and forth his lips claimed her nipples. She, in turn caressed his buttocks, pulling him deeper inside of her.

They climaxed at the exact same moment, something he'd only ever experienced with Trinity. Their bodies were wet with perspiration. Their breathing came in shallow gasps.

When she could catch her breath, Trinity said, "God, you're good, Davie." "I had a good teacher." He smiled.

She moved off of him. "I think we both could use a drink now."

He took her twice more, the foreplay more ingenious and drawn-out with each session. Emotionally drained, he struggled to return to reality, reluctantly facing the fact that he still had a job to do.

"I have to call Brad." He said. He strode, still naked, to the phone on the wall at the end of the bar. Brad answered on the second ring.

Before Dave could ask him anything, Brad bellowed. "You crazy son of a bitch.

You kidnapped Trinity St. John. Margaret is beside herself."

Dave smiled, aware that Brad couldn't see his amusement. "I see. And how is dear Margaret? And, dinner? She cooks a mean steak." He winked at Trinity.

"No good, Dave. You can't get away with stealing another man's wife from the hospital. Where in the hell are you, anyway?"

"If I don't tell you, you can honestly say that you don't know where I am. You're in enough trouble because of me. I'm taking full responsibility for my actions. Besides, I didn't kidnap her. She's a material witness."

"Then lock her up in a holding cell. St. John will be back tomorrow. Margaret called him. Just what in the hell are you going to say to the man?"

"The same thing I told you. Relax. It'll work out." "You coming back tonight?"

Dave looked over at Trinity. She lay on her side facing him. He didn't want to leave her. Tonight, may be all they had. "Tomorrow, Brad. I'll be back tomorrow."

"Back from where?"

Dave laughed. "Good night, Brad."

Dave called Sid Carter from the cabin as he prepared to leave. Sleep hadn't been a priority last night, but he'd never felt more alive or more invigorated. Trinity played with the hairs on his bare chest as he waited for Carter to come to the phone. He laughed and tried to push her away. She wasn't having any of it.

Carter came on the line. Dave explained Severn Wokowski's symptoms as he'd been told them. "What drug could cause all that, Sid?"

"You say the kid was an athlete?" "Yeah."

Sid signed. "Tough to make a real diagnosis without the cadaver." "A guess, then."

"Okay, a guess. Could have been steroids. I've heard rumors there's a new and lethal strain from Brazil. Haven't seen the results of that firsthand, though."

Steroids. Of course! So what was he looking for? A small supply bought on the black market, or something more ominous?

It would have to be something really big, he realized. Three people had died because of it.

CHAPTER 13

"Will you be back tonight?" Trinity asked, caressing the back of Dave's neck with her fingertips.

Hell, he didn't even want to leave! Dave shivered, mesmerized by her touch. "I want to come back."

"Then it's a promise?"

He smiled. "A definite maybe."

Dave pushed her away, willing himself to leave her. "I have to go. You promised not to get in my way, remember?"

She made a face. "A mistake. Besides, haven't you heard that it's a woman's prerogative to change her mind?"

Dave kissed the tip of her nose. "Not this time. I'll call you later."

"Just in case you do decide to come back," she yelled after him, "stop by my house and bring me a change of clothes. I'll tell Nellie you might come by."

Trinity second-guessed Dave's next statement. "Don't worry Davie. I won't tell her where I am."

He thought about her all the way back to Briarwood, wanting to turn his car around and forget solving Ellen's murder. He couldn't do that. His state of invigoration, and the sense of new life within him, disappeared as quickly as his view of the lake as he drove away from it.

His first stop was the Sheriff's office. Bromley scowled at him, ushering him into the same little room. He slapped a file on the desk. "Maybe you didn't understand me,

Kincaid. The Ellen Gray case is closed. Damn, you've got balls where your brains oughta be. What in the hell have you done with Trinity?"

"I have her someplace safe. She's a material witness." "A material witness, my butt," Bromley snorted.

Dave leaned across the desk. "What are you so upset about?" He stepped back. "I see Margaret couldn't wait to tell you Trinity was with me. Yes," he added, "with me. Not kidnapped, not coerced, not convinced. She asked me to take her away. For the record, she's afraid of St. John. You know, the same Steven St. John you seem to think is a paragon of virtue. Trinity told me some things that should interest you, and I've got a few things of my own that should be of interest to a lawman. A real lawman, that is.

Want to hear them?"

Dave sat in a chair and crossed his legs. He'd put out the challenge. A dangerous one. He held his breath. What if Bromley didn't bite?

Bromley pulled a cigar out of his desk drawer. He bit off the end, lit it and said, "All I want to do is retire, Kincaid. Nice, peaceful and inconspicuous."

"There's nothing inconspicuous about a town that's the center of a steroid smuggling operation. And there's going to be nothing inconspicuous about the Sheriff of that town. You have heard of steroids, Sheriff?"

Bromley grunted. "Sure, I have. You aren't talking illegal steroids? Not here in Briarwood? Who?"

"I see I finally have your attention. I think Severn Wokowski died because he was using steroids, probably a powerful and dangerous new strain. He went from healthy to dying in one hell of a hurry."

"You think? You come in here like Wyatt Earp at the O.K. Corral, and you THINK Severn died from using steroids!"

"Okay. So I don't have proof. To get it would mean exhuming his body. Before I put those nice people through that, I need your help to build a case. There could be other nice kids out there who're playing Russian roulette with their lives and don't know it.

When I first talked to Bill he told me he was grooming other promising athletes. Steroids make the difference between mediocre and super athletes. Ask Ben Johnson!"

"You still haven't said who you're trying to build a case against."

"Bryant and St. John. Bill is involved, too, I just don't know to what extent. I think he can be broken, maybe even hand us Bryant and St. John under the right circumstances."

Dave told him what Trinity had overheard the night Ellen left Briarwood. He also told him about the "loans" Bryant made. "Three loans, Sheriff. Loans to people without collateral, Ellen, Bill, and Gerard. I'll bet the farm that none of those loans show up on the books."

"Blackmail?"

Dave shrugged. "I think so in Ellen's case. The others were probably insurance." "So who killed Ellen and Bertha?"

"And Chris," Dave added. "Don't forget Chris. I don't know which of the two killed them yet, but with your help I hope to find out. Can I count you in, Sheriff? Can you find out about those loans for me?"

Bromley looked older, defeated. "I knew you was trouble the first time I laid eyes on you." He sighed. "Clara Newby has worked at the bank since it was built. She's a fixture there. She has access to all the files, and she's a good friend. She'll get me the information you need if I ask her to."

Dave stood and extended his hand. The older man ignored the gesture. "No promises, Kincaid, but I'll see what I can do."

Dave stopped at the St. John farm to get Trinity a change of clothes. It was, he knew, an admission that he was thinking about going back to the cabin. Then, he hadn't been able to put her out of his mind all day. He was impatient to be with her again. He felt a momentary sense of disloyalty to Laura, then dismissed it. She walked out on him. And to Katie. He hadn't given her a thought in days.

The housekeeper was noticeably miffed as she handed Dave a small suitcase. "Is Mrs. St. John all right?" She asked, peeved that she had to go to Dave for information on her employer.

Dave couldn't resist. "Better this morning, since I untied her."

The woman clapped a hand over her mouth. "You don't mean…?"

Dave grimaced. "I'm kidding, Nelly. I'm a cop, not a monster, for Christ's sake!

Mrs. St. John is just fine."

"What do I tell the mister?" she lamented.

There were a lot of things Dave would have liked to have told her to tell St. John. Instead, he responded with, "Tell him to call me if he has a problem with Mrs. St. John's temporary living arrangements."

She seemed to be heartened by the word "temporary."

Next, Dave stopped by his motel to get himself a change of clothes. Brad was out. Dave placed a call to Captain Herring.

When Herring answered, Dave said, "Before you get too pissed off at me, Captain, hear me out. This case is far from over. In fact, I seem to have fallen over a whole new case. Whoever killed Ellen Gray is into steroids, and on a large scale if I don't miss my guess."

You seldom do, Herring thought. "What about the Briggs boy's confession?" "A blind."

Herring sighed. "You got proof, Kincaid, or just another wild hair up your ass?" "Ellen Gray didn't prove to be a wild hair, Captain. Neither is this. I pulled the

Sheriff on my side this morning. Reluctantly, I admit, but he's on my side. He doesn't believe Chris Briggs killed Ellen Gray anymore than I do. He just isn't as open about it."

"And, Brad?"

"Is being a friend. I told him to go back to the city. He wouldn't listen."

There was a brief silence on the other end of the line. "Run through what you have."

Dave told him everything. Everything except that he had walked away from the hospital with one of his major suspect's wife.

"Two days, Kincaid. Then I want your ass and Brad's back here. No arguments."

Two days. It wasn't enough time, but Dave knew that Herring was sticking his neck out by giving him this much leeway.

"I'll take it."

There was a knock on Dave's motel room door. "I have to go, Captain.

Someone's at the door."

It was Brad.

"You decided to leave your love nest, did you?" Brad said.

Dave smiled. "For now. Sit down, Brad. I want to fill you in, then you can tell me about Margaret and Bryant." Dave started with Trinity's statement and then his own thoughts and findings. "Steroids, Brad. On a large scale. I think Briarwood is a proving ground for a new type of steroid, one so powerful that it killed a high school kid. This stuff is dynamite in the wrong hands. Even the cleanest-cut kid, who wouldn't think of smoking a joint, will take steroids, especially if he thinks it will separate him from the other kids. Bill told me he was grooming several promising athletes. I think he got caught up in something he couldn't handle. I don't believe he meant to hurt any of his protégés, especially Wokowski. My guess is that he was counting on them to be his ticket out of here. Coach at one of the bigger colleges, maybe. I'm going to see him after I talk with Gerard again. I want to shake Gerard's tree and see if anything falls to the ground. What happened with Bryant?"

"He's cool and unconcerned. If he isn't, he puts on a great act. If he's guilty of anything, he'll be hard to crack. You think he had something to do with this?"

"I think he had everything to do with it. Him and St. John." Dave grabbed his jacket. "I'll check back with you later."

"What am I supposed to do while you're gone?"

Brad checked his watch. It was still early. He could get Brad out of hot water and keep Herring happy at the same time. "Go back to the city and flash Bryant's picture around. See if anyone saw him with Ellen either the night she died or before that."

Brad looked puzzled. "I thought you were interested in this steroid theory." "I am. Ellen knew about the steroids, that much is obvious. Knowing got her

killed. It was the biggest mistake her killer could have made. If Ellen hadn't shown up on our doorstep and on our beat, maybe this steroid caper would have stayed under wraps. Try the motel where she stayed that first night." Dave smiled. "Take Sheila with you, if you like. Maybe you can turn things around for the two of you. Fact is, you can be of more help to me now in the city than you can be here."

He was almost out the door when he turned around and said, "That is, unless you have something going on here." He grinned. "I forgot to ask about Margaret."

Brad smacked his lips. "You were right about her. She's a hell-cat, all right.

And, no, I didn't sleep with her. You want to know why? She didn't offer. She was in a rage because you took off with Trinity St. John, and I don't think it was merely sisterly concern. The woman has the hots for you, Dave."

"Only because I had something going with her mother." "Had?"

Dave shook his head. "Even if I could answer that question, I wouldn't. I was going to see Margaret before I met Gerard and Bill to ask her if she knew about Bryant and Ellen, and if she's been hiding that vital piece of information. If so, why? On second thought, maybe you'd better do it. I'll call you tonight."

Fifteen minutes later, on the other side of town, Bill Lackland never saw the car that hit him as he crossed the street on his way to the gym. Because school was in session, neither did anyone else.

Gerard wasn't at the bank. He was home with a cold. Bill was at home too, according to the school, taking care of his wife who wasn't feeling well. Dave was on his way to Bill's house when he saw the ambulance and the crowd of people as he passed by the school.

His first thought was that another kid had fallen victim to steroids. He pushed his way through the crowd. The ambulance attendants were lifting Bill inside the vehicle.

He looked more dead than alive. Blood trickled from a huge gash on his dead.

Dave flashed his badge. "Is he dead?"

"Damn near," one of the attendants said. "We're taking him to Henderson. He's too far gone for the clinic."

Bromley appeared at Dave's side. Dave flashed him an angry look. "You don't want to call this an accident, do you?" His voice held yet another challenge for the older man.

Bromley tiredly responded. "No, I don't. Come on over to my office later and we'll talk."

"You bet we will," Dave said, "but first I have to check on Trinity."

∽ﾟﾟﾟﾟ∾

Dave used the phone in the school's office, making sure that no one saw him dial the number. Trinity didn't answer right away. The phone rang ten times. Dave was about to hang up and get in his car to check on her in person, when she answered. She was breathless.

"Where the hell were you?" He yelled.

"Outside, getting some air. Why? What's the matter?"

"Someone just ran Bill Lackland down. I was on my way to see him. Him and Gerard. I thought I could get one, or both of them to roll over on Bryant and whoever else may be connected with Ellen and the sale of illegal steroids."

"Steroids?" She paused. "Oh, My God. Severn! He was an athlete! That's what Ellen was so afraid of, isn't it?"

"Yes." Dave longed to be with her. To touch her, to see for himself that she was all right. "Listen to me, Trinity, I want you to stay in the cabin and don't go outside again. Don't answer the phone unless you know it's me. I'll let it ring twice, hang up, ring once, hang up, then call again. You got it?"

Fear crept into her voice. "You think I'm in danger, don't you?"

The thought had crossed his mind only about a hundred times since he'd seen Bill lifted into the ambulance.

When Dave reached the hospital in Henderson he was told that Bill was in surgery.

"You can wait," the nurse said, "in the waiting room with the other policeman."

Dave briskly strode into the waiting room. Bromley was putting out his cigar in a standard issue hospital ash tray.

"It's you," Dave said.

"Who did you expect? Guess you're here to see if Bill saw who plowed into him.

Assuming he makes it out of surgery, that is. I'm here mostly because Bill is one of mine. Imagine how you'd feel if it were your partner in that operating room. You'd be worrying, too. I confess, I feel guilty. I never wanted to follow this case of yours."

"Our case," Dave corrected him. He took a seat beside the sheriff. "How long to they expect Bill to be in surgery?"

"Another hour or so, if he lives." Bromley shrugged. "Sooner, if he don't make it."

"Anybody see anything?" Dave asked.

"Nope. Whoever did it got away clean. Figured you'd ask, so I had someone check on the whereabouts of Felix, Carey and St. John. I just heard. Carey was taking an early lunch, Felix was at home with a cold, or so he said, and St. John is unaccounted for. He left his hotel early this morning and is expected back in Briarwood sometime this afternoon. No one has seen him in town yet today."

"Ask me why I'm not surprised," Dave said. "Where's Bill's wife?"

"The shock of hearing about Bill sent her into early labor. She was already feeling poorly." Bromley frowned. "For the life of me, I don't know what Bill was doing at the school. He was supposed to be home taking care of her." Bromley shook his head. "Bill's been looking forward to being there with her, to seeing his kid come into the world. These past few days he's talked of little else. He even took those new-fangled breathing classes with Beth."

Together, Dave and Bromley kept an almost silent vigil. Dave kept looking at his watch, thinking about Trinity. He wanted to get back to her, admitting he intended to spend another night with her. He tried to chalk up his need to be with her as part of his job in protecting her, knowing full well he was white-washing the real truth. He was obsessed.

Almost an hour-and-a-half after Dave arrived at the hospital, a green smocked doctor entered the waiting room. Dave and Bromley stood expectantly. "Mr. Lackland made it through surgery," the doctor said, "and the prognosis is good. He's a lucky man. All his vital organs survived serious damage. He'll be in recovery for a while, and then you can see him."

Dave and Bromley looked over at one another. Maybe now they'd get some answers.

They were in the hospital cafeteria when the same doctor, no longer wearing his green smock, but a white jacket, approached the table Dave and Bromley were occupying. His face was grim.

The doctor took a seat at their table. "I'm sorry. Mr. Lackland expired ten minutes ago. We weren't expecting complications, certainly not a massive hemorrhage, but it happens sometimes. I called the Briarwood clinic to see if someone there could tell his wife."

Bromley looked older than time, his cup of coffee halfway to his mouth, momentarily frozen in space. "I'll tell Beth myself. After, she's had the baby."

The doctor sighed heavily. "Mrs. Lackland had her child at about the same moment we were fighting to save her husband's life. Ironic, don't you think, that Mr. Lackland's son entered the world when he was leaving it?"

Neither Dave nor Bromley saw any irony, only tragedy.

There seemed little for either man to say to each other, and yet the bond between the two men was being cemented by a powerful need to see justice done.

"Follow me back to my office." Bromley said, his voice gruff.

Dave shook his head. "I can't. I have to get back to Trinity. Now, more than ever, I'm afraid for her. There's less chance of me being followed from here, than if I leave from Briarwood. Besides, St. John is probably looking for Trinity, and that means he'll be looking for me."

Bromley nodded in agreement. "You're probably right." He pulled a folded piece of paper from his pants pocket and handed it to Dave. "I've been wanting to talk to you about this, but I was waiting until after we talked to Bill." He shrugged. "Now, we're going to have to do it the hard way."

Dave looked at the sheet of paper, a puzzled from on his face. "It's Chris's note.

So, what about it?"

"You sensed something was wrong with it, and you were right. You thought he was trying to tell us something, and you were right about that, too."

Dave read the note over.

I'M SORRY ABOUT ELLEN AND BERTHA. THEY GAVE ME NO CHOICE. I BURNED BERTHA'S DIARY AND HER NOTES. SHE GUESSED THE TRUTH. I COULDN'T LET HER TELL ANYONE, AND I'D NEVER SURVIVE PRISON.

CHRIS

Dave wearily rubbed his eyes. He was worried about Trinity. He couldn't think straight because he was obsessed with her safety. "If you know what's wrong with the note, Sheriff, tell me."

Despite his own weariness, Bromley seemed almost jubilant, pleased with himself for discovering something Dave hadn't been able to figure out. "What did you call Bertha? Not only when you was a kid, but when you came back here?"

"Miss Bartlett, of course."

"Of course!" Bromley responded excitedly. "You called her that out of respect, like everyone else in Briarwood, except for me and the Doc, cause she allowed us to call her Bertha, and there were times when even we called her Miss Bartlett, because it seemed more fitting. Her students never did call her anything else. Not Chris, nor any of them."

Dave slapped the sheet of paper against his side. "Then I was right! Chris's note held a message. He was trying to tell us it was a fake. And that means…"

"That it had to be someone who hadn't been around Briarwood too long. Else they'd have known what Chris was up to."

Dave thought about Chris's last moments. It must have been hell, knowing he was going to die, and that all he could do about it was try to tell someone it wasn't suicide. Just like Ellen, he thought. "St. John," Dave said. "He's a virtual stranger around these parts."

Bromley nodded. "That's why I ain't going to ask you where you're headed, Kincaid. I'll even go you one better. I'll make sure that no one follows you out of here."

Dave grabbed his lead. "Thanks, Sheriff."

"Sure enough," Bromley said gruffly. "You call in, you hear? I may need to talk to you."

"You got it," Dave said as he sped out of the building.

⁂

It was only a short drive to the lake, yet it seemed like an eternity. Dave had to see for himself that Trinity was all right.

A shiver ran down his spine. All those dreams. He'd had a dream about Bertha Bartlett and Chris before they died. Yet nothing, not so much as a sleepless night where Bill's death was concerned.

Since his father's death, Dave had hated his dreams, and now he was worried because he wasn't experiencing them! Bill's death, now murder, as far as he was concerned, had come straight out of left field. He was being contrary, he knew, because his dreams made little sense, but the fact that he hadn't had them recently seemed to make Trinity more vulnerable. Without his dreams to warn him, he was going to have to rely on his instincts if he was to keep Trinity safe from harm.

⁂

Dave pulled Trinity close to him, so close, she gasped for air. "I've been so worried about you," he said.

She pulled away from him and took a deep breath. "This is more than routine concern, Davie. You're beginning to frighten me."

"Bill Lackland's death was murder. No one saw the car that hit him, but there's no doubt in my mind it was intentional. For a while it looked like Bill might make it, but then…"

She paled. "Bill's dead!" "Yes."

"You were, no, you are afraid that I'm next! My God, how many more people are going to die? And for what?"

He sat her down and explained his steroid theory. "I think the stuff is being smuggled into the states and dumped in Briarwood for distribution throughout the country."

"Why, Briarwood?"

"Can you think of a better place? If Ellen hadn't been murdered, they might have gotten away with it indefinitely."

He told her about Chris's note. "Poor bastard," Dave said. "His only crime was in loving Ellen. Bromley thinks, and I agree, that Chris wouldn't have tried to leave us that clue if whoever killed him had been more familiar with Briarwood and the respect Miss Bartlett commanded. That narrows the field of suspects."

"Steven," she whispered.

"It looks that way, but Bryant is in this up to his neck. When we found Ellen in that alley, she had scratched out the initials BR. I thought she was trying to tell us she was from Briarwood. Maybe she was trying to tell us about Bryant, but died before she could finish scratching out his name."

The shocked look on Trinity's face warned him that he was being insensitive.

Sometimes he forgot Trinity was Ellen's mother. Or maybe, he thought, I just don't want to think that I could have been her father.

"Sorry, I'm used to thinking out loud."

"Don't be sorry. You have a job to do. I know that. Can you stay?" "Don't worry. Nothing is going to make me leave you tonight."

She kissed him, gently at first, then with more vigor. "Is it wrong to want you to make love to me, now, when there's so much for you to think about?"

Once again Dave was reminded that here and now may be all he and Trinity had.

He slipped her dress from her shoulders. "You talk too damn much."

She'd talked him into skinny-dipping in the lake, a crazy, foolish thing to do, and yet he found he couldn't refuse her. She was like a child, blissfully happy, unwilling to face danger though it lurked on every corner, and just as likely to pout if she didn't get her own way.

He marveled at the sight of her naked body; the body of a woman ten to fifteen years younger; and at the way the moonlight bounced off the water giving her silhouette the appearance of a goddess. She was as unreal in this setting as was the fact they were here together, romping in the water like naughty children, but when they made love, there was no doubt this was a grown-up sport they were engaging in.

Exhausted, they staggered to the edge of the lake and threw themselves to the ground.

"You're a crazy, wonderful woman," he said. "No wonder my life has seemed lacking since the day you…"

She placed her fingers on his lips. "Shush. One day, one moment at a time."

Dave reluctantly looked back at the cabin. "I promised the Sheriff and Brad I'd check in with them."

"Go ahead. I'll stay out here and dry off."

Dave shook his head. "I can't leave you here alone." He pulled her to her feet and kissed the top of her nose. "My God, you're beautiful."

She went to take a shower while Dave called Bromley at home. "Checking in," Dave said, his eyes straying to the open bathroom door where Trinity had just disappeared. Maybe they'd make love in the shower.

Bromley broke that chain of thought. "Your Captain called me. He said to give you a message, and I quote. "Tell Kincaid to get his ass back here first thing in the morning. The Ellen Gray case is closed, period. No arguments. Just tell him to get himself back here."

Dave couldn't believe he was hearing Bromley right. Herring was doing an about-face, and it wasn't like him. "This is beyond Ellen Gray's murder and Herring knows it. Did he say anything about steroids?"

"Only that as far as he and the department were concerned, you have an over- active imagination."

Dave was silent for a moment. "And you, Sheriff? Where does that leave you?" "Same place as you are, Kincaid. Nowhere. I was told to forget anything you and

I discussed as far as steroids were concerned."

"It sucks, Sheriff, and you know it. Something stinks."

Dave could almost visualize Bromley leaning back in his chair, a cigar halfway to his mouth. "You're right. I ain't smelled anything like it since the sewer system backed up in the middle of town in 1964."

Dave's breathe quickened. "What are you saying?"

"That if I was you, and I ain't, I'd hightail it back to the city, else you'll likely find yourself without a badge. But, I ain't you, and if you want to stick around and find out why someone is dumping death all over my town, I'll tell your captain to poke it where the sun don't shine, if you get my meaning."

Dave knew he was at a crossroads. He remembered telling Katie that if there were two paths to take and they'd always taken the hard ones. He realized this time was no exception.

"I get your meaning, Sheriff. I'll be back in town first thing in the morning." "Good. Oh, and by the way, St. John is here, threatening anyone who'll listen, mostly me, if you don't bring his wife back." "What did you tell him?"

"That I don't have a clue where you took her, which thank the Lord ain't no lie." "Thanks. I'll deal with him and my Captain in the morning."

Dave phoned Brad. He was out. He'd try to reach him in the morning. Surely Brad would know what in the hell was going on with Herring.

Trinity emerged from the bathroom, a towel wrapped around her hair. She wore nothing else.

She noticed Dave's agitated state and reached for a robe. "Something's wrong, isn't there?" Fear crept into her voice. "What is it?"

"I underestimated your husband and Bryant. I don't know how they managed it, but I've been ordered to return to the city."

He voice held a quiver. "You're going?"

He pulled her to him, his tone grim. "Of course, I'm not going back. Not until I've gotten to the bottom of this goddamn case."

CHAPTER 14

Dave arrived in town early, just in time to catch Bromley as he was entering the Sheriff's office. "I was going to call Brad and find out what that message from Herring meant," Dave said, "but I've decided I'd be better off facing Herring in person. I wanted to let you know I was going to the city. I'll be back late tonight."

"Where's Trinity?" Bromley asked.

"I'm getting tired of being asked that question. She's safe. What about St. John?

Where is he?"

"I put one of my deputies on him. He left town at first light." Dave frowned. "In what direction?"

"North."

The lake was to the south of town, but Dave was still uneasy. "Is there any way he could have found out where Trinity is?"

"Not unless you or she told someone. He asked everyone he could think of yesterday. To the best of my knowledge, he came up empty."

"Then, I guess she's safe. I didn't even tell my partner where she is, and Trinity knows better than to tell anyone, not even Margaret. I'm the only one she trusts right now."

"I hope you're right. About her only trusting you, that is." Bromley looked dismal and unconvinced. "Oh, I almost forgot. Clara came through for me. You were right. There are no loans on the books to either Ellen, Bill or Felix. I suppose that's good news for Beth. She won't have to worry about paying back a loan. Bill didn't have a whole lot of insurance. I saw her yesterday. She's taking Bill's death hard. She's not even interested in the baby. I'm worried about her."

Dave stared at the Sheriff in wonder. "You really are one of a kind, Sheriff. I know how easy it would be for you to walk away from all this. Herring gave you your way out."

"I don't see it that way, Kincaid. The way I see it is that your Captain dealt me a new hand, one I have to play. Now get the hell outa here and find out what's going on." His tone was gruff.

Go figure, Dave thought. I've played hell trying to drag the old bastard into this case, and all it took was for someone to tell him to stay out of it!

⌘

The city squad room reeked of sweat and stale smoke. Going back to Briarwood had given Dave a subconscious appreciation for a clean environment. Men and woman worked at desks overcrowded, with half-finished paperwork and full ashtrays. An aura of stress, frustration and overworked personnel filled the air. A knot formed in Dave's stomach. He loosened his tie, but it gave him little relief. It was still hard to breathe in here.

He threaded his way through the disorder to the tiny space that was allotted to him and Brad. It consisted of two desks pushed together, each with a phone on it. His own desk was a shambles. Messages and memos from days before were haphazardly strewn across the surface. He picked one of the messages and half-smiled, half-frowned. It was for Brad. It was from someone named Denise. Dave grinned. Apparently, Brad was bouncing back nicely from Sheila's rejection of him. He tossed the message on Brad's desk. No matter how many times he and Brad complained, messages for one or the other were always being placed on the wrong desk, or put through to the wrong extension. He sorted through the other messages and found two more that were misplaced and put them on Brad's desk, where he found a message that belonged to him.

Herring was in his office. Dave squared his shoulders, prepared for battle, and strode toward the Captain's open door.

Herring looked surprised. "Well, I'll be damned! I would have bet my pension that you wouldn't have listened to my telling you to get back here." Herring sifted through a mound of files on his desk. He picked up on. "Good to see you. We can use you. Let's see. This case here really could use your touch. Does Brad know you're back? You can work on this one together."

When Dave didn't respond, Herring sighed deeply. He moved across the room and closed the door to his office behind him, ignoring the curious glances from the occupants of the squad room.

"Take a seat," he ordered Dave. He fondled his moustache. "Shit! What made me think that you would lay down and play dead?"

Dave ignored the order to be seated. "I could have called you, in fact I almost did, but I wanted you to look me in the face Captain, when you told me why I'm off the case. We haven't always seen eye to eye, but in all the years I've known you, this is the first time you ever went back on your word. You gave me two lousy days, then you yanked them out from under me. I want to know why."

Herring didn't quite meet Dave's eyes. "We're short on manpower."

Dave leaned over Herring's desk. "We've been short of fucking manpower ever since I can remember. What is it that you're not telling me? Who has the kind of clout that makes you willing to give up what could be the biggest bust we've had in a long time?"

"Who said anything about clout?"

Dave hadn't been sure until this moment that there really was undue influence at work here. Herring had given himself away in just a fraction of a second by refusing once again to look Dave directly in the eye.

Dave stepped back from Herring's desk. He eased himself into a chair. "Son of a bitch! Who gave the order to pull me off?"

Herring sighed again. "The order came straight from the Commissioner himself." Dave whistled. "Whose payroll is he on?"

"You have no grounds for that kind of accusation." "The hell I don't!"

Herring seemed to be wrestling with himself. There was indecision and anguish on the Captain's face. Dave wasn't sure what he was winning Herring's conscience, or the goddamn book he lived by. Finally, Herring said, "Maybe I can clear things up for you. I don't care what the Commissioner says, you deserve an explanation. Wait outside."

Dave watched through the window of Herring's office as Herring reached for his phone and dialed a number. Whoever he was talking to was giving him a hard time, but Herring was fighting back. Dave wished he could hear what was going on in there.

Herring came out of his office a few minutes later. His expression was grim. "I hope I'm not making a mistake. Follow me."

Herring led Dave down the hall and opened up a door that led to a room that served as both conference and interrogation room. Inside, there were three men. One of them stood with his back to them looking out the window to the busy street below. He slowly turned to face Dave and Herring.

Dave sucked in his breath. It was St. John. Dave looked over at Herring. "What's going on here?"

"Sit down and shut up, Kincaid," Herring ordered.

If Dave was confused, St. John was just plain angry. "What the hell is he doing here?" he demanded, pointing at Dave.

Dave took a step toward him. Herring restrained him with great effort. "I'm doing my job, you son of a bitch," Dave yelled.

St. John shook his fist menacingly. "What have you done with my wife?"

"If she'd have wanted you to know where she was, she would have told you." Herring stepped in between the two men. "What's this about his wife, Dave?" "Ask St. John. I had to put her someplace safe. She's afraid of him. She had reason to be. She thinks he may want to kill her."

"Kill her!" St. John said. "Why would I want to kill Trinity?"

One of the other men, a formidable looking man who was over six-feet tall, his demeanor one of authority, said, "Why don't we all sit down?" He looked over at Herring. "I'm counting on you to keep your boy in line, Herring."

Herring gave Dave a warning look and said, "I thought I told you to sit down and shut up."

The tall man took charge. Dave had no doubt as to what he was. He had to be FBI. They had an attitude he could spot a mile away. The man quickly recognized that he'd been made. "That's right, Kincaid, I'm a Fed. So is my partner here." He indicated a shorter man. "I want to go on record as saying I'm against your being here, but, like your Captain, I see a certain logic it in. He's convinced me that if we shut you out, you'll take matters into your own hands, and we can't afford that."

Dave hadn't taken his eyes off of St. John since he and Herring had entered the room. "Is somebody going to tell me what he's doing here?" Dave asked.

The tall man gave Herring another warning look. "If he doesn't shut up, the deal's off." He nodded at St. John. "And that goes for you, too."

Dave took comfort in the fact that St. John was no more happy about being in the same room together as he was.

"You stumbled onto something we've been following for over a year now," the tall man went on. "Bryant has his fingers in a lot of pies. He's been using Briarwood as a drop off point for drugs for some time, trafficking the stuff across country. He's even laundered money on occasion. He just recently branched out into the steroid market.

Our sources tell us that he's getting his supplies from a relatively new distributor, Brazil. The stuff is virtually untested, so Bryant was using Bill Lackland and his athletes to test its effectiveness. We know all this because we have a man under-cover in Briarwood.

He got close to Bryant, then you came along and threatened his cover with a murder investigation. We would have stopped you then, but you came to town like Paul Revere, announcing foul play. To have stopped you at that point would have been tantamount to suicide. Our man advised us to lay low and see what happened." He gave St. John a stern look.

Oh Jesus! Dave stared at the man he knew as Steven St. John. He blanched. "Not him!"

"I'm afraid so. He was placed here and told to establish a life in the community.

He achieved that goal. Now, you threaten everything we've all worked for."

Dave felt like someone had knocked the wind out of him. St. John, or whatever his real name was, was heat! "If you know so goddamn much, why haven't you pulled Bryant in? Four people died because you didn't. Count them, gentlemen. Four. A young girl, a harmless old woman, and two guys whose only crimes was being in love with Ellen Gray."

"I understand your anger, Kincaid," the tall man said. "We didn't bring Bryant in because we don't have his colleague or colleagues. He isn't alone in this."

St. John spoke for the first time since his earlier run in with Dave. "Bryant didn't kill Ellen. I was watching him that night. He didn't leave Briarwood."

Dave's eyes narrowed. "You supposedly weren't in Briarwood the night Ellen was killed."

"A necessary deception. Most of my so-called trips out of town never happened.

Bryant didn't kill Bertha Bartlett, either." He shrugged. "I don't know about Chris Briggs or Lackland. I was kind of busy the night Chris died, if you recall. My wife was in the hospital. But you know about that, don't you, Kincaid? Just like you know where the hell she is. You should, you took off with her."

The tall man intervened. "I don't know what it is with you two, but you'd both better knock it off. There's more at stake here than overworked hormones." He addressed Dave, indicating St. John. "He's right. There's a missing link. Someone who commits murder. Bryant himself, may be guilty of murder. We haven't ruled it out." He tapped his fingers on the desktop. "How many people have you told about Bryant and the steroids?"

It was a question Dave had anticipated and waited for. "Four. Captain Herring, my partner, Brad, Sheriff Bromley, and…" he looked away from all of them. "I told Trinity St. John."

"Great! Why didn't you just take out an ad?"

Dave ignored the sarcasm. Under the circumstances he considered it justified. "I want to stay on the case," Dave said. "For reasons other than your own, but I want to stay on."

The tall man looked at Herring. Herring looked away. "I don't know," the man said. "You'd need to work with St. John. Can you handle that?"

Dave glanced at Herring. Herring shook his head and shrugged. This was a decision Dave had to make on his own, his look conveyed.

Work with St. John! Work side by side with Trinity's husband! Dave stubbornly refused to give up St. John as his prime suspect. If he did, that could mean losing Trinity all over again. Why let the son of a bitch off the hook, anyway? Who was to say he wasn't playing both ends against the middle? It wouldn't be the first time. Dave realized that his choices were narrowing. If he refused to work with St. John he'd be out, and Herring wouldn't be able to help him. If they pulled him off the case, Dave knew he would resist, and that could mean losing his badge. He was amazed that right now, at this minute, the thought of being kicked off the force didn't seem nearly as important as the chance to be with Trinity again.

Dave wasn't the only one in the room with doubts. St. John said, "Is it okay if I talk to Kincaid alone? There are things we need to discuss."

You bet your ass, there are, Dave thought. But do I really want to discuss them?

⚬∭⚬

They were alone in the room. Neither of them spoke right away. Animosity and distrust filled the air. No matter how the investigation turned out, because of Trinity, they'd probably never like each other, Dave knew.

It crossed his mind that the room might be bugged, and realized that he didn't care.

"I guess I should begin," St. John said.

"Good," Dave responded. "You could start with your real name." "My name isn't important."

"Or that you're a Fed?" "I'm not."

"What?"

234

St. John paced the room. "This isn't easy for me, Kincaid. I don't like you, and sooner or later we're going to have to deal with the reason I don't like you."

"Let's do it now," Dave said. "Your boss said you were 'placed' in Briarwood. Was Trinity was part of the plan? What a cover! Tell me, how long did it take you to 'fall in love' with her? A day, an hour, what?"

"Fuck you," St. John exploded. "I don't think our working together is going to pan out."

"That's the way I see it," Dave said, "but we seem to be trapped, don't we? You can't afford to have me running loose shooting off my mouth, and I won't walk away from Ellen's murder."

"Or my wife!"

"That, too. My relationship with Trinity goes back a long way, and at least what we had, or may have, is honest. I didn't crawl into her bed because my job demanded it."

"All right," St. John growled. "So, in the beginning it wasn't honest. It is now." Dave glared at him, unwilling to be convinced.

"Where the fuck do you get off judging me?" St. John asked. "You're going to hear how it was even if you don't want to. I'm not a Fed. I'm a cop, just like you. Four years ago I was investigating a drug Tsar. I was too good at my job, getting too close to nailing him. He had one of his goons put a bomb in my car. It didn't kill me, but it rearranged my face. That was a lot of operations ago. Don't feel sorry for me," he said with rancor, "I'm prettier now than I was before the accident."

That explains the plastic surgery, Dave thought. "Okay. I'm listening."

"When the Feds wanted someone to go under cover, my name came up. You see, I still wanted to be a cop, not just a name on a payroll or pensioned off, so I kept trying to get them to assign me to something. This job was perfect, for them, and for me. There was no chance of my being recognized as a cop." He smiled, showing perfect white capped teeth. "I don't even recognize myself in the mirror anymore. I was single with no close living family. I was a dream come true for the FBI. My job was to get married, settle down and get close to Bryant. They came up with three women who might be open to marriage. When I met Trinity, I knew she was the one."

"What's supposed to happen when the case is over? Do you leave a 'Dear St.

John.'" Dave smiled, but the smile never reached his eyes. "Forgive the pun." "That's the way it was supposed to play, yes, but something happened to me.

Along the way, I fell in love with my own wife, and I don't give a fuck whether you believe that or not."

Dave had no trouble believing him. None at all. It would have been hard for him to believe that anyone could get that chose to Trinity and not lose himself.

"You're sleeping with her, aren't you?" St. John asked. There was pain and resignation in his voice.

For the briefest of moments, Dave almost felt sorry for him, but the moment passed. "Yes, I am."

There was silence in the room. Dave could almost hear his own heartbeat.

The next words that came out of St. John's mouth threw him off guard. "Can you keep her safe until this is over, Kincaid? If you say yes, I'm going to hold you to it, and I'll come after you if anything happens to her."

This was going to be rougher than Dave had thought. St. John really was in love with Trinity. Dave nodded. "Yes, I can. I'd give up my life to save hers."

The challenge was unspoken, but it hung in the air refusing to go away. Like men from another time arranging a duel at sunset, they expected a showdown sooner or later.

"What about your money and the ranch? Compliments of the taxpayers?"

"Part of it, and some of it is my own. Bryant had to be impressed. We knew there were some bad loans on the books, and the bank needed temporary bailing out. You're like all the others! You think you have to be poor to want to be a cop. My grandfather was old money. When my father died, he reluctantly willed it all to me because I was the only one left to leave it to. He always hated it that I wanted to be a cop and not take over the business."

"You going to tell Trinity you're a cop when this is over?"

"I'll give you a gift, Kincaid. You tell her. She'll believe you. She has no reason to believe anything I say. I know and accept that."

Under different circumstances they might have been friends, Dave realized. He sensed that they were probably the same kind of cop, maybe even the same kind of men. There was a major difference. St. John was able to separate the job from the woman. He envied him that.

"How old are you?" Dave asked. "Your real age, that is." "Thirty-five."

Ironic. They were the same age. That, at least, will make us even, Dave thought. It could have been St. John at sixteen, instead of me. But it wasn't him, a voice inside of Dave murmured. That gives me and Trinity a history he'll never have. He smiled in satisfaction.

⌘

The other men, including Herring, returned to the room and they talked strategy and ground rules. Herring constantly glanced from Dave to St. John, shaking his head. His pessimism wasn't lost on Dave.

Finally, the tall man rose from the conference table signally that the meeting was at an end. Dave and Captain Herring remained in the room after the others left.

"You sure you want to do this, Kincaid? Or more importantly, I guess, are you up to it?"

"The truth?" "Yes."

"I really don't know."

Herring nodded. "At least that's honest. I'm going to count on your judgment to get out of this any time you know you can't hack it."

Judgment! Not much of a character asset as far as Dave was concerned lately. "I won't embarrass you, Captain."

Herring stood. "Can't ask for more than that, I suppose. You coming?" Dave shook his head. "No. I want to stay here for a while. I need to think."

After a while Dave gave up on getting any brainstorms. His thoughts were more about Trinity than the case itself. He made his way to the door and proceeded into the hallway.

A few yards away, talking to a guy he didn't know, was Laura. She was wearing a light blue suit that matched her eyes, a white blouse with ruffles, and light blue high- heeled pumps that accentuated her long legs. She hadn't seen him yet, so he took time to study her. She and the other guy were in a heated discussion. He smiled to himself.

Dave had seen Laura at work when she was out to make a point. She was a tiger when she thought she was right. He felt sorry for the other guy.

Dave swallowed a lump in his throat. He'd missed Laura.

The discussion over, Laura moved on down the hallway in his direction. If I had any character at all, Dave thought, I'd duck back into the room and avoid letting her see me.

She was coming closer, studying some notes as she walked. She looked up, and then it was too late to hide. She stopped a few feet away from him. Indecision crossed her face. Dave moved toward her.

"Hi," he said. "You're looking good."

She subconsciously checked her blonde hair with her fingertips. "I didn't know you were back yet, but I heard about the guy who killed himself. At least it's over." She bit down on her lip. "It isn't over, is it? It wasn't only a girl's murder that took you to Briarwood, was it?"

He wondered how much she knew, and if Brad had blabbed to Sheila about Trinity, and then Sheila had told Laura. It surprised him how much it mattered that she didn't think badly of him. "No. I'm trying to work it out. How about a cup of coffee or something?"

"No, I don't think so."

"Come on, Laura. It's only coffee."

"I know." Her smile was full of sadness. " I can't."

He hated himself for asking. "Are you seeing anyone?"

"No. That's not the problem, is it? You are." When he didn't contradict her, pain filled her eyes. "I didn't know till now how much I was counting on you denying it. I'd better be going." She glanced at her watch. "I have to go. I'm late for an appointment."

 He didn't want her to leave. He stared at her, a yearning in his eyes. Laura was marriage, children, a house with a white picket fence, taking out the garbage, mowing lawns. And Trinity was…well, she wasn't a white picket fence.

He knew there was nothing he could say to keep Laura here, and with that knowledge came a feeling that he'd lost something very valuable. "I'll call you sometime." he said.

"No," she said. "Don't do that. Please don't do that." Then she was gone.

An hour later, after failing to make a connection with Brad, Dave was on his way back to Briarwood and to Trinity. This time, his usual excitement at being with her was tempered by his meeting with Laura.

CHAPTER 15

Trinity rubbed his naked buttocks, teasing him by brushing her nipples against his back. "Turn over," she said. "I'll do your other side."

"Don't you ever get enough?" Dave groaned. "You complaining?" She laughed.

Dave rolled over, an erection in full bloom. He pulled her to him. "Do you know how really incredible you are?"

She smiled. "No. Why don't you show me?

Later, still naked, they lay interlocked before a dwindling fire.

If only this was all there was to life, Dave thought. The look on St. John's face when he'd admitted to sleeping with Trinity flashed across his mind. In any endeavor there were winners and there were losers. He frowned distractedly. And there were rules, and he wasn't following them.

Trinity caught his change of mood. "What is it? You're someplace else." "I was thinking about my trip to the city today."

She shifted away from him. "You're thinking that I'm getting in your way. I've been thoughtless. I should have asked you how your day went, but I wanted nothing to change for us, or be spoiled. Are you still on the case?'

"Yes, but with a new wrinkle." Dave sat up. "Tell me, Trinity, didn't you ever stop to ask yourself why your husband didn't seem to have a past?"

"Several times, but only once to him directly. He avoided the issue. You're leading up to something, aren't you? Something I'm not going to like, and it's to do with Steve."

Dave muttered curses under his breath. What the hell did he owe St. John? He told himself that what he was about to say, and do, was for Trinity, not her husband. "St. John was in the city. I met with him and a couple of other guys." Dave made a face. "Brace yourself, Trinity, you married a cop."

"Steve? Steve isn't a cop, he's a businessman."

"I don't like it any better than you do, but he is a cop. He was sent to Briarwood to do a job, to blend in, and take an active role in the community. He's after Bryant and whoever Bryant is working with."

Trinity placed her hands on her cheeks. "I don't understand. If he's a cop, then that means I have nothing to fear from him."

Dave sighed. "Maybe, maybe not. Cops have been known to play both sides before. I don't trust him, but then I'm biased. I don't like him very much, because of you. Whoever we're after is clever. Someone has been anticipating my every move since I arrived in Briarwood. Until I'm sure who it is, I don't want you telling anyone where you are." He shrugged. "I can't stop you from telling your own husband. All I can do is advise against it."

Trinity distractedly reached for a robe and slipped it on. Dave followed suit. "I can't believe that Steve is a cop," she said. "Placed here, you say. And me?

What does that make me? What role was I supposed to play in this charade?"

What was he to do now? He could crucify St. John with a few well-placed words and inferences, but he didn't want to win Trinity that way. "You'll have to ask him that."

"I don't know that I care to. How could I ever trust him after this? I'm his wife, and yet he kept something as important as this from me."

The night was ruined. Dave felt that both of them would benefit from some time alone. He'd been antsy since he'd left the city, as if he was on the verge of discovering who murdered Ellen, if he could only get his mind clear enough to think it through. He acknowledged that his mind was never clear when he was around Trinity. "I should go back to town," he said. "I don't want to leave you here alone, and I can't run the risk of taking you with me."

"I'll be all right." She was still troubled by his revelation concerning St. John. "I'll keep the door locked, and I won't answer the phone unless I know it's you. Two rings, then one, then you call again. Right?"

"Right. I gather from what you said earlier, I can be assured you won't be calling St. John."

"Why would I call him? I don't owe him anything? He's a fraud, and I don't even want to think about what that makes me. I don't know if I ever want to talk to him again."

Dave had never seen her really angry before. This was the moment that he could have revealed that St. John was in love with her. That his reason for marrying her, though bogus, was no longer of consequence. But, he didn't. Instead, he strode over to his jacket that Trinity had stripped from him and thrown to the floor. He reached inside and withdrew a package. He opened it up. Inside, was a small revolver. "Do you know how to use this?"

"Yes. I don't like guns, but I know how to use one. What about you? Don't you need a gun?'

"I have one. Police issue. This little piece is my insurance, and now it's yours." He placed it in her hand. "If anyone but me comes through that door, shoot to kill."

She paled. "You're serious!"

"Never more so. There's a killer out there who is systematically exterminating anyone who remotely poses a threat. I don't think you really pose a threat at this point, but he, or she, may not be convinced of that fact."

"She? It could be a woman?'

"Some of the best murderers are." He kissed her. "You'll be back?"

He kissed her again, this time with more fervor. "Of course, I'll be back. Only my death could stop me."

She clung to him. "Don't say that. I've gotten used to having you around. I don't want to think of a life without you in it."

"Then we have the same problem," he assured her. "I have to go. Remember what I said. Keep the doors locked, and don't…"

"Answer the phone unless it's you." She finished for him. "Thank you for caring so much." She tilted her head to one side. "I love you, Davie Kincaid."

She was making it difficult for him to leave, and she knew it. Think like a cop for a change, he cautioned himself. You'll have plenty of time when this case is over to put you, Trinity, and St. John in perspective.

"I'll call you when I get to town. If you have problems, I'll be at my motel for a while, and if I leave, I'll give the desk clerk my location. Don't leave your own name. Make one up."

"How about Mary Smith?"

Dave laughed. "Hardly original, but Mary Smith it is."

Moments later he left her. Eight hours at least until he would see her again. He wondered if he would ever stop thinking of her in terms of the time he spent away from her.

⌇

Dave parked his car by a pay phone outside of Briarwood and called Trinity to make sure she was all right. She seemed to be holding up better than he was. He drove to his motel and stopped by the office for messages. There were two. One from Brad, another from St. John. He called Brad first.

Dave filled Brad in on St. John. The tall FBI agent had told him not to tell anyone, but he'd already broken that rule by telling Trinity, and Brad was his partner.

Brad whistled. "What a turn of events. Puts you behind the eight ball, doesn't it? I know how badly you wanted him to be guilty. Where does this put you and his wife?"

Dave had thought of little else since he'd found out he and St. John were supposedly on the same side. Deep down, he felt that no matter how pure St. John emerged from this investigation, he himself had the edge. Trinity loved him. She'd said so. "I don't think it's going to make a difference. What happened when you flashed Bryant's picture? Did the motel clerk where Ellen stayed recognize him?"

"I didn't get to check it out myself, Herring put me to work on something else as soon as I got back, so Sheila took Bryant's picture around. She came up empty. The motel clerk never saw Bryant before. He could be wrong. He wasn't that close to the guy Ellen left the motel with."

Dave swore under his breath. "Another dead end. Bryant seems to be living a charmed life."

"Do you think he killed the girl?"

St. John says no, and he may be in a position to know. If he really was on him that night, I suppose we have to count Bryant out."

"Who the hell does that leave?"

It was a good question. One that Dave had no answer for.

Dave called St. John at the farm. He was told by the housekeeper that he was out. He thought about the gun he'd given Trinity. Would she use it if she had to? He had to believe she would.

Dave spread everything he had on the case out on the bed. Everything from Ellen's file, Bertha Bartlett's notes, to Chris's suicide note. He arranged and rearranged the paperwork, as if by doing so everything would come together like a giant picture puzzle.

He studied his own notes. Somewhere, either here on the bed or in his head was the answer.

He was deep in thought when the phone rang. It was St. John. "I think we should talk," he said. "Can you come by the farm?"

"When?"

"How about now?"

Dave agreed to meet him there.

The housekeeper answered the door, unable to keep the disapproving look off her face. She led him to St. John's study.

St. John offered Dave a drink. Wondering if he was going to need it, Dave accepted. He looked around the room while St. John fixed them drinks. It was real class. The best that money could buy. He could never offer Trinity anything like it.

St. John handed Dave his drink. He perched himself on the edge of a huge oak desk. Dave took a seat across the room.

"It's all falling apart, Kincaid. I think you fucked it up so that we can't win."

Dave took a swallow of his drink, asking himself whether St. John was refereeing to Trinity or to the case. He waited for him to reveal himself.

"I just came from Bryant's house. He was distant. I think he knows we're onto him. More importantly, I think he knows I might not be what I claimed to be, a rich man more than willing to get richer if the stakes were high enough. He was starting to come around. Then, you started opening your mouth about steroids. I think he's going to stop his operations. If he does, we're in trouble. We don't have enough to take him down and make it stick."

"That,s why you asked me here?" Dave asked. "To chew me out? Or did you ask me here so as I couldn't be with Trinity? You should have asked me about my plans on the phone. I could have saved myself a trip, and you the hassle. When I leave here, I'll be going back to her," Dave lied. "Don't have me followed. I can spot a tail a mile away."

Dave hoped that would end the discussion, but it didn't. "How is she?"

"Great. Just great."

"Did you tell her about me?"

So, that was why he'd really asked Dave here. He should have known. "I told her."

"How did she take it?"

"Like a woman who's been fucked and not told thank you. What did you expect?"

"I should have told her myself."

Dave downed his drink and placed his empty glass on the desk. "Well, you'll get your chance to plead your case when this is over, assuming, that is, that you come out of this as clean as you claim to be." He smiled. "Of course, by then it may be too late."

St. John was quick to react. "Something for you to think about, Kincaid. You can't make me the bad guy just because you want me to be. When this is over, I intend to fight you for her."

"Ask me if I'm worried," Dave said with a lot more conviction that he felt.

✦

Dave headed out of town, making sure he wasn't followed, then set his course for his motel. Everything was just as he'd left it, papers still strewn all over his bed. He stared at them for a minute, then ran his hands across them and pushed them to the floor. By now, he knew almost every word on every piece of paper by heart.

He resisted the urge to get in his car and go to Trinity, or to call her. He turned out all the lights in the room and flopped down on the bed. He placed his hands behind his head and closed his eyes, thinking back to the day he and Brad had found Ellen in the alley. He relieved every moment since.

Motive! Who had one besides Bryant? Who stood to lose or gain from Ellen, Miss Bartlett, Chris and Bill's deaths? Who knew every move he was going to make before he made it? Who would Ellen have left the motel with so willingly? Why was she kept alive for a few days before she was killed? Who hadn't known Bertha Bartlett well enough to know that Chris would never have called her Bertha? Or did it go deeper than that? Was he dealing with someone so damn clever that was what he was expected to think? Who had ready access to heroin? Who could be of such use to Bryant that he'd cut them in on the action? Had Bill known the name of Bryant's connection?

The questions kept rolling around in his head. He flipped on the light by his bed, lit a cigarette, and turned off the light again. He took a deep drag of and watched the circle of smoke hover in the air, then vanish. His mind went back to the beginning again, and to everyone he'd been in contact with since he'd found Ellen.

An hour and a half a pack of cigarettes later, he had his answers. He was down to two suspects. One of them was guilty of murder, and something else that was almost worse.

The dream was so real he could reach out and touch her. Trinity was naked, floating on a cloud. Dave extended his hand, but instead of taking it, she smiled. "Where are we?" he asked her.

She didn't answer him. Instead, she beckoned to him.

He was running after the cloud but it was gathering speed, taking her further and further away from him. The distance became so great she was a dot on the horizon. And then she was gone.

Dave shot up and wiped sweat from his eyes. He leaped out of bed and threw on his pants and shirt. He reached for his cell phone.

The code! What the fuck was the code he'd worked out with Trinity? Two rings, then one, then connect, that was it!

He rang the cabin number twice, hung up, no answer. Rang once, no answer. He rang the number again, and on the third ring Trinity answered. Her voice was sleepy. "Davie?"

Thank God! "You're all right?"

"Yes, I'm fine. You don't sound so good. What is it?"

"I had a dream. I was afraid that something had happened to you. Listen to me and don't argue. There's a hotel in Henderson called The Golden Spoon. I want you to go there."

"When?"

"Right now. Call a cab. Just pack what you need and go. Take the gun." "Will you be there?"

"No. It should take you about an hour to get there. Call me on my cell the moment you arrive. Check in under another name and have the hotel operator place the call for you. Don't come on the line until you hear my voice, then say, 'It's done.' Leave a sealed envelope for me at the desk with your room number in it. I'll be there as soon as I can."

"You know who killed Ellen, don't you? That's what this is all about, not some dream."

He didn't feel like explaining the importance of his dreams, and truthfully, the significance of this one was escaping him. Unlike his other warning dreams there was no violence, implied or real. It was probably just a normal dream. Not unusual, considering how much Trinity was on his mind.

"You know, don't you?" she persisted. "Who is it?"

"You wouldn't believe me if I told you," he said. "Please, just do as I say."

The housekeeper led Dave to a covered patio where St. John was having breakfast. St. John wiped his mouth with a linen napkin. "Kincaid. To what to I owe this visit?"

It hadn't been an easy night for Dave and coming here to St. John for help was hardly palatable. He handed him a sheet of paper. "I'd like you to call your boss and get me information on the two names written there. It's important that we know if either of them knew Bryant before he came here, and if so, in what connection. I'd like one of your people to go to the address I've written down and dust it for prints. Whoever killed Ellen and the others was probably smart enough to wear gloves, and in the case of one of them, we'd expect to find their prints. They wouldn't have been questioned. What I'm hoping is that whoever killed Ellen wasn't worried about us looking for her fingerprints. If I'm right about our murderer being one of the two people on that list, we're looking at someone who thinks they're above the law."

"Why come to me? Why not use your own people?"

"The FBI moves faster."

"You got a warrant to search at this address, or can you get one?" "No."

"Then it's breaking and entering. I don't know if I can sell that." He tapped the piece of paper Dave had handed to him. "Why one of these two?"

"It was easy once I put all the pieces together. Whoever killed Ellen, Bertha Bartlett, Chris, and Bill, knew everything I did. More than I did in Ellen's case.

Whoever killed them knew that Ellen was onto the steroid racket, that Miss Bartlett was onto how Severn died, knew where Chris was the night he was killed, and that Bill might turn over. Once I came to that conclusion and quit trying to hang it on you, these were the only two people who came to the surface."

St. John stared down at the names on Dave's list, and then stared up at Dave. "It took a lot for you to come here this morning and say what you just did. I'm glad we finally agree that we're on the same side. Sit down and pour yourself a cup of coffee.

Have you had breakfast? I can have the housekeeper fix you a plate." "Thanks, but I don't eat breakfast. I'll take that cup of coffee, though."

"Go ahead and pour yourself a cup. While you're drinking your coffee, I'll make a call to see if I can get your requests granted and in motion."

Twenty minutes and two cups of coffee later, St. John returned. "Checking backgrounds and any connection with Bryant was a piece of cake. Getting a blanket search warrant, was another matter. I couldn't get them to do it. The FBI has gotten some bad press in the past few years, they won't risk it. I did get them to agree to get a search warrant just to look for Ellen's prints. It wasn't easy." He grinned. "I had to threaten to blow my own cover. I got my way, but I think I just made a powerful enemy."

Dave paced the floor. "We'll lose the element of surprise. With warning, there could be no prints left to find."

"It's their way or nothing," St. John said. "Besides, without a warrant, anything we find we can't use."

That had already occurred to Dave, but he'd been afraid that any evidence of Ellen being at that address would be gone before the authorities could get to it. He didn't like the way things were turning out but realized there was nothing he could do about it.

"When will they go in?"

"Tomorrow. They'll have their search warrant at noon." He gave Dave a searching look. "You seem real sure they'll find something."

It was something Dave didn't want to think about. Not this morning. "What are you going to do until I hear from my people?" St. John asked.

"Look out for Trinity. I moved her last night for insurance. I don't really think it was necessary, but I wanted to be sure no one could get to her. I'll bring her back here to you, in the morning. Now that she has nothing to fear from you, it's a logical place to put her. I've been so vocal about your hurting her, this is the last place anyone will think to look for her now."

There was admiration in St. John's voice. "I wish we could have been friends, but I'll settle for your conviction that I am what I say I am, just a cop doing his job. As for Trinity, I'd be foolish to think that if you want her, I'd stand a chance."

Dave knew he spoke the truth. All that did, was make the road ahead much harder.

⟩∞⟨

Dave picked up the sealed envelope addressed to him from the desk at The Golden Spoon. Inside, there was a sheet of hotel paper with the number 311 written on it. Dave moved to the house phone and asked the operator to ring room 311. Trinity answered immediately. "Davie, is that you?"

"Yes. I'm on my way up. Are you dressed?"

"Do you want me to be?" Her laugher filled his ears.

"Later, Trinity. Pack whatever you brought with you. We're leaving." "Where are we going?"

"Back to the lake. I'm still paying for the cabin." "What's going on?"

"Nothing. Just get ready. As long as you're with me you'll be safe."

"You're coming to the cabin with me?" She didn't try to disguise her pleasure. "Yes."

Her laughter rang out again. "Then I'll pack light."

⌾

A year before his father died, Paul Kincaid had taken his son to the lake and shown him his "secret" place "You can fish from here and no one will ever know you're around," Dave remembered him saying.

Dave rented a pontoon and took Trinity to the spot his father had shared with him.

He smiled when as he rounded a curve in the lake, he spied his father's "secret" place.

After all, it had been eighteen years. The landscape could have changed. Over the years boats had come to this spot in the lake and wended their way around the curve, bypassing the towering willow. Dave steered the pontoon through the overhanging leaves.

"We're going to crash into the bank!" Trinity shrieked.

Dave smiled and ignored her warning. Beyond the sheltering leaves was an open area of lake, large enough to conceal two boats the size of the pontoon. Dave switched off the engine. He turned to Trinity. "Like it?"

She wore a mini-cover-up over a one-piece bathing suit that fit her like a glove.

Slit at both sides, the black nylon material barely covered her breasts. The bikini cut showcased her legs and slender thighs. Tanned to perfection, she took his breath away.

She removed the cover-up. "How on earth did you find this place?"

"I didn't. My father did. He said no one knew about it except him, and then me. Since my father and I both fell in love with you, it seems appropriate to bring you here."

She drew in her breath. "Your father never loved me, Davie. I told you that." Dave felt differently, no longer angry about his father's involvement with Trinity.

"It doesn't matter, now. The important thing is that no one can see us here." "No one?"

"No one."

A huge smile swept across her face. "Then why waste that kind of privacy?" She lowered the straps on her suit and peeled it off.

If he was breathless before, now he was overwhelmed. No matter how many times she exposed herself to him, he could never seem to get enough. He stripped off his shorts and tee-shirt, pulled her to him and lowered her to the floor of the boat. He took each hardened nipple into his mouth as she reached for him and took him into her hands. His lips moved to hers, and they hungrily kissed, their tongues meshing. He ran his hands through her dark hair. She, in turn, entwined her fingers through his own sandy strands. Moving his lips downward, he hungrily suckled her breasts, while his fingers explored her softness. His lips moved to that softness. Her hands gently turned him so that she could take him into her mouth without disturbing her own pleasure. He probed her softness until she felt like a part of him, and he a part of her. When he finally entered her, the crescendo that proceeded their climax was like a firework display going off in his head.

Afterward, they lay naked on the pontoon's roof, stroking each other until the tender foreplay precipitated another round of love-making. They were oblivious to the odd passing boat or two that never knew they were there behind the willow tree.

Much later, she said. "I don't suppose you thought to bring food or drink." "Oh ye of little faith," he said. "I had the lodge pack us a basket."

Sated sexually, and now nourished, they reluctantly headed back to shore. As the dock came into sight, Dave was grimly reminded that while this interlude with Trinity had blocked out reality, there was a murderer out there, and that he still had a job to do.

He started a fire when they settled in at the cabin. It would be dark soon. He was reasonably sure that no one knew where they were, and even if they did, Trinity was safe as long as he was here with her.

Tomorrow, if was possible he would find out which one of his two suspects was guilty of murdering Ellen Gray. And tomorrow, he would hand over Trinity's safekeeping to Steven St. John.

⌘

It was a wet and windy morning, in complete contrast to the glorious sunshine of the day before.

Trinity was angry. "Suppose I don't want to go back to the farm!" "You'll be safe there."

"I don't feel safe. How can you be so sure that Steven is innocent? You still haven't convinced me of that, because you still haven't told me who you think killed Ellen."

254

"I can't. Not until I'm sure. Do you trust me, Trinity?" "Of course, I do."

"Then believe me when I say that the farm is the best place for you to be. St. John won't let anything happen to you."

"What do I say to him? He lied to me, and he used me." "He loves you. That alone will keep you safe?"

She clung to him. "Well, I don't love him, I love you. I don't want you to leave here."

It took a supreme effort to push her away from him. "You have to. I may have to go to the city today. I can't leave you here alone. Don't ask me to, and don't make this any harder than it already is. Do you think I want to deliver you to St. John? Do you think if there was any other place, I would take you to him?"

As they drove away, Dave and Trinity glanced back at the cabin, as if to savor and commit to memory the magic that had taken place there.

CHAPTER 16

It was a bittersweet moment for Dave when he took Trinity to the St. John farm, but his consolation lay in the fact that it was certainly no moment of triumph for St. John.

Trinity sailed past her husband without a word, her expression of disgust and indifference statement enough.

St. John was visibly shaken. "Until this moment," he told Dave, "I didn't know I cared this much."

Dave was anxious to be gone from here for a variety of reasons, not the least of which was St. John himself. "You have something for me?" he asked impatiently.

St. John produced the paper Dave had given to him yesterday. "This one here," he said, pointing to one of the two names on it, "has at least a plausible connection to Bryant, though it's not much more than circumstantial. The other guy so far, looks clean. I guess we'll know more when they look for Ellen's prints later today."

Dave took a deep breath and exhaled. It was almost over, but he felt no elation. "Yeah, I guess so."

"I think you should stay here at the farm until we know the results of the search." "Why?"

"I have a lousy feeling that you're about to take the law into your own hands. "If I was, and I'm not, what makes you think you could stop me?"

St. John stared at him deep in thought. "I keep wondering what I'd do in your shoes. Sometimes, I think that you got closer to Ellen in death that I ever did while she was alive."

"I wouldn't want to admit that if I were you. Especially around Trinity. Speaking of which, shouldn't you be making sure she's secure?"

St. John was torn between his desire to protect Trinity and his desire to keep an eye on Dave. Trinity won. Then, she always won.

"Done. Where can I reach you?" "I'll reach you."

"Why do I get the persistent feeling that you're about to screw things up, Kincaid?"

At about the end of his tolerance, Dave said. "I don't know. I'd say that's your problem."

Dave made a few phone calls, and then he left Briarwood.

Traffic was light. Dave arrived in the city in good time. He'd told no one he was coming.

He went to his apartment. He drew in his breath. This place was Laura.

Somehow, she'd managed to leave something intangible, but overpowering of herself here, even though everything material that was hers was gone. He entered the kitchen, half-expecting to see her there, sitting at the table, a cup of coffee in her hand. He was met inside with a cold, sterile, unpleasant, unlived-in sensation.

He moved to the phone and dialed a number, tapping his fingers on a nearby table. He mumbled under his breath. "Be there."

Brad answered on the fourth ring. "Hey, pal, what's up?" Brad asked. "I'm at my apartment. Can you come over? Say in a half an hour?"

"What are you doing in the city?" And when Dave didn't answer. "Okay, but make it in an hour."

Dave had killed a half bottle of scotch when the doorbell rang an hour-and-five minutes later.

Brad looked at the almost empty bottle and the full glass in Dave's hand. "A little early for that, isn't it? What the hell!" He reached for the bottle and a nearby glass. "I won't tell, if you don't." He poured himself a generous helping of Scotch. "What's so damned important? Brad fell into a chair.

Dave remained standing. "I asked you here, because you, more than anyone else, knows how hard this Ellen Gray case has been on me. I lost perspective and direction so many times and in so many ways. Some of it was Trinity, but a lot of it was Ellen herself. I cared about her, and all that did was confused me. When I started to get it together, and began thinking like a cop, it was like daylight on a dark night."

He turned to face Brad. "If feels good to think out loud again. I used to do it all the time with Laura, and with you, of course. Where was I? Oh, yea. I asked myself some very important questions. Like, why wait to kill Ellen? Why not kill her that first night? Who knew every move I was making, because I gave them a roadmap? Who, besides me, knew where Chris was the night he was killed? Was Chris's bogus suicide note a double cross, not only for Chris, but for me? Who could get enough heroin to dope Ellen up for days, kill her, and then kill Chris the same way? Why kill Bertha Bartlett? Or Bill, for that matter? Because they knew too much, or because in time they'd have figured things out?"

Dave swallowed the last drop in his glass and refilled it. He stared at the now empty bottle as if willing it to replenish itself. "I started to answer my own questions. Ellen wasn't killed right away because whoever murdered her, didn't have a natural stomach for murder, just for greed and self-preservation. Killing her must have been painful in the end." He shrugged. "After that, killing came easy, I suspect. From the moment I met Clyde Bromley, I told him everything. He was the one who couldn't wait to tell me what Chris's clue to his own murder was. As a lawman he could have gotten dope. Why Miss Bartlett and Bill? Bertha Bartlett was a tough one to figure out. She and Bromley were cut from the same cloth. Then, I figured, that could be the reason she had to die. Chris called three numbers the night he was killed. One of them was Bromley's home phone number. I only had Bromley's word for the substance of that conversation, which put me where it was supposed to, incidentally, on the defensive."

"You with me, so far?" Dave asked.

Brad nodded, uncharacteristically silent, waiting for Dave to continue.

"Ellen was supposed to have come to the city to ask for my help. Trinity sent her here to me. Ellen didn't connect with me. Bromley is a kindly old bastard on the surface, so it was reasonable to believe she might have gone to him for help, instead. A lot of the pieces fit. I made a short list of suspects who met the criteria to be Ellen's murderer.

Only two names came to mind. Bromley made the list."

Brad stood. "The Sheriff! It's circumstantial, Dave. You'll never make it stick.

I wish I could be more enthusiastic, but if this is all you have, conjectures…" he shrugged. "It won't work. But, if you're right, it's over, isn't it? There's no one left to eliminate. I hate to say it, Dave, but it's time to put this case to bed. For God's sake, let it go."

"You'd like that wouldn't you?"

"Hey, Buddy, don't take it out on me. I didn't make the rules, I just play by them."

Dave opened up a cabinet and found what he was looking for, another bottle of scotch. "Should have known Laura wouldn't have let us run out." He poured himself a drink and set the bottle on the side. Brad helped himself to another drink, too.

Dave lifted his glass. There were no signs of inebriation, only controlled and unleashed anger. "To you and me, Brad. Partners, but better yet, friends."

Brad lifted his glass in wary response. "I don't think I've ever seen you like this." "You never will again. I keep thinking about Ellen's last few days. Hard to

imagine what those days were like, but I can't stop trying. Did she suffer? I want to say no, but my heart tells me she did."

"If she did, you can't change it, Dave. When are you ever going to learn you're not God, though sometimes you act like you are." He shook his head in disgust. "What are you going to do? About Bromley, I mean. Don't say nothing, because I know you better than that."

Dave gave him a hard look. "You're wrong. I'm not going to do a damn thing about Bromley." Dave took a healthy swig of his drink. "Because he didn't kill Ellen or the others. You did."

⚬⚬⚬

The drink in Brad's hand spilled to the floor. "That's a lousy joke."

"Except we both know it isn't a joke, don't we? There were two names on my list, Brad, Bromley's and yours." He stared into space. "Believe me, I wish it had been Bromley. As incredibly preposterous as it seemed, it always came back to you, and even now that I think I know how it all went down, I still ask myself why you did it."

"You're crazy, Dave. I don't fit the picture of your murderer at all."

"Oh, but you do. You gave yourself away twice, but I was too absorbed with Trinity for it to sink in. You talked about Miss Bartlett's pictures on her bedroom wall. You couldn't have known about them unless you'd been there. Then, you said that the motel clerk was too far away to have seen the guy Ellen left there with. Only the guy she was with could have known that."

"You're cracking up," Brad said. "It's understandable. You're stressed out. That's why I'm going to make allowances for you. You told me about the old lady having pictures of her students on the wall. Don't you remember? As for the motel clerk, that's really groping."

Dave shook his head. "I didn't tell you about the pictures on Miss Bartlett's wall."

"You must have."

"No. There's more. The additional information on Gerard and Bryant that Sheila called me about, should have come from you. You deliberately neglected to send it to me."

"Bullshit! I gave you everything I had."

"No, you didn't. Only what you wanted me to have." Dave poured himself and Brad another drink. "Sit down, Brad, and I'll try to reconstruct how it went, and if I miss anything, you can fill in the blanks. Ellen was told to call me when she reached the city. I think she tried. By then, I suspect that Bryant had called you in a panic because she was blackmailing him about his illegal activities. Maybe he wouldn't pay her enough, or maybe she just got tired of covering up, I don't know, but I think she told him she was going to turn him in. He must have been beside himself wondering if she'd really go through with it. It's possible that when he called you, he may not have known at that point that Ellen had left Briarwood."

Dave paced the floor. "Then something unfortunate happened, for Ellen, anyway. When she tried to reach me, she was put through to your extension instead. It happens all the time. You get my messages and calls, and I get yours. I can imagine you thinking what a wonderful stroke of luck someone else's error was. It was you who picked Ellen up at her motel. She would have trusted you, because of me. You took her somewhere. Your place, probably. You didn't kill her right away, Brad. You filled her full of heroin, stolen from the property room, or held back from a bust; I don't know which. An inventory check of the property room will likely reveal a bag of powdered sugar instead of heroin. The next step, I admit, is harder to figure. You kept her three days before deciding to kill her. Maybe you'll oblige me, and tell me why. Then, you dumped her in the alley, hoping she'd go down as a hooker and a junkie. It was a reasonable gamble. It might have worked." He looked over at Brad. "How am I doing so far?"

Brad yawned. "As stories go, it's rather boring. It's certainly far-fetched." "Wait, it gets better. I don't think that in your wildest dreams you figured on us

being the ones to find her. We were supposed to be off duty that night, but thirty minutes to an hour after you killed her, we got a call to replace Rogers and Chernak. Now, the best you could hope for, was that I would see her death as an O.D. I not only didn't do that, there was something about the girl that haunted me. I didn't know it then, but it was because she was Trinity's daughter."

"I think you've been hit it on the head, Dave. God knows you're under a strain, what with Katie, Laura leaving you, this thing with Ellen's mother, and your obsession with the girl, but this is insane."

Dave ignored Brad's outburst. "Bertha Bartlett was next. Something either myself or Bryant said put the wind up you. By now, killing for self-preservation's sake was becoming easier. Right? Don't bother to answer, I think it's a given. Chris was next. Bromley could have known where he was, but you definitely knew. You were there when he called me. I wrote his cabin number down. You saw it. What was killing Bill all about? Final insurance? Not long after I talked to you about him rolling over, he became a victim of a hit and run. Coincidence? I don't think so. That left Trinity, but this was the only time you weren't able to outsmart me. I spirited her away and told no one where she was. Finally, I told you about St. John's undercover status. The next day Bryant treated St. John like he had the plague, or more appropriately, like he was a cop."

Brad reached for the bottle of scotch and filled his glass again. "Where's your proof? Even if I was guilty of what you're accusing me of, which is ridiculous, you wouldn't have a shred of proof. You know, of course," he said, lifting his glass to his lips, "that we can never work together again. Not after today. I guess I can be charitable and forget to mention this incident to Herring, but that's all the slack I can give you Dave."

He was playing his hand well, Dave gave him that. Dave glanced at his watch. Soon, he would know if his gamble was going to pay off. It was 2:19 p.m. "By now, an FBI team should have been through your apartment, legally," Dave emphasized, "looking for signs that Ellen was there. Finding her prints would wrap this case up, don't you think?"

One of Brad's more noticeable traits was his cockiness. Women found it irresistible, men, often grating. There was none of that cockiness visible now. A thousand doubts crossed Brad's mind and were easily read on his face, doubts that were replaced by sheer terror.

Dave had borne witness to similar expressions when a suspect knew there was no way out. He took no pleasure in witnessing it in Brad. He was sick to the depths of his soul. It took all his willpower to keep from running to the bathroom and spilling the contents of his stomach into the commode. He felt tears of anger rush to his eyes. He brushed them away, afraid Brad might mistake them for weakness.

"You did that to me?" Brad said, disbelief in his voice. "You sicked the Feds on me?"

It was the last straw for Dave. His fist took on a life of its own as it smashed into Brad's handsome face.

Brad, taken off guard, staggered backward, falling to the floor, knocking over his chair as he fell. Dave took advantage of the moment. He straddled Brad, took the gun from Brad's holster from under his sports jacket, emptied it of shells and seized the collar of Brad's shirt. His fist connected with flesh once again.

Brad spit out blood. "You're a dead man, Dave." He struggled to get out from under Dave's weight, bringing up his own fist, hard. It caught Dave on the corner of his chin.

They fought like crazed animals, breaking furniture, glassware, and everything else in their path. Brad fought valiantly; he was fighting for his life, but, Dave fought harder, because he was fighting for something much more compelling. He was fighting for Ellen, Bertha, Chris and Bill, because they would never be able to do it for themselves, and for being taken in and used. He fought the better fight because he desperately needed to avenge Brad's act of betrayal, not only to a partner and to a friend but to a police force that was, for the most part, worthy. Dave only stopped his anger- driven abuse when it was painfully clear that Brad was beaten.

He pulled Brad to his feet, pushed him toward the kitchen, took a pair of cuffs from his pocket, and chained Brad to a chair. He passed a mirror on his way and took stock of his own wounds. His lip was sliced, one eye was threatening to close, and his head felt like a brass band had taken up residence there.

Dave moved to the sink and ripped a paper towel off the rack. He wet it and dabbed at his face. He ripped off another few sheets and wiped the blood from Brad's face. "I'm not a dead man, Brad. You are. You know how they treat cops in prison."

"You won't find anything at my apartment, Dave."

Dave had a sinking feeling. Finding anything at Brad's apartment had always been a long shot. He had to know just how long of a shot it really was. He dialed St. John's number. St. John answered the phone himself. "It's Kincaid," Dave said. "You hear anything?"

He listened while St. John responded. He placed the receiver back on the hook. "They found a print and a partial print belonging to Ellen at your place. It's all we needed to subpoena your phone records. If you made just one call to Bryant, it'll be more nails in your coffin. There's a warrant out for your arrest."

"Oh, hell, I can explain the prints. I didn't want to tell you, but Ellen really was a hooker at heart. I picked her up in a bar, took her to my apartment, and let her stay there because she had no place else to go. I turned her out after one day. I don't know where she went after that."

Dave hit Brad with the back of his hand. "Bastard. She's dead. I won't let you pull her down in the gutter with you."

"You're going to pursue this, aren't you? I guess I'm going to have to get me a good lawyer."

"You'd better get yourself a damned good one. Bryant will turn states evidence, branding you as a murderer, I guarantee it. St. John is on his way over to Bryant's place now. It's open and shut, Brad. You're going away for a long time, to a place where your charm will have to be parlayed against gang rape and every con in the place looking to put you six-feet under because you're a cop." He shook his fist. "What a waste. Why, Brad? Fuck you, tell me why?"

Brad sighed. "Let me loose and I'll tell you." Dave shook his head.

"Have it your way. I want you to know how it was. I didn't want to kill her, Dave. You were right, Bryant did call me. He was already half-packed to leave and go underground. I was curious about the girl who had the power to get a stranglehold on Bryant's heart and a hammerlock on his life."

"Back it up, Brad. We were able to establish a slim connection between you and Bryant. You came from the same neighborhood. What we didn't find was evidence of a lasting friendship."

Brad ran his tongue across his lips. "I could sure use a drink."

Dave reached inside a cabinet, took out a glass, and filled it full of water. He hand fed the liquid to Brad.

"That's because we didn't have one," Brad said. "I never really knew Bryant when I was growing up, but he must have seen me around. I ran into him when I worked vice. He stopped me in the street as I was leaving the stationhouse. Aren't you from the neighborhood? He asked. You know how hard I try to avoid my roots, but he wouldn't give up.

He looked back at the stationhouse, and said, "No! You're putting me on!

You're a cop?" He told me if I ever wanted to make some real money, to call him. I forgot about him and the incident until I ran into him again, a year ago, here in New York. He extended another invitation. He said he needed someone above suspicion." He ran his tongue across his parched lips. "I could sure use another drink."

Dave held the glass to Brad's mouth and waited for him to finish drinking. "Go on."

"You remember that hooker we found in little pieces? That was the day I started to ask myself what my life as a cop was all about. Scum mongers, that's what we are.

Every day a little bit of that filth rubs off on you until you start to wonder why we do it, and what fucking difference we make. How many of the slime bags that we pulled in this last year made it to trial, much less did any time? When Bryant approached me this last time, I was ready to listen."

"Why, you?"

"Maybe he saw the underlying weakness in me. Something you never did. Part of it may have been that he remembered how it was when were kids, how easy it had been to cross the line. Some things you never leave behind. You know what they say? You can take the crook out of the ghetto, but not the ghetto out of the crook." He smiled weakly. "Sorry. Re-arranging an old adage. The way Bryant laid it out, I was going to be able to split from here in another six to eight months with enough loose change to write my own ticket. It sounded good. Damn good. I swear, I never figured it would lead to murder."

"What exactly did you do for Bryant?"

"More than he bargained for in the end," Brad said ruefully. "More than I bargained for, that's for sure. I wasn't hired on as a hit man. I was his token cop. Every smart crook has one of the payroll. The steroids came to a warehouse here. Since it was a new strain and a new source, Briarwood was to be a proving ground. I mailed them to Bryant at the bank in small, regular packages. They were labeled as bank supplies.

Wokowski was the first and only casualty that I know of. Bryant thinks that Lackland doubled up on the dosage because the kid was star material, and Lackland didn't want to screw up his second and last chance at being a part of pro ball."

"Why did you kill Ellen?"

Brad sighed. He strained against the cuffs. "I didn't want to, though Bryant was pushing me to get rid of her. It's hard to believe she was only eighteen, she was so worldly and sophisticated. It didn't take me long to realize what Bryant had seen in her." He looked up at Dave. "She wasn't what you think she was, or what you wanted her to be. Then, that's your problem. You think if you squeeze people into the niche' you've mentally designed for them, that they'll fit. Truth is, I wanted her, and she let me know it was all right."

Dave clenched his fist and resisted the impulse to beat Brad senseless. "You raped her?"

"Grow up, Dave. It wasn't rape. I never forced myself on a woman in my life. She was no exception. But, now, I had real problems. I had to carry on as if nothing was happening, which meant working, which also meant I had to leave her alone in my apartment. I tied her up that first day, but she almost broke loose, so I kept her spaced out after that, which solved one of my problems, but gave me another. Heroin made her sick at first. I'd come home and find her laying in her own vomit." He shrugged. "In the beginning, I don't know what I thought I was going to end up doing with her. I couldn't let her get to you, that was for sure."

A burning sensation lingered in Dave's chest, unexploded anger, eating away at him as it threatened to erupt. "Did it occur to you that she might have let you sleep with her so she could stay alive? No, of course it didn't. How did you get her to leave the motel with you?"

"That was the easy part. I told her I was bringing her to you. She had some cockamamie story about you being her father. At least, I thought it was a cockamamie story until I found out about you and Trinity. She told me all about Bryant and his questionable activities. That's when I took her to my place for safekeeping."

"Some safekeeping," Dave retorted.

"I'll give you that one, Dave. I've never been in love, so I don't know how it feels, but I think I could have loved this girl." For a moment, Brad was back with her. "She was something. Really something. The best lay I've ever had. Of course, when I started shooting her with heavy doses of heroin, that stopped. She couldn't handle the stuff and me, too."

Dave clenched his fist tighter. This time, he gave into his impulses. When flesh hit bone, the sound seemed to bounce off the walls.

Brad spit out a tooth. "That's right, Dave. Beat me up again. See, there's a devil in all of us. Who would have guessed you'd hit a man who can't defend himself?"

Just in time, Dave realized Brad was baiting him to take off his cuffs. He moved across the room, putting as much space as he could between the two of them.

"You want to hear how it was or not?" Brad asked.

Dave nodded, afraid to open his mouth for fear of what might come out.

"It was painful to have to kill her. You were right about that, too, but I couldn't trust her to keep her mouth shut. It was her, or me. I went out and bought a cheap black dress, fancy underwear and all the trimmings. I made her wear them, and I made her put on heavy makeup. I did a good job. She looked like a hooker. To everybody except you," Brad added bitterly. "I took her to the alley, gave her enough heroin to kill her, and left her there. She was alive when I left. I couldn't stand to watch her die. Strange, a small part of me wanted her to survive. Crazy, isn't it? She would have sent me to the chair."

"She still may, Dave said. 'BR.' For Briarwood, was what I thought. And maybe it was. We'll never know now if she meant to lead me back to Briarwood, or to you."

"She couldn't have known you would be the one to find her! Who the hell else would have cared? I figured that by the time we came on duty the next day, finding her would be hardly worth a mention. I doubt that Rogers or Chernak would have given her a second thought. When the call came in, and we rolled on it, it was the beginning of the end. You had that look on your face that told me you were going to jump all over my well-planned O.D., like steel to a magnet. I knew I was living on borrowed time after that night."

"Did you kill them all?" Dave asked, anxious to get off the subject of Ellen. Suddenly, his fascination about knowing what kind of person she was, had become a mission he wanted to abandon. In a pathetic and almost irreversible way, she'd set the stage for her own murder long before Brad came on the scene.

"Yes, all of them. The old lady never expected it. When I snuck into Briarwood on that seldom used back road and told her I was your partner, she welcomed me. She showed me the pictures on her bedroom wall, pointing you and Ellen out to me. She told me she could hardly wait to tell you about her theory concerning the Wokowski kid's death. Some kind of drug killed him, she told me. Chalk another one up for you, Dave. Killing her was easy." A faraway expression passed over his face. "After Ellen, anything was easy."

"And, Chris?"

"You handed him to me. I couldn't let the chance to silence him pass me by.

You were convinced he knew something. Like Ellen, he trusted me because of you. No one saw me there or heard me. I made sure of that by parking my car down the road and going around the back of the cabin. I tapped on the window and told him that you'd changed your mind and wanted to move him that night, so he let me in, after I explained that I hadn't knocked on the door of the cabin because you didn't want to take a chance on anyone seeing me, in case someone had followed him to Duncan. I showed him my badge and that took away the last of his apprehensions. It should have ended there, but you wouldn't accept his death as a suicide." He sighed. "It would have been so fucking simple, Dave. Then there was Bill. You were talking about him rolling over. He was always the weakest link. He didn't know about my involvement, so I called him at his house; told him that we wanted to meet with him at the school, and that if he didn't come, we were going to charge him with Ellen's murder. I waited till he showed up, ran him down and left town. It was almost too simple. Nobody saw me. It was at that moment I believed I was going to get away with everything. There was Trinity, of course, but that was a gamble I had to take. You wouldn't let anyone within miles of her."

The really tragic part of all this, Dave thought, is that in the end Brad had really expected to get away with murder, and might have.

He dialed the precinct number. "What are you doing?" Brad asked.

"I'm having you taken in. I admit, it occurred to me to kill you, but all that would do is put me on your level. I suppose there's an outside chance you might walk

Away from a death or life sentence, but I'm willing to let the courts decide your fate." His smile was forced. "You see, Brad, I don't always play God."

Dave spoke into the receiver, asked for Herring, and when he was connected, he asked that someone be sent to his apartment to make the arrest. After he hung up the phone, he turned back to Brad. "They'll be here for you in a few minutes."

CHAPTER 17

The media turned out like sharks in a feeding frenzy. A crooked cop was news enough, but Brad was more than just crooked, he was an alleged murderer.

Dave, with Herring's help and finally his blessing, gave credit to St. John for nailing Brad and Carey Bryant.

"No guts," Dave told him.

Herring, devastated by Brad's actions, said, "No guts? You've got more guts than this whole goddamn precinct. I know how tough this was on you. I admit I didn't like it when you asked me to go to the brass for permission to pass on cleaning up our own mess, at least as far as the public was concerned. In the end they, like me, went along with your need to keep a low profile. Like me, a few of them even understood why you wanted it that way. I liked Brad," Herring went on. "hat only makes what he did even harder to swallow. I heard he got himself a sharp criminal lawyer." Herring stroked his bushy moustache. "Monroe will make one hell of a witness on his own behalf. He might get off with life, and only do seven to ten years." Herring balled up one fist and punched the palm of his other hand with it. "It'll be a real travesty of justice if he does."

"He has to live through it," Dave said. "Ten years is a long time for a cop to stay behind bars and stay alive."

Herring nodded agreement, his expression melancholy.

Dave, anxious to escape contact with the press or anyone else, went into retreat. He ignored calls from both Trinity and Laura. The only call he accepted was Bromley's.

"Sorry," Bromley said. "I always said it was a city slicker. Bad stuff that, though. I ain't never had a partner, but if it was one of my deputies, I'd be feeling mighty bad right about now. How'd you figure it was Monroe? Don't say it was St. John who put it all together. The newspapers might buy that line, but I'm not buying it for one moment."

"Process of elimination, Sheriff. I was hoping it would turn out to be you." "The hell you say!"

Dave told him about the case he'd built against him and then tossed out. There was silence on the other end of the line. Then, "come see me when you get this over with. This town could use you."

"As what?"

"I think you know."

"You can't mean sheriff of Briarwood?"

"You bet your boots. Don't say no before you've had time to think about it."

⚬⚬⚬

Dave threw a rock into the water. He watched the water ripple in a widening circle. Earlier in the day, he'd debated on taking out a boat. Fishing was for thinking, his father had said. That was Dave's problem, he didn't want to think anymore, he just wanted to get on with his life.

He knew she was there before she revealed herself. It wasn't only her perfume, musky and inviting, it was the overpowering way she filled space.

"How'd you find me?" He asked without turning around.

"It wasn't difficult once I believed that you really weren't in the city. Where else would you come?"

He turned to face her. He'd told Brad that she was like daylight on a dreary day.

That hadn't changed. Only he had.

Dave kicked at the dirt at his feet. "I was going to call you, Trinity. I just haven't felt like talking to anyone."

They stood in silent reflection. One had lost a daughter, possibly both of them, the other, a trusted friend.

She stared at the bruised flesh around his eye at his cracked lips. "What happened?"

"I lost control." He smiled, attempting levity. "You should see the other guy." "Brad Monroe?"

"Yeah."

"This is painful for both of us, Davie, but I have to know. Did Ellen suffer? You must have asked."

It was a question he'd known he'd have to answer sooner or later, 'No, she didn't suffer," he lied. "He didn't want to hurt her, it just happened."

"Thank you, for that. I won't ask you for details, but if you want to talk, I'll listen. Can we go inside?" she asked.

Every fiber of his being wanted to say yes, but if he did, he knew he was lost.

He'd been lost for too long.

"I'd rather talk out here."

Trinity sighed. "I guess that's what I expected you to say. We had some great times here, Davie." She laughed. The sound echoed across the nearly deserted lake.

"You have nothing to fear. As much as I like sex, I know when it's the wrong time and the wrong place. This is the right place, but the wrong time."

"I don't know what to say, Trinity."

"Sure you do." She moved to a nearby tree trunk and sat down, her brief sundress hiked past her thighs. Dave smiled inwardly. She wasn't doing it on purpose, she just couldn't help herself.

"I'm sure you have a lot to say to me, Davie," Trinity said. "More than I want to hear, probably."

She was right, of course. Since he'd arrived back at the lake two days ago, he'd thought about little else than what he was going to do where she was concerned, or what he was going to say to her. He turned away from her and threw another rock into the surface of the water. "This is a great place to think," he said. "I've been thinking back to when I first returned to Briarwood. I was looking for background on Ellen, as if by finding out more about her, I could find out who killed her. My search for Ellen led me unwittingly, and reluctantly, to a search for myself." He turned to face her. Damn, she was so beautiful. His voice when he spoke, was hoarse. "I've loved you for eighteen years, Trinity, and I'll never in my life love anyone this way again, and for that I'm screwed, but I'll get over it. No one should love another person as much as I've loved you. You've been my addiction. When I'm not around you, I get withdrawal symptoms, and I've been on an eighteen year withdrawal that almost sucked me under.

No matter where I went or what I did, you were in my blood, my head, my thoughts. Maybe you always will be. Did you know that recovering alcoholics and dope addicts never stop wanting another drink or another fix? Those that make it, get by one day at a time. I'm going to make it, just like they do, one day at a time."

A sad smile played around her lips and lingered there. "I assume this is goodbye, then," Trinity said.

The weakest part of him, the part of him that had kept him chained to her all these years, wanted to scream out, "No," over and over again. He reached deep inside himself for the strength to overcome that weakness. "There was a moment last week when I saw myself," he said. "I mean really saw myself, and what it is that I want. Don't laugh, but I want a white picket fence, snot-nosed kids, backyard barbeques, bowling on Tuesdays, and a mortgage."

She wrinkled her nose. "That doesn't sound like us, not me anyway. It's that girl, isn't it? It's Laura?"

"It's not that simple, Trinity, or even that complicated."

"I could stay I'm surprised, but I'm not. Please don't look so damned guilty.

We've been lucky, you and I. How many people get to relive the best part of their lives, or get the chance to make their fantasies come true? We did that, and I won't apologize for it, and I'll never regret it."

Neither will I, he thought.

"What will you do about you, and St. John?" he asked.

"There is no me, and St. John. His name, incidentally, is really Mark Peters, but I suppose you know that by now."

Dave hadn't known.

"There could be something for us later. I'm not ruling it out. He says he'll never give up on me." She laughed. "Perhaps I should have him talk to you. Look what that kind of thinking did to you!"

"What will you do?"

"Margaret was offered a new job at the American Embassy in Rome. She asked me to go with her. I admit the invitation floored me. God knows we have fences to mend. I think I'll surprise her and accept." She looked out at the water. "I'm finally getting the good sense to leave Briarwood and I won't be back. I should have left years ago."

Dave took her hand in his. The chemistry between them was strong, like a fast moving current after a torrential downpour. He gently withdrew his hand so that she wouldn't see the effect she still had on him. But of course, she knew. "God help those Italians," he said. "Italy will never be the same."

She looked back at the lake. It was near dusk. Lights from summer homes on the far shore danced off the water's surface. "I love it here, but I'll never come back here again, either. It wouldn't mean anything without you." A wistful expression passed across her face. "We could still have tonight, you know."

The thought had occurred to him. The temptation to have this night with her was the biggest challenge he'd ever faced. In the next few seconds he was going to find out if he was up to it.

It was like being in the Garden of Eden, he thought. She, the serpent, her offer of a night's lovemaking, the apple. He licked his lips. He'd come too far in the last two days to falter now. "I can't. If I did, I'd be hooked again. It would be like taking another drink, or needing another fix. I envy the next guy who says yes to you," he said with fervor.

"No, you don't, Davie," she whispered. "Eighteen years ago I sent you away because it was wrong for me. Now, you're sending me away because it's wrong for you. We had everything except timing," she said, sadness and regret in her voice.

She kissed him on the cheek. His flesh felt like it was on fire. Desperate for diversion, he offered to walk her to her car. He opened the car door for her, managing somehow to resist the urge to touch her one last time. The look that passed between them would be etched in his memory forever. He watched her drive away and out of his life.

The dust from her tires flew up in his face, but he hardly noticed. As her car became a dot on the landscape, he was reminded of his dream about her floating away on a cloud.

He took a deep breath, held it for a few seconds and exhaled. He smiled. For the first time in eighteen years, despite his inner yearning, he felt at peace with himself.

⚬≈≈≈⚬

Bromley shook Dave's hand. "Sorry to see you leave, Son." Dave grinned. "You wouldn't have said that last week."

"Well, things change. So do people. You will think about what I said?" "Yeah, I'll think about it."

"Good. This town could do worse. So could you. You can pull up your roots, but you can't deny them. Look at your friend."

"I'm not making excuses for Brad, Sheriff, but he was a victim as much as Ellen and all the others."

Bromley lit a cigar. He scowled. "Damn things taste better every day. Call me Clyde. God knows you earned the right. You got Briarwood blood in your veins, Boy, that's what makes you unique. Now, St. John, or whatever the hell his name is, got all the glory, but you're the real winner. You came outa this in one piece."

Dave shook his head. He didn't feel like someone in one piece. "There were no winners. Only different degrees of losers." He extended his hand. "Thanks Clyde, and goodbye."

Bromley stared after him. "You'll be back," he yelled.

⚬≈≈≈⚬

Dave was about to open his car door when a familiar voice rang out. "Hey, Dave, were you going to leave without saying goodbye?"

Funny, he thought, now that you've made the final break with Trinity, Margaret poses no real threat to you.

She put out her hand. Dave took it. "We're leaving for Italy tomorrow. If you're ever in the neighborhood…"

"Thanks, but I don't think so."

"A girl can always hope. I don't suppose you want to tell me what happened between you and my mother? She won't say."

Dave shook his head. "If Trinity wanted you to know, she'd have told you. I think it's good that you two are trying to bridge the gap."

She laughed. "Gap? More like a divide." She sobered. "I want it to work. I don't want to hear someday that my mother died and end up hating myself for not really knowing who she was. You were wrong about a lot of things, Dave, but you weren't wrong about me and Ellen. I loved her, yes, but I also resented her, and that made me feel horribly guilty when she was killed. She, more than I, was like my mother. More than anything, I wanted to be like my mother. Now, all I want, is to be myself, whoever that is." She shrugged. "Who knows? Maybe I'll even like who I am."

In a fleeting moment, Dave had his first really clear glimpse of Ellen Gray. Like Margaret, she'd resembled an opal whose many facets changed colors depending on the setting. Ironic that in their efforts to emulate Trinity they'd become more like each other. Margaret was nobody's angel. Neither was Ellen. "I hope the Italians are prepared. You and Trinity represent a small, but formidable invasion team."

She grinned. "I don't know whether to say thank you, or be angry at that remark." Her smile faded. "I'm sorry the way things turned out. Your partner, I mean."

"Yeah, well, those are the breaks. Tell you what, I hear there's a fountain in Rome that's supposed to bring you luck if you toss a coin into it." He reached inside his pants pocket and took out a dime. "Throw this in for me."

She took the coin from him. "My pleasure." She winked. "You know, I think I'll like Italy. I understand they have more titles there than you can shake a stick at." She tilted her head to one side and placed her forefinger on her cheek. "Countess Margaret? It has a ring to it, don't you think?"

Dave found himself liking her. She's come a long way, he thought. Like me, she's walked through fire, and, like me, she hasn't always escaped the flames.

◌▦▦◌

A white-coated attendant led him to the garden area. Katie sat in a wheelchair, a rug covering her legs.

Dave nodded at the attendant and took a bench next to his sister.

He took a deep breath and exhaled. "Okay, kiddo, I talked to your doctor today. I called him last week to discuss a theory that Laura had. She believes that much of your problem lies in your desire to hurt me. She's also convinced that you've been putting on one hell of an act. Seems like she was half-right. You've been closely observed this past week. You need help, but you no longer need expensive babysitting. I paid for one more month of care in this facility, and then you're going to have to go on outpatient status. I talked to mother. You can stay with her. You just can't stay here anymore, and vegetate."

Katie stared blankly ahead of her.

Dave stood. "It's a wonderful act, Katie. You ought to take it on the road." He turned to leave.

"Wait!" Her voice quivered, a result of long misuse.

With his back still turned to her, Dave allowed a smile to come to his lips. When he turned to face her, his expression was stoic. "Did you say something?"

The words when they came were faltering, unsure, and as pathetic as they were selfish. "I don't want you to marry Laura."

"I don't care what you want, Katie, but I do care about you. I want you to live a full and wonderful life, separate from mine, but that doesn't mean I want to separate myself from you. Am I making sense? "He sighed. "I guess I'm not. As for Laura, we split up a while back."

"Did I do that?"

"Sorry to disappoint you, Katie, but I lost Laura all by myself. It's a long and depressing story."

She reached out her hand. Dave took it in his. A smile, the first he'd seen on her lips in over two years, lighted up her face. "I'd like to hear it."

Dave kneeled down beside her and took her in his arms. She clung to him. Tears wracked her slender body. Moisture filled Dave's eyes, and emotions, long submerged, rushed to the surface. Sobs filled his throat. Their tears mingled, as they sobbed out loud together.

✺

Dave sealed the top of yet another cardboard box. All that remained to be packed were some books and his personal belongings. He sat on one of the boxes, thinking how little actual space it took to compile everything a person owned.

He was deep in thought when he became aware of another presence in the room.

He looked up to see Laura.

She held a key in her hand. "I rang the bell. It must be broken, and I still had my key. Why didn't you return any of my calls?"

Dave slapped the side of the box he was sitting on. "What would have been the point?"

"You're angry, Dave. You have a right to be. I thought it might help to talk to someone who knew Brad almost as well as you thought you

280

did. It wasn't hard enough for you finding out that Brad killed all those people? You had to go through it alone?"

"It seemed like the right thing to do at the time. Besides, dealing with what Brad did wasn't all I had to work through."

Laura tested one of the other boxes for stability. Satisfied that it would hold her weight, she sat down on it. "She must have been special to have kept a place in your heart all these years."

"Brad told you about her?"

Laura nodded. "I went to see him. He's frightened." She threw up her hands. "I don't know why I went, really. Maybe I just wanted to hear why he messed up his own life, and so many others from his own lips. He wouldn't talk to me about the murders, even though I assured him I wasn't there on behalf of the D.A. He did want to talk about you. He regrets that he lost your friendship and your respect. He maintains that you were the best friend he ever had. He believes that, and so do I. He hates himself for what he's done." Sadness filled her voice. "That doesn't help you, does it?"

Dave shook his head. "It also doesn't matter anymore."

Laura looked like she didn't believe him. Because she didn't, she weighed her next words carefully. "There are rewards to working for the D.A. You get to hear a lot of things firsthand. They won't be putting Brad on trial on all four counts of murder, Dave, only one, the girls. There's nothing to place him at the scene of the other murders except Bryant's statement. The D.A. doesn't think they can win on all four counts, so he's going for what he hopes is a sure win. Brad is going to stick to his story that he picked Ellen Gray up in a bar and didn't see her again until you and he found her in the alley. It's a weak defense, but he's got a great lawyer. The D.A will tear holes in his story. He'll ask why Brad didn't mention he knew the girl when you found her. Then, of course, there's still the girl's connection to Bryant, and Bryant's own statement. In spite of that, there's a chance he may get off with second-degree murder, maybe even manslaughter. There's been talk of plea bargaining because there's a high priority on getting those steroids off the streets, and out of this country. After Brad gets through this trial, he'll face charges on his involvement with Bryant and the steroid smuggling, so he will do time."

"I already heard about a plea bargain," Dave said. "I can still hear Brad asking me how many of the slime bags we picked up pay for their crimes. It looks like he may become one of the miscarriages of justice he claimed to hate. There's nothing you or I can do about the outcome of his trial, is there? Personally, I'm not going to lose any more sleep over it. This case is over for me."

Laura stared at him, her mouth open in surprise. "Is this the same Dave Kincaid I lived with? The same Dave Kincaid who shouldered all the world's ills? What happened to you?"

"Maybe I just grew up."

"Does she have anything to do with your transformation?"

"She? She has a name. It's Trinity. She was Ellen Gray's mother." It was amazing how much better he felt now that he was able to say her name out loud to Laura.

She nodded at the packaged boxes. "You're going back to Briarwood, and to her?"

"I was offered the job of Sheriff there. Bromley is retiring early. I fought going back until I realized it was what I really wanted to do. I can't live in this jungle we call a city anymore. Katie and my mother may come later. You were right about her, you know, and you were right about me."

Laura stood and brushed away a tear. "You seem to have it all worked out. I'm happy for you."

She was all the way to the front door of the apartment when Dave said, "Trinity is out of my life, Laura. I just wanted you to know that. She is leaving Briarwood and won't ever be back"

She froze, her hand on the doorknob. "What are you trying to say?"

He stood and shuffled his feet on the rug. "I don't know what I'm trying to say. I know that I love you, but I also know that I'm not good enough for you. Trinity may be out of my life, but like a lingering disease, she's a virus I may have to fend off for the rest of my life. I can't ask you to put up with that, and I sure as hell can't ask you to give up a promising career to bury yourself in a small town."

"We don't choose the people we fall in love with, it just happens. I still love you." she said.

She moved away from the door and came back to stand close to him. "Ask me, Dave. Ask me to share your life, and in return you can share mine, problems and all. Ask me."

"I don't want to hurt you, ever again."

"You won't, because now I know what I'm up against, and I can win."

He stared at her in disbelief and wonder, a smile slowly spreading over his face. "How do you feel about a white picket fence, snot-nosed kids, backyard barbeques, bowling on Tuesdays, and a mortgage?"

Her smile matched his. "You stole my dream. All it needs to complete it, is you." She stamped her foot impatiently. "Are you going to ask me or not?"

Dave felt a wave of warmth flow through him. He'd never loved her more than at this moment. "I'm one lucky son of a bitch, and you're crazy. But, here goes. Will you marry me, Laura, and be a small town Sheriff's wife?"

She threw her arms around her neck. "I was beginning to think you'd never ask."

THE END